continued . . .

"A wonderfully delightful story that has all the romance and drama any reader could want . . . This book should top everyone's must-read list for the summer."   —*Eye on Romance*

"Funny, energetic, and loads of fun, *With a Twist* is a tale readers shouldn't miss . . . Once you start reading *With a Twist*, you won't want to put it down."   —*Romance Reviews Today*

Power Play

"A wickedly fun and steamy hot contemporary romance . . . [I] could not put it down . . . *Power Play* is a definite keeper."
    —*Romance Junkies*

"A sheer delight from the first page till the last . . . Contemporary romance doesn't get much better than this."
    —*All About Romance*

"This is a book you won't want to put down."
    —*The Romance Studio*

"Deirdre Martin has another hit on her hands."
    —*Romance Reader at Heart*

"Sparkling banter and a couple with red-hot chemistry . . . [If you] enjoy a funny, hot romance that sizzles, then you won't go wrong with *Power Play*."   —*Romance Reviews Today*

Just a Taste

"Another victory for Martin."   —*Booklist*

"Be prepared to get a little hungry . . . Pick up *Just a Taste* for a tempting read you won't want to put down."
    —*Romance Reviews Today*

Chasing Stanley

"Martin has a way of bringing her dissimilar characters together that rings true, and fans and curious new readers won't want to miss her latest hockey-themed romance."   —*Booklist*

The Penalty Box

"[Martin] can touch the heart and the funny bone."
—*Romance Junkies*

"Martin scores another goal with another witty, emotionally true-to-life, and charming hockey romance."   —*Booklist*

"Fun, fast rink-side contemporary romance . . . Martin scores."
—*Publishers Weekly*

"Ms. Martin always delivers heat and romance, with a very strong conflict to keep the reader engaged."
—*Contemporary Romance Writers*

Total Rush

"Deirdre Martin is the reason I read romance novels."
—*The Best Reviews*

"Martin's inventive take on opposites attracting is funny and poignant."   —*Booklist*

"A heartwarming story of passion, acceptance, and most importantly, love, this book is definitely a *Total Rush*."
—*Romance Reviews Today*

Fair Play

"Martin depicts the worlds of both professional hockey and ethnic Brooklyn with deftness and smart detail. She has an unerring eye for humorous family dynamics."   —*Publishers Weekly*

"Makes you feel like you're flying."   —*Rendezvous*

Body Check

"Heartwarming."   —*Booklist*

"One of the best first novels I have read in a long time."
—*All About Romance* (Desert Isle Keeper)

"Deirdre Martin aims for the net and scores."
—*The Romance Reader*

Titles by Deirdre Martin

BODY CHECK
FAIR PLAY
TOTAL RUSH
THE PENALTY BOX
CHASING STANLEY
JUST A TASTE
POWER PLAY
WITH A TWIST
STRAIGHT UP
ICEBREAKER

Anthologies

HOT TICKET
(with Julia London, Annette Blair, and Geri Buckley)

DOUBLE THE PLEASURE
(with Lori Foster, Jacquie D'Alessandro, and Penny McCall)

Icebreaker

Deirdre Martin

BERKLEY SENSATION, NEW YORK

THE BERKLEY PUBLISHING GROUP
Published by the Penguin Group
Penguin Group (USA) Inc.
375 Hudson Street, New York, New York 10014, USA
Penguin Group (Canada), 90 Eglinton Avenue East, Suite 700, Toronto, Ontario M4P 2Y3, Canada
(a division of Pearson Penguin Canada Inc.)
Penguin Books Ltd., 80 Strand, London WC2R 0RL, England
Penguin Group Ireland, 25 St. Stephen's Green, Dublin 2, Ireland (a division of Penguin Books Ltd.)
Penguin Group (Australia), 250 Camberwell Road, Camberwell, Victoria 3124, Australia
(a division of Pearson Australia Group Pty. Ltd.)
Penguin Books India Pvt. Ltd., 11 Community Centre, Panchsheel Park, New Delhi—110 017, India
Penguin Group (NZ), 67 Apollo Drive, Rosedale, North Shore 0632, New Zealand
(a division of Pearson New Zealand Ltd.)
Penguin Books (South Africa) (Pty.) Ltd., 24 Sturdee Avenue, Rosebank, Johannesburg 2196,
South Africa

Penguin Books Ltd., Registered Offices: 80 Strand, London WC2R 0RL, England

This is a work of fiction. Names, characters, places, and incidents either are the product of the author's imagination or are used fictitiously, and any resemblance to actual persons, living or dead, business establishments, events, or locales is entirely coincidental. The publisher does not have any control over and does not assume any responsibility for author or third-party websites or their content.

ICEBREAKER

A Berkley Sensation Book / published by arrangement with the author

PRINTING HISTORY
Berkley Sensation mass-market edition / February 2011

ISBN: 978-0-425-23979-7

BERKLEY® SENSATION
Berkley Sensation Books are published by The Berkley Publishing Group,
a division of Penguin Group (USA) Inc.,
375 Hudson Street, New York, New York 10014.
BERKLEY® SENSATION and the "B" design are trademarks of Penguin Group (USA) Inc.

PRINTED IN THE UNITED STATES OF AMERICA

10 9 8 7 6 5 4 3 2 1

In memory of Nan Beytin

Acknowledgments

My incredibly patient husband, Mark.
My *extremely* patient editor, Kate Seaver.
My wonderful agent, Miriam Kriss.
Binnie Braunstein, Eileen Buchholtz, and Dee Tenorio.
The Left Wings Improv Group and AWI.
Rocky, Mom, Dad, Bill, Eli, Allison, Beth, Jane, Dave, and Tom.

1

"There's a twenty dollar tip in it for you, Ashok, if you get me there in ten minutes. Step on it."

Sinead O'Brien was rarely late, no matter where she was going. The only female partner at the law firm of Callahan, Epps, and Kaplan, she was known not only for her punctuality but also for her sharp intellect and history of getting successful outcomes for her clients. Sinead believed whatever success she had came from working her tail off, which is what she'd been doing today, despite it being Sunday. Her parents called it "workaholism." Sinead called it dedication.

Despite her usual attention to detail, time had gotten away from her. One minute, she was in her office reviewing depositions for a new case; the next she was fifteen minutes late for her family's traditional Sunday afternoon dinner. Annoyed with herself, she'd packed her briefcase and hurried out onto the street, impatient for the car service, which seemed to take forever to come. Sliding into the backseat of the black Cadillac, she'd directed the familiar driver to speed to Eleventh Avenue and Forty-third Street, where the

Wild Hart, her parents' pub, was located. She could hear her mother's voice in her head. *Why are you working on a Sunday? Why haven't you started dating again?*

Her parents' lack of appreciation for her dedication baffled her. Irish immigrants, they'd broken their backs for years—seven days a week, year in, year out—to make the Wild Hart a success. She realized part of their concern stemmed from worries about her health (she suffered from debilitating migraines and had high blood pressure despite being only thirty-two), but she was a big girl and could take care of herself.

Sinead checked her watch. The ride to her parents' apartment seemed to be taking forever. She told Ashok to take Thirty-fifth Street across town to Tenth Avenue, thinking it would be quicker than heading uptown on Park Avenue. She settled back in the seat, wondering what wonderful dish her mother would be making. Sinead savored these Sunday dinners because she usually lived on takeout. It wasn't that she didn't know how to cook (God knows you couldn't be Kathleen O'Brien's daughter and not know how to cook); it was that she was too exhausted to make dinner for herself at ten or eleven o'clock at night when she got home. She tried to eat healthy, but every now and then a big, fat, juicy burger or a couple of donuts were the only thing that satisfied.

Ashok pulled his Cadillac up in front of the Wild Hart, and Sinead hurriedly paid him, unlocking the pub door and heading toward the kitchen, where steps led to her parents' apartment. She'd grown up here in the cozy flat above the bar: she and her sister, Maggie, crammed into one small bedroom; her brothers, Quinn and Liam, in another; her parents in the third. The apartment never felt small—until adolescence hit and she and her siblings began getting on each other's nerves, tripping over one another and finding little space for much-craved privacy. Yet somehow they'd survived.

Sunday dinner together stretched as far back in her memory as she could remember. The whole family would go to Mass and then come home for a large, early afternoon meal. Now that she and her siblings were grown and living their own lives, it was a way for them to come together once a week and catch up with one another.

She walked into her parents' kitchen, girding herself for a steely glance from her mother. Everyone but Liam, her younger brother who lived in Ireland with his wife, Aislinn, was there: her older brother, Quinn, a successful journalist, and his French wife, Natalie; her sister, Maggie, and her husband, Brendan. Their baby, Charlie, sat in a high chair between them. Sinead ducked her head sheepishly as she slid into the sole empty seat at the table.

"Sorry I'm late," she said, reaching for the steaming bowl of mashed potatoes. She was famished.

"I thought maybe you weren't coming," said her mother coolly.

Admittedly, she had missed a few Sunday dinners over the past couple of months. But she'd always called ahead to let her mother know not to expect her.

"I would have called."

"I hope you weren't down with a headache," her father said, concerned.

"No, I had a little bit of work to catch up on, and time got away from me."

Quinn feigned shock. "Time got away from *you*? *You*?"

"Shut up, Jimmy Olsen."

"I don't like when you work on Sundays," said her mother.

"It's the Lord's day of rest," Sinead, Quinn, and Maggie chimed in unison.

"Will you listen to that?" her mother said to her father with mock indignation. "Making fun of their own mother."

"If you can't mock your mother, who can you mock?" asked Quinn.

For a split second, Sinead's eye caught Maggie's, and Maggie smiled tentatively. So did Sinead. Their relationship had cooled a bit since Charlie was born. Sinead desperately wanted children; her ex-husband, Chip, was initially on the fence about the issue. When they were finally in accord and ready to start a family, Chip, who came from a wealthy family, had very traditional ideas about child rearing, namely that Sinead should give up her career. Sinead disagreed and proposed a number of compromises, all of which Chip rejected. They started to fight vehemently—about everything. Eventually, they both admitted that their differences were irreconcilable, and they divorced. But that didn't mean Sinead's hunger for a child went away, and seeing how happy her sister was with Charlie made her envious. It was painful.

Sinead turned to Quinn. "So, what are you working on?"

"A story about a woman with a rare form of cancer. There's an experimental drug that's had some success, but of course, her insurance company won't cover it."

"That's terrible," said Sinead.

"It is," said her father. He studied her face. "You look tired."

"Dad, you say that every time you see me," Sinead said, amused. "I've looked tired for years. There are circles under my eyes in my first Holy Communion picture."

"You need a holiday," her mother declared. "When's the last time you had a holiday?"

"It's been a while, but I'm fine," Sinead replied defensively.

"And when's the last time you were up at your weekend place?" her mother pressed.

Sinead was silent as she speared two pieces of ham and put them on the plate.

"Thought so," said her mother.

When she and Chip had first separated, Sinead had

made an effort to go up to their country house in Bearsville as many weekends as she could. Taking hikes made
her feel calmer and more balanced. She liked hibernating
and licking her wounds in private.

"Maybe you should go visit Liam and Aislinn," her
mother continued.

"I'll think about it," Sinead promised.

"That means 'Get off my arse, Ma,'" her mother said
with a sigh.

"Yup, it does."

Maggie cleared her throat nervously. "I was wondering," she began, looking at Sinead, "if Brendan, Charlie,
and I might use the house one weekend? Just to get away
for a bit."

"Of course," said Sinead. "Just let me know when, and
I'll call the caretaker to come air it out and clean things
up a bit."

"Thanks."

Sinead had always let her siblings and friends use the
house. In fact, Quinn and Natalie had their wedding there.
It made her feel better about spending all that money on a
place she didn't use as much as she should.

Dinner conversation turned to the usual subjects: gossip about relatives and pub patrons, chat about favorite TV
shows and various familial health ailments, the occasional
heated political discussion. And of course now that baby
Charlie had joined the family, everyone, especially Sinead's
parents, focused a lot of attention on him. It made sense: he
was their first grandchild after all. Sinead thought Charlie
was cute, but she didn't know how to *connect* with him,
exactly. She was awkward with him. It made Sinead wonder if she was cut out for motherhood at all. Shouldn't this
stuff come naturally?

When dinner finished, Maggie went off to nurse Charlie, and the men went into the living room to watch the

Jets game. Typical. Sinead and her sister-in-law Natalie helped her mother clean up.

"How's it going at the restaurant?" Sinead asked.

Natalie's face lit up. "I love it."

"Good. I keep meaning to stop by and have a meal. I promise I will when I get the chance."

"That would be the twelfth of never," her mother muttered under her breath.

Eventually it was just Sinead and her mother alone in the kitchen as Natalie went off to annoy Quinn with questions about football.

"You know, I noticed something at dinner," her mother continued.

"What's that?"

"You didn't hold Charlie. Not once."

"I'm not good with babies, Ma, okay?"

"I think you're afraid to hold him."

Sinead swallowed painfully. "Could we not talk about this?"

"Maggie misses you."

"Stop meddling, Mom. Please."

"I just worry about my girl. You seem so unhappy."

"I'm fine, Ma. Honestly."

"But you must be getting a bit lonely, no?"

"Don't start," Sinead begged. "Please."

"Don't you think it's time to find a good man?"

"I'm not sure there are any," Sinead lamented. "And I'm certainly not going out looking for one."

"Stubborn thing. You've always been a headstrong, stubborn thing. You and your sister."

"Gee, I wonder where we get that from."

"Is it because you're afraid of getting hurt again?" her mother pressed on. "So you made a mistake. Big deal. Live and learn, I say. Onward and upward and all that. Every pot has its lid, my mam used to say. I want you to find yours."

"If it's meant to happen, it will, Mom," said Sinead, hugging her mother tight. "Now stop fretting and hand me that dish."

* * *

"Guys, I'd like you to welcome our new captain, Adam Perry."

Adam stepped forward from where he stood between the New York Blades' GM, Ty Gallagher, and head coach, Michael Dante. Nodding curtly, he glanced around the locker room.

To say Gallagher and Dante were disappointed with the team's play in the prior season was an understatement. In Ty's estimation, they'd gotten soft. Michael believed their previous successes had led to the loss of the burning hunger needed to propel a hockey team forward. Ty and Michael both felt the Blades needed a strong physical presence on the ice; someone whose will to win would carry the team through the moments when skill wasn't enough. Someone who would inspire effort in his teammates and fear in his opponents.

"Adam? Anything you want to say?" Michael asked.

Perry had a league-wide reputation of being a man of few words who only spoke when necessary. He didn't disappoint. Once again he glanced around the locker room, as if searching for something inside each of his new teammates. The tension was thick. Finally he spoke. "I'm here to win a Stanley Cup," he declared firmly. "I hope that's why you're all here. Nothing else is good enough."

The looks on the faces of the other Blades ranged from awe to fear. Perry was known for more than just being taciturn. A powerfully built back liner, he'd won the rookie of the year award for his offensive production as well as his defense. But over the years, he'd evolved into a primarily defensive defenseman known for being the hardest hitter in the league. His specialty was a dying art: the open-ice body check. It was a hit he delivered with such force and ferocity that more than a dozen players had suffered concussions when their heads met Perry's shoulder at the blue line. Adam's hits were perfectly legal but always ferocious. No one had retaliated against him in years, thanks to his reputation for being just as brutal and effective when he dropped his gloves. In a sport in which players prided themselves on their fearlessness, the one person players readily admitted to each other that they feared was Adam Perry.

A brief moment of awkward silence followed Perry's pronouncement as everyone waited to see if he would say anything else. When it was clear he was done, Michael Dante spoke up, breaking the tension. "Right, let's get dressed for practice."

Ty Gallagher left, and Adam sat down and began unlacing his shoes. While the team talked and got ready, there was a definite psychic, if not physical, distance between Adam and the other players. They were giving him as much space in the locker room as they usually afforded him on the ice. It was something he was used to: the mixture of fear and respect that often made him a man apart, at least until they got to know him. He was not an easy person to get close to; he didn't like to be emotionally vulnerable, which was often a roadblock when it came to friendship. Aloof was safer. Aloof allowed him to focus fully on the task at hand.

Adam hated to admit weakness, even to himself, but deep down, he was afraid of never winning the Cup. The truth was, he needed the Blades as much as they needed him. Despite being an all-star for most of his career, Tampa Bay had only made the playoffs once in the ten years he'd played there. The Blades were probably his last shot at Stanley Cup glory.

Adam looked around as he pulled on his practice sweater. He'd faced most of these guys on the ice for years. Jason Mitchell knew what it was like to butt heads with him; Adam couldn't count the number of times they'd hit each other. He'd had his run-ins with Jason's brother Eric as well. Ulf Torkelson downright hated him. That was okay. All he cared about was that they produced on the ice.

The one wild card in the bunch was Esa Saari, a Finnish-born defenseman who it was rumored the Blades intended to pair with Adam. Saari was Adam's opposite on the ice: an offensively minded, fast skating defenseman whose lapses in his own zone sometimes hurt the teams he'd played on.

As if on cue, Saari spoke up. "Hey, Coach Dante, I hear your brother makes killer meatballs."

Everyone laughed. Adam knew from chatting with Michael that his brother, Anthony, owned an Italian restaurant in Brooklyn called Dante's. Players ate there all the time. In fact, Michael and Ty were making plans to take Adam there one night soon. Apparently it was a tradition: take the new guy out for a meal.

"Best in New York," Michael boasted.

Esa grinned. "I'm going to have to check them out."

With a model hanging off each arm, Adam thought scornfully. Saari was one of those athletes known as much for his lifestyle as his style of play; you couldn't open the paper or watch celeb TV without there being some piece about Esa and who he was seen with, or what hot new restaurant he was at, or what club he was hanging out at. Unfortunately, the guy was a hockey rock star, and he knew it, too.

"All right, you putzes," said Michael. "Let's get out on the ice."

Adam got up to leave with everyone else, but Ty popped his head in the door. "Hold on a minute, you two." He waited until the team had cleared out. "Michael: work your usual magic, kicking their asses till they break down and cry like little girls. Adam: make it clear to these pussies that you're not going to take any shit from them both on *and* off the ice."

Adam grinned wickedly. "Will do."

2

"*Oh my God,* did you sleep here?"

Unlocking the front door to the law firm's offices, Sinead found her coworker, Oliver Casey, lying on his back on one of the posh leather couches in the lobby, blinking at the ceiling. It was clear that he'd just woken up. It was also clear that he'd slept in his clothing.

Oliver sat up with a yawn. "What the hell are you doing here at this hour? Let me guess: working."

"What the *hell* are you doing sleeping on the couch?"

Despite their different temperaments, Sinead adored Oliver, and the feeling was mutual. He was manic, guzzling diet colas all day like they were water, while she was even-tempered. He flew by the seat of his pants, while she planned everything carefully. He was a womanizer who slept with half his clients, something Sinead found inconceivable. But he was a brilliant litigator, which was the reason the managing partners in the firm were willing to turn a blind eye to his "shortcomings," as one of them put it. It was different for her: all it would take was one Oliver type lapse of judgment on her part, and she'd be fired. She hated that there was a double standard, but there was nothing she could do about it.

"Had a little bit too much to drink last night, and when I got in the cab to take me home, this was the only address I could remember."

Oliver yawned again, running a chunky hand through the thick tangle of his black hair. He wasn't what you'd call traditionally attractive: he was slightly overweight, and his nose was a little too big for his face. Yet he bagged any woman he wanted to, mainly because he was one of those effortlessly charming men who could flatter the clothes off even the most resistant female. He was smart as hell, and funny, too.

Sinead sat down next to him. "How's the hangover?"

Oliver's eyes rolled up in his head dramatically. "Ever wonder what it's like to have an ice pick driven into your skull repeatedly?"

"I don't have to wonder: I get migraines, remember?" She patted his shoulder. "C'mon, I've got some aspirin in my desk drawer."

"Sinead O'Brien: always prepared. I bet you were a Girl Scout."

"Shut up."

With Oliver wincing every step of the way, they walked down the long, carpeted hall to her office.

"Do you have to be in court this morning?" Sinead asked.

"Stop yelling."

"I'm not yelling. Do you have to be in court this morning?" Sinead stage-whispered.

"Yep."

Oliver peered at her with disdain. "What are you so chipper about this morning?"

"I got a call from Kidco Corporation, the company that owns the New York Blades. They asked me if I'd be interested in defending one of the team's star players, Adam Perry, in an assault case."

"What's the dude being charged with?"

"Assault causing bodily harm of another player. A suburban Philadelphia DA who's up for reelection brought the charges. Kidco wants to meet with me ASAP to discuss the case further."

"Sounds like it could be primo." Oliver looked her up and down. "You look devastatingly beautiful today. Have I mentioned that?"

"Shut up."

"You do. How come you and I have never gone out?"

"I don't date coworkers."

"For now." Oliver sighed dreamily. "Ever hear of Tina Andreas?"

"No."

"Some socialite gazillionairess. She's divorcing a real schmuck. Unfortunately, they didn't sign a prenup, so this putz is going after half her money. She's retaining me, of course. Anyway, she's gorgeous."

"You've slept with her already, haven't you?"

"Hell yeah."

"How did you lure her into your bed?"

"Drugged her."

"Oliver!"

Oliver grinned. "How do you think, babe? I turned on the charm. Explained to her how we were going to demolish this guy in court. Told her if she needed anything—*anything*—I was there for her. Apparently she needed a good shtupping."

"Charming."

"Well, I am known for going above and beyond for my clients," Oliver wisecracked.

"In a manner of speaking."

Even though Oliver's "relationships" were purely sexual,

they still reminded Sinead of how she awoke in an empty
bed day after day. "What if I never find anyone else, Oliver?"

Oliver looked dumbstruck. "You kiddin' me? With your
killer bod and great big brain? You will. Trust me."

"If you say so." Sinead kissed his cheek. "You always
make me feel better. Thank you."

"You're very welcome, Sinead. And screw the aspirin.
Can I have one of your migraine pills?"

* * *

Sinead strode confidently into the offices of Kidco Corporation. Unlike the rest of her family, she'd never been a sports
fan. Her father had fallen hard and fast for baseball the
minute he'd set foot on American soil from Ireland. Sinead
remembered him bringing the whole family to a Mets
game when she was about six, and being bored senseless.
Both her brothers liked football as well as hockey. In fact,
the Wild Hart had actually become the New York Blades'
new hangout. Every time Sinead visited her parents' pub, a
group of players could be found occupying a bunch of the
tables in the back, downing pitchers of beer and looking
like they were having a good time. Sinead never paid them
much attention, though she sometimes heard the occasional appraising murmur when she passed to get to the
kitchen. It made her uncomfortable. Auburn-haired Maggie was the beauty of the family, not her.

After presenting her ID at the desk in the lobby, she
was ushered up to the fifty-third floor into a windowless
conference room, where she found six men seated around
an oblong teak table. They all rose as she entered. Sinead
proffered a hand to the man nearest her for a handshake.
He was squat and overweight, a splat of dry ketchup on
his tie.

"Hello. I'm Sinead O'Brien from Callahan, Epps, and
Kaplan."

"Lou Capesi, head of PR for the team," the man said, his fingers as plump as the Irish bangers her mother cooked. Lou gestured to the thin, gray-haired, distinguished-looking man in an expensive black suit sitting across from him.

A small man with a pinched face seated next to Lou cut in, reaching past him to shake Sinead's hand. "Larry Welsh, NHL commissioner."

"Nice to meet you."

"This is Justin Barry, our in-house counsel," Lou announced, referring to the man in the black suit.

"Nice to meet you," said Sinead. Barry echoed the sentiment.

"Ty Gallagher, the team's GM," Lou said next, pointing to a well-built man with dirty blond hair and an extremely serious expression on his face.

Ty nodded curtly. "Pleasure."

"Michael Dante, our team coach," said Lou, his gaze falling on a handsome Italian man with a friendly face sitting next to Ty.

"Thanks for coming," said Michael.

"My pleasure."

"And this is Adam Perry," said Lou, gesturing at a ruggedly handsome man with light brown hair and hazel eyes at the end of the table.

Adam was unsmiling. "I'm the one being charged."

"Pleased to meet you, Mr. Perry," said Sinead.

Lou Capesi pulled out a chair for her and offered her coffee, which she declined. She sat down, pulling out a yellow legal pad and pen from her briefcase. "So, gentlemen, how can I help you?"

"Three nights ago, the Blades played Philly on their home ice," Justin Barry began. "Adam here, one of the best defensemen in the NHL, made a hit on one of Philly's defensemen, Nick Clarey. Guy was knocked out cold and taken off the ice. The next day, Philly released a statement saying Clarey had suffered a fractured cheekbone and had a concussion. Serious injuries for sure, but nothing unusual."

"We suspended Adam for two games," said Commissioner Welsh, glancing at Adam with an unmistakable look of displeasure.

"Despite his not being penalized during the game," Ty interrupted with a glare.

"The next day," Barry continued, trying to regain control of the conversation, "we were informed that Adam was being brought up on charges of assault causing bodily harm by Patrick Dobbins, Philadelphia's DA—"

"Who just happens to be running for reelection," Michael interrupted disgustedly.

"According to Dobbins," Barry continued with a touch of annoyance, "Adam's hit was outside the accepted norms of the game, constituting assault."

Sinead jotted all this down, all the while aware of Adam Perry watching her intently. "Why did you contact me?" she asked Justin Barry.

"We were told you were one of the city's top litigators."

"Well, I'm certainly one of the city's top female litigators," Sinead noted. "And I'm assuming you believe having a woman defense attorney could be beneficial." Before Barry could respond, Sinead deftly continued, "That's neither uncommon nor a problem for me. However, I've never defended a hockey player before."

"Why are you telling us this?" Ty asked.

"Full disclosure, for one thing. It also means I'll have a slight learning curve when it comes to the intricacies of the game." She tapped her pen lightly against her pad. "For example, I assume it's uncommon for hockey players to be brought up on assault charges?"

"Fuck yes," Lou Capesi blurted, immediately looking sheepish. "I mean—yeah. Sorry for cursing."

"That's okay," Sinead assured him. "I've heard every

curse in the book, most of them coming from the mouths of Wall Street executives."

There was something about Capesi's rumpled look and bluntness that reminded her of Oliver; it was actually somewhat charming. The fact that the team had someone in-house who could spin the story would be a big boon.

"You play in the NHL, you know there's this kind of risk of on-ice contact," Ty Gallagher explained. "Guys have been charged a few times in the past, but it was always for hits outside the norms of the game: either cheap-shot punches or hits in the head with a stick. This kind of check is just part of the game. The charges are just bullshit politicking. As we've said, Dobbins just wants to be reelected."

Sinead nodded thoughtfully. Six pairs of eyes were assessing her reaction to the information, especially Adam Perry's. She looked at him. His expression betrayed nothing, which was curious. Usually defendants exhibited some level of anxiety. But there he sat, as unreadable as the sphinx. Sinead found it slightly unnerving.

"There's footage of the hit?" she asked.

Welsh nodded. "Of course."

Sinead put her pen down and looked around the table. "I would be happy to defend Adam," she said, her eyes again drawn to him. No reaction to her statement, just that intense, inscrutable gaze. What was he feeling? Was he upset about the charges? In shock? Pissed? Brainless? She couldn't tell.

Lou pulled a giant chocolate chip cookie wrapped in a napkin out of his jacket pocket and began munching on it. "Thank God," he said.

"You know how a case like this works, right?" Sinead asked them.

"Yeah," said Michael, smiling good-naturedly. "We pay you tons of money, and you pin Dobbins's ass to the wall."

Sinead chuckled. "I wish it were that easy. No, in assembling the case I'll definitely have to interview the three of you"—she gestured at Adam, Ty, and Michael—"numerous times, as well as talk to other players and referees as potential witnesses." She forced her attention back to Adam. "I'll have to look into your past conduct. Gather autobiographical info. Talk to people who will testify to your character, things like that." She looked around the table. "Have any NHL players ever been convicted of assault?"

"One," said Welsh.

"Have there ever been any charged with assault who were acquitted?"

"Two," said Barry.

"Well, like I said, I would be happy to take this case on," Sinead repeated, putting her legal pad and pen back in her briefcase.

"What happens now?" Welsh asked, once again glancing down the table at Adam with resentment.

"You have the appropriate party from Kidco call my firm, and they'll discuss fees, contracts, etcetera," said Sinead. "It's pretty straightforward." She stood. "Anything else, gentlemen? Anything you want to ask me?"

All the men nodded no, including Adam. Sinead took six business cards out of the pocket of her blazer, handing them to Lou to pass around. "Please don't hesitate to call me if you have any questions. In the meantime, I look forward to working with you all."

"I'll walk you out," said Lou, launching himself out of his chair.

"You just want to hit the vending machines," said Michael.

"*Va fungool,*" Lou replied affectionately.

"Not nice to talk like that in front of a lady," said Michael.

"Again, apologies for my mouth," Lou said to Sinead.

"It's all right."

Sinead nodded politely to everyone as she left. She was excited about taking on the case; it was something new and different, a challenge, which she loved. She'd be able to bury herself in it, forget her loneliness.

She found herself thinking about Adam Perry. Was it possible he was a brainless goon who had been instructed not to speak? She got the sense that part of the challenge with this case was going to be Perry himself. She had her work cut out for her.

* * *

"Well, that was relatively painless," said Justin Barry, draining his coffee cup.

"Until you get the bill," Welsh snapped with a frown.

Ty looked irritated. "You get what you pay for."

Lou walked back into the room. "I like her. No-nonsense broad. Smart."

"What did you get from the vending machine?" Michael asked eagerly.

"Snickers Bar," said Lou, holding it up for Michael to see. "Want some?"

Ty raised an eyebrow. "Remind me: how many heart attacks have you had now?"

"It's dark chocolate! It's good for your heart!" Lou protested, breaking the bar and giving half to Michael.

Ty just shook his head.

"What do you think of her, Adam?" Michael asked.

Attractive in a cool, corporate sort of way, he thought, *with that long, sleek, brown hair of hers pulled back and her flawless makeup,* but that wasn't what Michael was asking about. Adam noticed that she made a point of frequently looking at him. He wondered if she was expecting more input from him, since he was the one being brought up on charges.

"All I care about is that she wins the case," Adam

replied. He couldn't believe it when he'd opened the sports pages of the *New York Sentinel* the morning after the game to read he was being charged for the hit. He sat there at his kitchen table, staring at the article with incredulity. Him being charged with assault causing bodily harm? What bullshit. It would be laughable if the prospect of losing the case didn't mean his career could come to a screeching halt.

Lou and the league office had arranged a press conference almost immediately after the article appeared, featuring Commissioner Welsh, Ty, and one of the suits from Kidco. Welsh stated that the NHL supported Adam 100 percent, and that they'd be supporting the Blades in fighting the charges. It was short and sweet; Welsh took no questions. Adam knew he himself wouldn't get off the hook as easily: the sports press would be all over him at the next game, sticking their mikes in his face, which he hated. Lou had told him to "No comment" them to death. Even if Lou had advised otherwise, that's what Adam would have chosen to do.

Everyone except Welsh stood to leave. "Adam, Michael, Ty," he said, "please sit back down. I have a couple of things I want to talk to you about." He looked at Justin and Lou. "You guys can take off."

"I'll pop upstairs, tell the big kahunas we're going with Callahan, Epps, and Kaplan," said Justin, gathering up his things.

"Lou?" Welsh said politely.

"I'm goin', I'm goin'," Lou garbled as he chewed. "Jesus H., can't a guy even finish his candy bar?"

"By all means, take your time," Welsh said sarcastically.

Lou did just that. Adam looked down at the table, stifling a laugh. When Lou was done, he wiped his hands on his pants. "That was delicious." He patted Michael's shoulder. "See you boys."

Welsh closed the door as Lou departed.

Ty eyed Welsh warily. "What's up?"

There was no love lost between these two men, or between Welsh and any NHL player, for that matter. Welsh didn't have a hockey background; he was a sharp lawyer whose previous sports experience was as senior vice president of the National Football League. He'd been brought in by the owners to help increase the league's revenues which he did, by forcing through a salary cap, much to the players' chagrin.

"What's up is this lawsuit," Welsh replied with a frown. "These assault charges couldn't have come at a worse time."

"Why's that?" asked Ty.

"Because the league has decided it's time to clean up hockey's image."

Adam was skeptical as he folded his arms across his chest. "What does that mean?"

"It means what I said. The league wants to tone down the on-ice violence in the belief it'll make the sport more appealing."

Michael snorted. "To who?"

"We're trying to grow the sport," said Welsh. He looked directly at Adam. "Look, the league will obviously support you in public when it comes to fighting these charges. But off the record, we want to phase out this kind of violence."

"Violence?" Ty echoed, looking at him like he was a moron.

"He's got to cut back on the mid-ice hits."

"I'm in the room," Adam pointed out curtly. "You can talk to me directly."

"Mid-ice hits are part of hockey, Larry," said Ty as if he were talking to a child. "I know it's a dying art, but it's an integral part of the game, and Adam is one of the best ever at it. It's part of the reason we acquired him."

"It's like fighting. It turns people off," Welsh insisted.

"No, fighting turns people *on*," Michael countered. "You get rid of fighting and the hardest checking, and you lose the essence of the game."

Welsh sighed. "Look, I understand this isn't what you want to hear, but for the league to grow, we believe we have to reach beyond our usual fans and bring in new people: young people, parents with little kids, specifically young American parents with little kids who don't like their children to be exposed to too much violence. From now on, Adam, we're going to be watching how you play very closely."

"*Madonn'*, are you fucking kidding me?" Michael turned to Ty, incredulous. "You hear this shit?"

"Calm down," said Ty. His expression was resolute as he looked at Welsh. "Larry, do what you think you gotta do. But I can tell you right now: the Blades aren't changing a damn thing about the way they play."

"Understood, Ty. I respect you a great deal and just wanted you to understand the big picture. I'll do what I have to and you do what you have to. Gentlemen." Welsh rose. "Good luck on the ice tomorrow night."

* * *

As Michael had advised, Adam asked for the players' attention before they went out on the ice the next night to warm up—all the players except Esa Saari, who was late. *Well, this will give me the chance to kill two birds with one stone*, thought Adam. *Assure the guys that the lawsuit was nothing to worry about, and then tear Saari a new one when he turns up.*

"Obviously, you all know about the lawsuit," Adam began.

"It's bullshit," Eric Mitchell blurted.

"Yeah, it is," Adam agreed. "Which is why none of you should worry about the case, because I'm not. I intend to keep playing the way I always have, and I expect all of you to do the same."

"Sorry I'm late." Esa Saari came flying through the locker room door, breathless.

"Nice of you to join us," Adam said sarcastically.

"I—"

"You can tell me your bullshit story in a minute," said Adam. He resumed eye contact with the rest of the team. "Any questions?" There were none. "Get out there and start warming up, then. Esa and I will be with you in a minute."

One by one, the players filed out of the locker room. Adam noticed a couple threw Esa a dirty look. He deserved it. It was disrespectful to his teammates to arrive late when the rest of them made the effort to arrive there on time. Short of the death of a family member, lateness wasn't tolerated.

"Well?" Adam asked when it was just the two of them.

"Subway delay," said Esa as he frantically began dressing for the game.

"No excuse. If you're taking the subway, you should leave extra early just in case something like that happens. Not to mention the fact you earn enough to use a car service."

"Sorry."

"Me, too. Because you owe the locker room fund five hundred dollars. If you're ever late again, you'll owe a thousand."

Saari muttered something under his breath.

Adam narrowed his eyes. "What did you say?"

"Chill, okay? I'm here now."

Adam slowly walked over to him, grabbing him by the collar. "I don't give a shit if you have no self-respect, but as long as I'm the captain of this team, you better start showing respect for your teammates and the game. Do we understand each other?"

"Yeah, yeah, I got it," Saari muttered, eyes darting away.

"Good. Now get your ass out there on the ice."

Arrogant little prick, thought Adam. *You're not going to be so smug by the time I get through with you.* He strode out of the locker room, his anger energizing him. Time to go out and do his job.

3

"Holy shit."

Sinead sat on the couch in her office beside Oliver, showing him the footage the NHL had sent her of Adam Perry's hit on Nick Clarey. She knew nothing about hockey violence, but the force of the hit shocked her. It was brutal. She found herself wincing every time she watched Clarey's head snap back before his body crumpled to the ice.

She'd decided to show the footage to Oliver as a way for her to gauge whether she'd overreacted to the hit. But she hadn't: Oliver's eyes popped out of his head the moment the hit was made, his body leaning forward as if he couldn't quite believe what he was seeing.

"Holy shit," he repeated. He turned to Sinead, incredulous. "He hit the guy so hard he was unconscious before his head hit the ice."

"Yeah, I noticed that," Sinead said grimly.

"I can't believe the dude isn't paralyzed. Let me see it again." Sinead showed it to him again. "Poor bastard. It was like he was taken down by the Incredible Hulk."

"So you agree that hit was incredibly violent?"

"Well, yeah, but I'm not a huge hockey fan, so I don't know if it was above and beyond the usual level of hitting. I mean, these guys really beat each other up on the ice."

"I've deduced that."

Sinead turned off the footage.

"Did the league suspend him?" Oliver asked.

"Two games."

"Has Clarey said anything?"

"No."

"Perry ever been charged with anything before?"

"No, thank God."

"What's your strategy gonna be?"

"Right now? That professional hockey players give their explicit consent to the risk of this kind of on-ice contact, and that this hit was not outside the norm."

Oliver nodded approvingly. "You're gonna have to interview enough hockey insiders to prove those points to jurors, who may be as surprised by the violence of the hit as we were."

Sinead grimaced. "I know. Believe me, I've already started compiling a list. Referees. Sportswriters. Retired players. Active players." She rose, riffling through some papers on her desk. "He's from a small town in western Canada. Claresholm. I'll have to go up there, too."

"That'll be riveting," Oliver deadpanned. "You talk to Perry himself yet?"

"He'll be here soon."

The thought made her nervous; she kept thinking back to her meeting last week at Kidco, his silent watchfulness, the way his hazel eyes betrayed nothing. There was something unnervingly *primal* about him.

"How's it going with the socialite gazillionairess?" Sinead asked.

"She dumped me."

Sinead was shocked. "*What*? Who's she getting to handle the case instead?"

"She didn't dump me as counsel. She dumped me as her boy toy."

"No offense, but you're too old to be a boy toy Oliver."

"All together now: *ouch*."

"Well . . ."

"It's probably for the best," Oliver said with a regretful sigh. "I mean, what if she'd fallen in love with me?"

"They all fall in love with you."

"Too true." He studied her face. "You look tired."

"Do I ever not look tired?"

"Come to think of it, no. But I want you to know it in no way detracts from your beauty."

"Thank you." She picked up the coffee cup on her desk and took a sip. Stone-cold. She'd gotten so involved in starting to assemble things for the case she'd forgotten all about her coffee.

"How's it going with the baby bonding?" Oliver asked.

"I've got bad baby juju, Oliver. I think Charlie hates me. I've had him on my lap a couple of times, and both times you would have thought he was being lowered into a cauldron of boiling oil."

Oliver laughed.

Sinead scowled at him. "It's not funny."

"Yes, it is."

"At any rate, I'm going to keep trying, not just for me, but for Mags. I've hurt her, and I don't want to lose her." She sighed. "Maybe the universe is trying to tell me I'm not mother material."

"It's just a matter of finding the right man."

"I'm not looking."

"There's always me. If you want a kid with none of the fuss of having to deal with a partner, I'll gladly donate my sperm. That way, you'd know the kid would have superior intelligence, as well as wit and charm. *And* we could take turns watching it here at the office."

Sinead shook her head affectionately. "You always make me laugh."

Oliver looked mildly wounded. "You're rejecting my sperm?"

"In a word, yes. I don't really think you're father material. Sorry." She checked her watch. "I need you to go so I can get ready to talk to Adam Perry."

"Sperm rejection, and now you're throwing me out. You're a hard woman, Sinead O'Brien."

"That's the rumor."

"Maybe we can catch a drink one night this week. I haven't been to your folks' pub in a while."

"Sounds good," Sinead said distractedly.

"All right, I can see you're done with me," said Oliver. "Good luck with Perry."

"Thanks. I have a feeling I might need it."

*   *   *

He was punctual; she'd give him that. At exactly ten a.m., Sinead's assistant, Simone, informed her that Adam had arrived. Usually Sinead was unfazed meeting clients, but she found herself a little uneasy, imagining that intense, unwavering gaze of his pinning her.

She checked her makeup and smoothed her skirt, waiting for Simone to bring Adam into her office. Simone knocked once and then ushered him inside. Sinead came forward, extending her hand to shake his. "Thank you for taking the time to come in, Mr. Perry. The sooner we get the ball rolling, the better."

He seemed a little stiff. "I agree."

God, he's huge, Sinead thought. She hadn't realized at the Kidco meeting, with him sitting down at the opposite end of the table, how big and broad he was. Strapping, her father would say. A strapping man. *An unnervingly handsome, rugged, strapping man.*

"Would you like any coffee?" Simone asked Adam.

"No thanks," he said.

"Water?"

"I'm fine."

"Okay, then."

"Thanks, Simone," Sinead said gratefully.

Sinead gestured to the couch. "Please, sit. I appreciate your punctuality. One late client, and the whole day's schedule gets thrown off."

"Someone wants a meeting at ten, I'm there at ten."

"Well, like I said, I appreciate it."

She could feel his eyes on her as she walked to her desk to get her laptop. She straightened her back a little. She wondered: was he mistrustful of her, and that's why he was watching her? Or did he find her attractive? *God, this is probably the way Oliver started*, she thought self-deprecatingly. *Get a grip.*

She joined him on the couch, opening her laptop. "Have you ever been interviewed by an attorney before?"

"No."

"Well, basically I'm just going to ask you a few preliminary questions, and then we'll talk about the incident."

Adam just nodded. No questions for her. No anxiety-filled eyes. No glancing around her office nervously. This was a new experience.

"Have you ever been arrested?"

"No."

"Have you ever testified in court?"

"No."

"Ever been a plaintive or defendant in another lawsuit?"

"No."

"You're thirty-five?"

Adam's eyes narrowed suspiciously. "How do you know that?"

"You're my client. I've done some research."

"You could have just asked me." He looked irked, as if she'd somehow invaded his privacy. "What else do you know?"

Sinead glanced down at her computer screen. "I know you're from Claresholm in Canada. I know you've been in the NHL since you were eighteen. I know you previously played for Tampa Bay. I know you have a reputation as a hard hitter, having caused a number of concussions in opposing players over the years. And I know you're being brought up on charges of assault causing bodily harm."

"That about covers it."

Sinead gave a short laugh. "Hardly."

Adam looked displeased. "Hardly?"

"The more I know about you, the better I can defend you."

Adam sat back, coolly assessing her as he folded his arms across his chest. "And do I get to know about you?"

Sinead was taken aback by the challenge in his voice, even though his face still betrayed nothing.

"What would you like to know?" Sinead asked. She gestured at the shelves to their left. "There are my degrees. I've been with this firm since I was twenty-five. I'm a full partner. I take my job seriously."

"So do I."

"That's good to know."

Do you know how unnerving your gaze is? she wanted to ask him. He probably did. That was why he used it.

Adam looked wary. "Anything else?"

"Tell me in your own words what happened on the ice with Nick Clarey."

"We were playing Philly, and I made a hit on Clarey. Philly released a statement saying Clarey was concussed and had a fractured cheekbone. I was suspended for two games. The next day I found out I was being brought up on charges of assault causing bodily harm. Kidco has hired you to defend me."

Sinead waited for more, but after a few seconds, she realized that was it, that was all he had to say. *He's a caveman,* she thought. *A simpleton.*

"Could you elaborate a little?" she prodded.

"What's there to say?"

"Do you and Clarey have a long-running, acrimonious relationship?"

"Not particularly."

"Was he trash-talking to you or doing anything to incite you?"

"No."

"How did you feel when you saw what your hit did to Mr. Clarey?"

Adam looked baffled. "How did I *feel*?"

"Let me rephrase that," said Sinead, since *feel* clearly wasn't a word he was comfortable with. "What did you think?"

"I felt sorry when I saw he was hurt. I hoped his injury wasn't severe. That was never my intent. But I knew it was a clean hit. We're professional hockey players. He was doing his job. I was doing my job. End of story."

"Except it's not the end of the story, because you're now being charged with assault. Tell me about 'your job,' as you call it."

"I'm a hockey player."

Sinead closed her eyes for a split second, trying to ward off the frustration building inside her. "Elaborate."

Adam looked genuinely perplexed. "What do you need to know?"

"Anything you care to tell me beyond 'I'm a hockey player' and don't tell me there's nothing beyond that, please."

She knew she sounded aggravated, but she couldn't help it. She needed him to let down his guard a little and give her more to work with. Unless he was unable to, because he wasn't the brightest bulb in the makeup mirror.

Adam was starting to look as frustrated as Sinead felt. "I don't know what you're looking for."

Sinead rubbed her right temple. She was dealing with a bonehead. It was that simple. Or not so simple, since dealing with a one-brain-cell wonder was going to make her job that much harder. It wasn't a good sign when you had to pull teeth to get the person you were defending to talk.

"Look, I'm not a hockey fan, and—"

"You don't know anything about the game, as you said in the Kidco meeting." Adam looked dubious. "I have to be honest with you: that doesn't exactly inspire confidence."

Sinead kept her expression neutral. "Are you saying you'd prefer someone else to handle the case?"

"No. If they say you're the best, then you must be the best, right?"

"Would you like me to recite my track record to you?"

"No need. But I would feel better if you learned about the game."

"I intend to. Now, may I finish what I was saying before you interrupted me?"

"By all means."

He probably thinks I'm a bitch, Sinead thought, *but who cares? Arrogant jerk.*

"The judge and jurors hearing the case might not be hockey fans, either. The prosecutor is going to show video of the hit, and for people who don't know hockey and who don't understand the game, it might seem excessive. Maybe even criminal."

"I'm a defenseman," Adam said, with a bit of annoyance.

"I know," Sinead said with a touch of frustration. "But what does that mean?"

Adam closed his eyes and lowered his head for a moment, as if gathering himself. When he lifted his head back up, his expression had changed; he looked more cooperative.

"Every player on the ice has a job," he said patiently. "The job of the goalie is to prevent the puck from going across the goal line. All of his efforts are focused on that one task. Wingers, by and large, are supposed to score goals. Their aim is to put the puck in the net. Generally, everything they do is with that end in mind. Centers are supposed to facilitate the forwards in goal scoring, while also assuming some defensive responsibilities. I'm a defenseman," he repeated.

"My job is to keep other players from scoring and from threatening my goaltender. Unlike everyone else on the ice, a defenseman's role is to oppose another player. To a goalie, winger, or center, the puck is primary. To a defenseman, the puck is secondary. My job is to physically deter and impede other men—strong, fast, determined men—any way I can, within the rules. When you look at the video of that hit, you see me doing my job—very well, I might add."

Sinead nodded. Clearly, Adam Perry was many things: Egotistical. Stoic. Attractive. Guarded. Physical. But one thing he was not was a bonehead. He seemed to possess a certain thoughtful eloquence. Sinead realized she had lost focus and quickly brought the conversation back to more mundane matters.

"Thank you for that explanation," she said gratefully. "Now, I'll also need to speak with some family and long-time friends. Who do you recommend I interview in your hometown?"

Adam looked irked. "Why do you have to talk to anyone in my hometown?"

"As I explained in the meeting last week, the more people we can get to attest to your character, the better for you," she said slowly in an effort to stop herself from speaking sharply. He was beginning to try her patience.

Adam looked angry. "You don't have to speak slowly. Just as you don't understand why I do what I do for a living, I don't understand why you do what you do for a living."

"You're right, I'm sorry," Sinead apologized. "But back

to my question: any recommendations as to who I should talk to in your hometown?"

Adam sighed wearily. "Call my brother, Rick."

"I'd prefer to interview him face-to-face."

"You can get the same info over the phone."

"May I have his number, please?"

Adam gave her the number, frowning with displeasure. He checked his watch. "Anything else?"

Sinead just stared at him. *Oh, gee, am I taking up your precious time?* she longed to say. *I'm just your attorney, that's all. Sorry for the inconvenience.*

"I'll call you. In fact, you should get used to talking to me. A lot."

Adam didn't look happy.

"I guess that's all for now." Sinead rose, extending her hand. "Thanks for coming in."

"No problem. I can see myself out."

She watched him go. Distractingly handsome. Distractingly taciturn, too. But intelligent and thoughtful in a way that wasn't obvious at first. As Adam's attorney, his being taciturn was problematic. As a woman, though, the combo made him seem mysterious and enigmatic to her. The strong, silent type, as the cliché went. Sinead hated that she was attracted to him. It was inconvenient. Unsettling. She'd had handsome clients before, but there was something about him . . . She made herself stop thinking about it.

She'd start interviewing people in New York later this week. As for his brother, well, she'd talk to him on the phone initially, but she fully intended to speak with him in person, whether Adam liked it or not. She was the one in charge here, not him. The sooner he realized it, the better.

4

"Is this the latest lamb you two are leading to the slaughter?"

Adam laughed, shaking Anthony Dante's bear paw of a hand. As per tradition, he was eating dinner with Ty and Michael at Dante's, the Italian restaurant in Brooklyn that Michael's brother owned.

Michael looked up at his brother, a refrigerator-sized version of himself. "Got anything good tonight?"

"Like what?"

"Veal parm?"

"Already out of it. You should know by now, Mikey: if you don't get here before six thirty, you don't get any veal parm."

"But I'm your brother."

Anthony scowled. "What am I, a freakin' psychic? I didn't know you were coming."

Michael turned to Adam. "See the bullshit I have to put up with?"

Anthony flashed him a dirty look. "You want some appetizers or what?"

"What have you got?"

"The tortellini stuffed with chard, prosciutto, and ricotta is out of this world, or so I'm being told," Anthony boasted.

Michael looked at Adam and Ty. "Wanna go for it?"

"Sounds great," Adam concurred.

Anthony headed back to the kitchen.

"You got a brother?" Michael asked Adam.

"Yeah, an older brother named Rick."

"Then you know what the ragging on each other is all about."

Adam smiled, but the mention of Rick brought on a twinge of guilt. He missed his brother; missed his niece and nephew, too. He'd called Rick twice; neither call was returned. Neither of them was particularly good on the phone, and now that Rick had lost his job at the Chevy plant, he was even less talkative. Adam made a note to check his schedule; maybe he could fit in a visit home soon.

Ty bit into a breadstick. "How'd it go with Sinead O'Brien?"

"Short but sweet." Adam took a sip of water. "She thinks I'm a moron. I don't appreciate it."

"Why would she think you're a moron?" Michael asked.

"I don't know," Adam replied, irked just thinking about it. "She was becoming increasingly frustrated with me, and I have no idea why. She'd ask a question, I'd answer it, but it wasn't enough for some reason. She asked me what I *felt* when I hit Carey."

Michael peered at him confusedly. "Wha? What were you supposed to *feel*? You were doing your job."

"Exactly," said Adam. "But she kept pushing me to 'tell her more' about everything."

"Well, it was the first time she was talking to you, and she is your attorney, not your pal," Ty pointed out.

"True. She doesn't seem the type for small talk," Michael noted.

"She's not," said Adam. "Total tight-ass. Überprofessional. Icy."

"Who the hell cares?" Ty groused. "As long as she gets them to drop the case."

"Ty's right," said Michael to Adam. "When are you talking to her again?"

"Not sure. I think she might talk to all you guys first, then maybe get me to fill in the blanks."

"She's a good-looking woman," Michael noted.

"What the hell, Michael." Ty gave him his famous scowl. "Are you encouraging him to date his attorney?"

"I don't want to date her, guys," said Adam. "She's too uptight."

"She was meeting you in a professional capacity," said Michael. "Maybe after hours, she's—"

"Can it," Ty interrupted, looking steamed. "He's here to bring us the Cup. He gets into a relationship—"

Michael groaned. "Jesus Christ, will you change the script? You've been spouting this crap for years. Being involved with someone has never affected anyone's play. Happy players make good players."

Adam stifled a laugh. They were bickering like an old married couple.

"Admit it, Ty."

"Yeah, yeah, yeah," Ty muttered. "I guess if he finds a girlfriend, it'll be okay."

"Uh, guys, could you not talk about me like I'm not here?" Adam asked. That had happened at the meeting, too. Was it something about him, or were Ty and Michael so enmeshed they sometimes failed to notice the presence of anyone else?

"Sorry," said Michael. He reached for a breadstick, broke it in two. "How's it going with Saari? You tear him a new one for being late?"

"Oh yeah. Little prick actually had the balls to tell me to chill out."

Ty shook his head in disbelief. "These young guys

now . . . Can you imagine ever saying that to your captain? Jesus Christ."

"No shit," said Michael. "If we'd ever talked to you that way, maintenance would have found our body in the Dumpster the next day."

"Damn straight."

"He wasn't happy when I pointed out a few mistakes he made on the ice against Philly," said Adam.

"Arrogant kid," said Michael. He turned to Ty. "You know who he reminds me of? Paul van Dorn."

Ty nodded in agreement. "Yup. But we got him to toe the line, didn't we? And that's exactly what's going to happen with Saari."

Wine was brought to the table. Michael raised his glass high. "To Adam. May the season end with him skating the Cup on home ice."

"I'll drink to that," said Adam. He wondered if Sinead O'Brien ever let her hair down and drank a glass of wine now and then. Probably not. She seemed the workaholic type, no play. Too bad Michael was right: she was a very attractive woman. Not that it mattered. The important thing was that she got Dobbins to drop the case. He steered his wandering mind back to present company, intent on enjoying the evening.

*   *   *

Midway through what was turning out to be an outrageously decadent meal, Michael's brother, Anthony, sat down at the table to shoot the breeze with them.

"Food okay?" he asked.

"Quit fishing for compliments, you loser," said Michael.

"It's amazing," said Adam. "I spent years in Florida. You couldn't get Italian food like this."

"'Cause this is the real thing, bro," said Anthony. "You must have been able to get some amazing Cuban food, though."

"Totally," said Adam.

He noticed Anthony kept staring at his brother's head. Michael noticed it, too. Finally, Michael snapped, "What? What are you staring at?"

"What the hell did you do to your hair?"

"Nothing. I went to Mario, as usual."

"You look like Shemp from *The Three Stooges*."

"Fuck you," Michael said to Anthony. "This is why you have no friends; you insult everyone."

"I have friends," Anthony protested.

"Name one."

Anthony rattled off four names.

"They're all chefs who are as batshit as you," Michael countered. "Name one non-chef friend."

Anthony glared at him. "Bite me, Mike."

"At least I don't look like Moe," said Michael.

Anthony shook his head sadly. "Pathetic comeback. Totally pathetic." He stood up. "Adam, it was nice to meet you. Ty, it was good to see you again. Mikey, you're not even worthy of uttering the name of Moe."

Anthony returned to the kitchen.

Michael touched the top of his head worriedly. "Do I really look like Shemp?"

"Nah, you don't," Adam assured him. "He was just yanking your chain."

"He's such an asshole," Michael uttered under his breath.

*   *   *

Dinner finished, Ty and Michael left to go home to their families. Adam, not tired and not particularly eager to return to an empty apartment, told them he'd call a cab later and went to sit at the bar. He ordered a single malt scotch, taking in the surroundings as he savored his drink. He liked this place; it had a real family feel, with pictures of customers past and present on the walls, as well as a few pieces of undeniably tacky art (paint by number gondolas? The Leaning Tower of Pisa?). It reminded him of one of the restaurants in his hometown, Robkey's Bar and Grill: unpretentious, good food, decent prices, and a place people could bring their kids. He'd heard through the Blades' grapevine that the team's watering hole, the Wild Hart, had a warm feel to it as well. He'd yet to check it out, but a drink with the team might be a good idea; it would give them a very small taste of his human side. Even so, he wouldn't let his guard down too much. It was too big a risk to the "awe" element Ty wanted him to cultivate.

Adam lifted his eyes to the TV above the bar to watch *Monday Night Football*. The game wound up going into overtime, and by the time it was done, there was only one other guy at the bar, nodding off over his whiskey. Adam felt a clap on his back as Anthony Dante pulled up the barstool beside him.

"You survive your initiation by pasta?"

"Apparently so."

"I hear my brother's a good coach," said Anthony, telling his bartender to pour him a scotch.

"Haven't been here long enough to tell, but that's the rumor."

"Helluva hockey player in his day," said Anthony proudly. "Tough."

"He was," Adam agreed. "I went toe-to-toe with him more than once on the ice. He was a real grinder."

Anthony took a sip of his drink. "No family to rush home to, huh?"

"Nope. You?"

"I'm married to another chef. In fact, she owns and operates the French bistro across the street, Vivi's. She'll probably be over in a few minutes; then we'll drive home together."

Adam nodded thoughtfully. "Married to someone in the same profession. That must be interesting."

"That's a polite way of putting it," Anthony chortled. He

threw scotch down his throat. "Put it this way: there's never a dull moment at our house."

"Telling your brother he looked like Shemp really got under his skin," said Adam, still amused by the comment.

"I knew it would," Anthony said with a smirk. "He's such a vain bastard."

"I take it you're a *Stooges* fan."

"Huge," said Anthony.

"Me, too."

"Yeah?" Anthony looked pleasantly surprised. "Ever notice women hate the *Stooges*?" he asked philosophically.

"I have noticed that."

"They think it's mindless crap. They don't have an appreciation for the art of physical farce." Anthony shook his head despairingly. "I've got the complete DVD collection, right? But I can only watch it when Vivi's not around. She hears one 'Nyuk nyuk nyuk' and she goes mental."

"Totally doesn't get it."

"You should come over one night to watch. I'll make a pizza, crack open a few brews . . ."

"That'd be great."

Anthony drained his drink. "I gotta get back in the kitchen. Gimme your number, I'll shoot you a call."

Adam gave Anthony his number.

"Great meeting you," said Anthony.

"Ditto."

"See ya."

"Yeah."

Adam gave the bartender a nice tip and asked him to call a cab. It had been a pretty good night. Great food, good company, and to top it all off, he'd hit it off with someone who wasn't a hockey player. He wondered what Sinead O'Brien would think of his liking the *Stooges*. She'd probably think he was a cretin. A vision streaked through his mind of her all prim and proper in her office, asking him, "I hear you like *The Three Stooges*. Do you think their violence influenced the way you play hockey at all?" The image amused him greatly. She wanted more info on him? Wanted to peel back the layers of his life? Maybe he'd volunteer the info himself. "Don't know if this will be helpful, but I really love *The Three Stooges*." He smiled, imagining her expression. That's when he realized: he sure as hell was spending a lot of time thinking about Sinead O'Brien.

5

"*So, tell me* all about Captain Perry."

"They all think he's the second coming of Christ."

Sinead wearily cleared away the mountain of papers obscuring Oliver's couch and flopped down. She'd spent three days at Met Gar talking to virtually every player on the Blades about Adam—his reputation, their encounters with him off the ice, if they knew anything about his personal life that could help the case. To a man, all they had was praise. Adam's a great player. Adam's the best at what he does. The charges against him are bullshit. Adam, perfect Adam. All ideal for her case, but she found the lack of information on other aspects of his personality frustrating.

Even so, she did find three things particularly interesting: no one seemed to know anything about his personal life, past or present; he was taciturn to an extreme, only speaking to the players when absolutely necessary; and everyone seemed a little frightened of him.

Oliver was behind his desk, can of cola in one hand and a pastrami sandwich in the other. He held up a hand, indicating Sinead should let him finish chewing, then took a long slug of his drink before putting it down with a resounding thud.

"Nothing? Seriously? Nothing?"

"Nothing."

"Hmm. Gotta be some skeletons somewhere. Always are."

"Well, if there are, these guys don't know about it."

"Who else you planning to talk to?"

"Guys he played with in Tampa. Sportswriters. Anyone I can find."

"Still planning to go to his hometown?"

"Definitely, even though he told me he didn't see the point."

"Maybe he's got a few illegitimate kids running around up there. Secret wife."

"Why keep them a secret? God knows there are enough professional athletes with illegitimate kids, and everyone knows about it. It's not considered a character flaw. And forget talking to *him*; it's like pulling teeth. At first I thought he was a moron. Now I realize he's just very, very guarded."

"Pot meet kettle!"

Sinead was shocked. "What are you talking about?"

"Sinead, we worked together for a year before I even knew you were divorced or came from a large Irish family. It took you forever to open up."

Sinead squirmed. "I just liked to keep my private life private, is all. Keep things on a professional level. His being so guarded is a detriment to me. My being guarded with you wasn't a detriment."

"Yes, it was. We could have become friends sooner. We lost a whole year of intimacy. Think of the things we could have shared. Think of the nights—"

"Shut up, Oliver. The point is, I did open up eventually."

"Once you trusted me. This guy just doesn't trust you yet."

"Good point."

"Some people need to be wooed. Coaxed into telling their story. I'm the client whisperer; I know these things."

"So do I," said Sinead, somewhat annoyed. "My coaxing method is just different than yours: it doesn't involve Grey Goose and garter belts."

"Maybe it should," Oliver murmured, raising one eyebrow seductively. He studied her closely. "You're hot for him."

"What?"

Oliver leaned back in his chair, tenting his fingers. "You're talking to a man who can smell female pheromones from a mile away. You're interested in this guy."

"As a client."

"Bullshit."

"He's a *challenge*. I'm not used to clients who don't display even the slightest bit of anxiety and who don't tell me their story, true or not, in the hopes it will help them out of a jam. It was like interviewing Lurch."

"A studly Lurch."

"An egotistical Lurch. He actually asked if I was really the best attorney for the case because I didn't know hockey," she said, smarting at the memory.

"Maybe he's uncomfortable being represented by a woman."

"Well, he has no say in the matter. His employers hired me. End of story. I'm hopeful that when I understand the game to his satisfaction, he'll be more cooperative."

"You care what he thinks of you," Oliver said slyly.

"As a client. Even if I was attracted to him," Sinead said with a sniff, "it's not like I would do anything about it."

"Why not?"

"Ethics, Oliver."

"Screw ethics. Has dating a client ever prevented me from being amazingly brilliant in court?"

"I love your humility."

"Well?" Oliver prodded.

"*No*, but I'm not you."

"Too true," Oliver said with a sigh.

"You're such an ass," Sinead said affectionately.

"What are you doing tonight?"

"Why?"

"I've got nothing going on, and I know for a fact *you* don't, so why don't we go have a drink at your parents' pub?"

"Okay." She'd call Quinn and see if he wanted to join them, since he and Oliver got along well. Going to the Hart would let her see her folks, too, so if she needed to bow out of Sunday dinner, her mother couldn't bitch that they hadn't seen her all week.

"What time do you think you'll finish up here?" Oliver asked.

"Sevenish," said Sinead.

"Perfect. We can head over there together."

"There's a new part-time bartender now, you know. Christie. She's actually a firefighter."

Oliver's eyes lit up. "Hot?"

"Yup."

Oliver looked mischievous. "Maybe I'll set my head on fire, and she'll throw herself on me to put out the flames."

"Bit extreme. I'm sure if you just exude your normal, manipulative charm, you could talk her into a date."

"Your faith in my abilities never fails to move me."

"See you at seven."

*　*　*

Mission accomplished, Sinead thought to herself. Leaving poor Christie to deal with Oliver, she popped back to the kitchen to chat with her folks. She loved them, but they worried about her too much. *You look tired. How's your blood pressure? Here with Oliver, hmm? Why don't you go out with him? He's nice. He makes money.*

She walked out of the swinging doors of the kitchen, wishing she could turn right back around. There, sitting at the bar next to Oliver, was Adam Perry. *Shit.*

The smile on Oliver's face was unmistakably impish as Sinead joined them.

"Ah, here she is, the lovely Ms. O'Brien," he said jovially. "I was just telling your client that your folks own this place."

Adam nodded approvingly. "Nice. Has a real neighborhood feel. Do you spend a lot of time here?"

Not anymore, Sinead thought. If she could have gotten away with pinching Oliver hard, she would. She knew him: any minute now he was going to claim he had some work to finish up and he'd leave her alone with Adam, a ploy so painfully obvious that Mr. Ego would probably think she'd told Oliver she was attracted to him.

"I'm usually here to visit my parents," Sinead told him. "And I waitressed here with my sister when we were in high school."

"You guys play Toronto tomorrow night, right?" Oliver asked Adam.

"Yeah. It will be a tough game," said Adam, accepting the beer Christie handed to him.

"Bullshit," Oliver responded, shocking Adam. "Toronto blows."

"You a hockey fan?"

"Not hard-core, but yeah," said Oliver. "I was there when the Blades won their last Cup. Amazing night."

Adam regarded Sinead. "I can explain to you why it was such an amazing game, if you'd like."

"No thank you," Sinead said politely. "I'm in the process of figuring out the game on my own."

"You should go to one," Adam continued helpfully.

"Will there be a quiz afterward?"

Adam cracked a small smile. "No. I'm sure you'll figure it out on your own."

"I appreciate the vote of confidence."

Sinead ordered a martini for herself, uncertain of what to do. She had never been in a social situation with a client before. *Ever.* It felt wrong somehow. Unprofessional. But her instincts were sharp enough to realize that casually chatting with Adam outside her office might loosen him up a bit and make him more willing to talk about himself. Maybe Oliver was right; maybe this was the way to go— *sans* seduction, of course.

"Can I ask you a question?" Adam asked.

"It depends."

"Why is there an urn with a picture of a parrot next to it behind the bar?"

"That's Rudy. He came in here for years and years with one of the regulars, Mrs. Colgan. When he died, she asked my folks if his ashes could be put behind the bar, and they said yes."

Oliver glanced around the bar, disappointed. "None of the regulars are here tonight. Pity. Usually there's quite the group," he explained to Adam. "The parrot lady, a guy who won't shut up, some novelist who hit it big with a book about leprechauns and salmon . . ." He turned to Sinead, alarmed. "Wait. Where's the Major?"

"He passed away three months ago," said Sinead sadly.

"Bummer." Oliver turned back to Adam. "Anyway, if you turned the regulars into fictional characters, no one would believe it."

Adam looked disappointed. "Sorry I'm missing them."

"Yeah, me, too," said Oliver. "One night with them, and I think to myself, 'Maybe I'm not so fucked-up after all.'"

Adam laughed.

"They've all started going to bingo together," said Sinead. "Except PJ, the novelist. The rest of them could use the extra money."

Just as Sinead predicted, Oliver drained his glass and stood up. "Sorry, kids, but I've gotta run. I've got a ton of paperwork to do back in the office." He wouldn't look at Sinead. "Adam, good to meet you. You're in good hands with Ms. O'Brien handling your case, believe me." He winked at Christie behind the bar. "Call me, babe," he said, putting his business card on the bar next to a twenty dollar tip.

Christie snorted. "Yeah right." But Sinead saw her casually slip Oliver's card into the pocket of her jeans.

I'm going to kill him, Sinead thought, as she watched Oliver leave.

"Seems like a decent guy," said Adam.

"He's a great attorney."

She was hoping that Adam would turn his attention back to the hockey game on TV, allowing her to make an excuse to slip away. But no: he was studying her like she was a pinned butterfly under glass. She didn't like it one bit.

"Can I help you with something?"

Adam shrugged. "No." He took a sip of his beer. "How'd the rest of your interviews at Met Gar go?"

"As far as I can tell, you've got no flaws and can walk on water."

Adam laughed. "Divinity is a bitch."

"There were two things I found very interesting, though."

Adam turned guarded. "What?"

"First, they all seem a little scared of you."

"Yup." Adam looked pleased.

"Why is that?" Sinead prodded, running an index finger along the rim of her martini glass. "Do you threaten them or something?"

"Of course I don't threaten them. I just refuse to stand for subpar playing, and they know it. I've got zero tolerance for lack of focus. Zero."

"I can identify with that." She sipped her drink. "Here alone?" *Oh, shit. Did that sound like a come-on?*

"Yeah, thought I'd check it out for myself."

"I would have thought you'd come in with the rest of the players."

"I might one night, just for a quick beer. I wasn't brought to New York to be their pal. I was brought here to provide toughness and determination."

"Aren't you lonely?" Sinead blurted.

She could tell by the steely expression in his eyes that she'd crossed a line.

"No."

Liar, Sinead thought. Anyone so singularly focused on their job usually let friendships fall to the wayside. She should know; her only friend in the world was Oliver.

Adam changed the subject. "What's the second thing that jumped out at you when you talked to them?"

"How come none of them seemed to know anything about you personally, apart from the fact you're Canadian?"

"There's nothing to know."

"I find that hard to believe. Everyone has a backstory. I need to know yours."

"Good luck with that," said Adam, taking a slug of beer.

"Can I point something out?"

"Sure."

"I know we're not in a professional setting right now, but I *am* your attorney. There's no reason to be antagonistic. I'm on your side."

Adam looked grim. "Right." He rolled his beer bottle between his hands. "All right, since we're on the same side, what's your backstory? You need to know so much about me? How about you tell me a little bit about you?"

Sinead's guard immediately went up. "It's not necessary for you to know about me in order for me to do my job."

"True, but I think it only fair. A quid pro quo."

Sinead hesitated, and then acquiesced. If this banter was the way to get him to trust her, then what was the harm?

"I like jazz," she said.

"You can do better than that."

"I love kids."

Adam dropped his guard momentarily as his face lit up. "Really? So do I."

Sinead tried hard to hide her shock, but obviously she was doing a poor job of it: Adam looked insulted. "Why do you look so surprised?"

"I'm not," Sinead insisted.

Adam changed the subject. "What else have you got on me?"

"You're pretty demanding."

"It's my job."

"Even off the ice?"

Their eyes caught and held. Sinead saw something behind the steeliness but couldn't quite put it into words.

"I'm divorced," she told him.

Adam's expression softened. "I'm sorry to hear that."

"Don't be. He was a jerk." Sinead's heart was pounding. She was a private person. Why was she revealing something so personal so quickly?

She sipped her martini. "Your turn."

"I love *The Three Stooges*."

"More than kids?" Sinead teased.

"No," Adam said without hesitation. "But I've sworn allegiance to the *Stooges*. I'll always be a fan."

"I'll try not to hold that against you."

Adam smiled.

"*You* can do better than that," Sinead continued. She put her drink down on the bar, folding her arms in front of her chest expectantly. "I'm waiting."

"I was engaged once," he revealed.

"Really? What happened?"

Adam shrugged. "Just didn't work out. We wanted different things." He turned his attention to the TV, an obvious signal he didn't want to discuss it further.

Sinead made a show of checking her watch. They were

dancing a little too close to flirting for her liking, even if it was under the guise of trying to get more comfortable around each other as attorney and client. The problem was, she was enjoying it.

"I should leave. Much like Oliver, I still have a ton of work to do, too."

"Do you ever slow down?" Adam asked.

"Not pertinent to your case."

The urge to flee was overwhelming. Sinead could easily imagine herself spilling her guts to him. *Stick to business,* she told herself. *Stick to safety.*

"We'll talk again soon," she told him. "In the meantime, if you can think of anything—"

"That would be helpful to the case, call you," Adam recited in a monotone. "Got it."

"Good night," Sinead said.

"Night," Adam replied, turning back to the TV.

Sinead walked out of the pub somewhat shaken. Adam could be charming. Still guarded, but charming. She found herself wishing he *was* a bonehead; he was stirring up feelings in her she hadn't had in a long time, and it was worrisome. From now on, she was going to play it strictly professionally. She had to.

6

Adam was annoyed with himself. There were rituals he needed to perform before every game to ward off potential injury and increase the odds of a win. First, he needed to put every piece of equipment on, as well as his uniform, from left to right. Then, he needed to find a quiet place, close his eyes, and picture the whole game in his head. The ritual didn't always work, but it helped focus him so intensely that by the time he hit the ice, all his mental energy was centered on one thing and one thing alone: winning.

Tonight, however, as he readied himself for a Blades home game against Los Angeles, Sinead O'Brien kept intruding on his thoughts, his mind going over their conversation at the Wild Hart. Polite talk had given way to banter, and then to personal info. He was shocked at her willingness to drop her guard for even a minute. Shocked at his own willingness to drop his guard, too. It was more than a professional exchange of information, though maybe he was wrong.

He couldn't help wondering about the circumstances of

her split from her husband. Was it because she was a work-aholic? She'd said he was a jerk; maybe he didn't like a wife with such a high-powered career. He wanted to know more.

But what right did he have to info if *he* wouldn't open up more to her—which he wouldn't. This wasn't good. He was brought here to win, not make friends or think about the life his attorney led outside her office. He'd have to watch himself.

Adam headed into the locker room, nodding curtly in acknowledgment to whichever teammates made eye contact with him. Michael and Ty were pleased with the way things were going. The Blades were battling Jersey for first in the division, and they were playing tough, defensive hockey. Their offense wasn't great, but the sense on the team was that it was just a matter of time before they started scoring more and took control of the division. Adam hadn't changed his game in the least and was as much a physical presence on the ice as ever before. Following his lead, the Blades were finishing more of their checks and not missing any opportunity to hit.

As always, Michael handled the pregame talk, with Adam adding a short comment here and there when needed. Finally, it was time to hit the ice to warm up. Adam was pumped, until he walked out of the locker room to find the hockey commissioner waiting in the hall, motioning him over.

"What's up?" Adam asked.

"Blades are doing well," Welsh noted.

"You called me over to compliment me?"

Welsh chuckled. "No. I just wanted to remind you of what we talked about in the Kidco meeting."

"Refresh my memory."

"We've been watching you, just like I told you we would. I'm still seeing a lot of mid-ice hitting. It's amazing you didn't concuss Toronto's Gil the other night. And dropping the gloves with Fraccia in the third period—did you really think that was going to help your case?"

Adam shrugged unapologetically. "I play the way I play."

"That's certainly true. But the league needs to change, and its players need to change along with it. You know the deal, Adam. We want a faster, higher-scoring, less violent game. The future is coming, and it looks a lot more like your teammate Saari than it does you," Welsh said icily.

Adam took a very small, almost imperceptible step toward the commissioner. It was so subtle that no one would think it premeditated, just an effort to maintain his balance, standing on skate blades on a carpeted floor. But it was intentional. Welsh was less than half Adam's size, especially with Adam in pads and on skates. He could tell the smaller man was intimidated. That was the point. Adam was using personal space to send a very clear message: *don't screw with me*. But since Welsh wasn't a player, he might need it spelled out for him more explicitly.

"I play the way I play," Adam repeated. "End of story. Now, if you'll excuse me, I've got a game to play."

Adam left Welsh and headed down the hall to join his teammates on the ice. *The future looks like Saari? Then to hell with the future. All that matters is today.* At least his conversation with the commissioner had one positive side effect: his anger was fueling his adrenaline, and he was ready to take no prisoners.

* * *

The morning after Oliver abandoned her at the Wild Hart, Sinead marched into his office and read him the riot act. Oliver was unrepentant.

"Riddle me this, Batgirl: did you or did you not find that chatting to your client outside the office made him open up a little bit more?"

"Oh, he opened up, all right," Sinead said scornfully. "He told me he liked *The Three Stooges*."

Oliver put his hand on his chest, feigning a swoon. "A man after my own heart!"

"You have got to be kidding me! Only adolescent boys and morons like *The Three Stooges*!"

"I'm disappointed in you, Sinead. Attorneys shouldn't stereotype. I have it on good authority that Mayor Bloomberg is a huge Curly fan."

"Shut up, please."

"You give him any info about yourself?"

"I told him I liked jazz," Sinead mumbled.

"That must have really turned him on," Oliver said dryly.

"I have no interest in turning him on! Can you please get that through your thick head?"

She decided to withhold from him that they both professed to liking children. Oliver would be all over it, torturing her endlessly. He already was.

"Whatever." Despite it being only eight a.m., Oliver was already guzzling his second cola of the day. "But seriously, lamb chop: don't you think spending time with him in an informal setting helped grease the wheels a bit?"

"Yes," Sinead grumbled.

"I'm telling you: meet him outside the office as much as you can and eventually, silent Moe will cough up all the info you need." Oliver took a long slug of Coke. "Seems like a nice guy, by the way. Good-looking."

"I suppose."

Oliver smirked. "Like you haven't noticed."

Sinead waved a hand in the air dismissively. "Not relevant to the case."

Oliver rolled his eyes as if he'd heard it a hundred times before. "What's next on the agenda?"

"I'm going to a Blades game with my brother. That will definitely make Adam happy."

"Plus you'll get to see him being all manly on the ice."

"I hate you, Oliver."

"Nah, you love me."

"I do," Sinead admitted. She stifled a yawn. "Time to go to work."

"Remember," Oliver called after her as she walked out the door. "Casual settings with hockey boy. Informal."

"Why don't you tell me again? I didn't hear you the first fifty times you said it."

She knew he was right. But she didn't want him to be.

* * *

"I'm having a really hard time following the puck."

Sinead was growing increasingly frustrated as she watched the Blades play against Toronto with Quinn. She'd read as much as she could about the sport and had been fairly confident that when it came time to watch the game, she'd know what was going on. But she wanted a bona fide hockey fan with her just in case. She was fast discovering that reading about a sport and watching it were two very different things.

"Don't fixate on the puck. Look at everything happening on the ice. Try to think of them skating in patterns, and visualize where you *think* the puck is going to go," Quinn advised distractedly. Sinead shot him a sideways glance; his eyes were glued to the ice.

Sinead tried to do what he advised, but it was hopeless; things were simply moving too fast. It bugged her. She was used to understanding things right away. That she couldn't grasp what was being played out in front of her eyes was incredibly irritating.

Perhaps she couldn't discern patterns because her attention kept being drawn to Adam. From the moment he stepped out onto the ice, there was something compelling about him. It wasn't just his size; it was his sheer physical presence. The other players seemed to react in accord with or in opposition to everything he did, even if he didn't touch the puck. They all seemed to be acutely aware of where Adam was and what he was doing.

He'd be pleased she'd come to watch the game. It would increase his confidence in her as his attorney. Oliver's taunting words from a few weeks back echoed in her head—*you care what he thinks*—but Sinead dismissed them. Just because Oliver had bedded half the female population of Manhattan didn't mean he was good at reading women.

Sinead was so deep in her own head that she jolted in surprise when the Met Gar crowd started booing loudly, her brother included.

"What just happened?"

"Your client was just given a penalty. The ref says he elbowed a Toronto forward."

"Did he?"

"No. From the replay the hit was with his shoulder. His elbow came up after to keep himself from smashing his face into the boards."

Sinead looked down at the ice. Michael Dante was arguing vehemently with one of the referees, who was shaking his head obstinately. Adam had skated to the penalty box.

Sinead's heart sank. This was exactly the sort of thing that wouldn't help his case. It was safe to assume that most of the jurors would not be hockey fans, so they wouldn't be as discerning as Quinn about whether penalties were justified. She needed to do more research, find out about clean hits, dirty hits, what was considered legal under the rules, and what wasn't. She had foolishly thought this case was going to be straightforward. Now she realized it had the potential to be anything but.

Play continued. Sinead didn't even try to pay attention to the game at large anymore; she focused only on Adam, sitting in the penalty box or on the bench, but mostly when he was out on the ice. He made skating look so effortless;

they all did. It was fascinating to watch such physically formidable men being so graceful and fluid. And God, they were all so fast.

"You wanna go say hello to your client when the game is over?" Quinn asked.

"Sure." It made sense: he'd see that she was serious about knowing all she could about his job, so she could build the best case to defend him. But that wasn't the only reason she wanted to see him. She forced her gaze back to the ice.

* * *

The Blades had won 4–3, so the mood in the packed Green Room outside the locker room was upbeat.

Sinead was on her way back from the banquet table, where she'd grabbed some bottled water, when Lou Capesi's voice cut through the din. "Hey, hey, number one attorney."

Sinead turned, smiling. "Hi, Lou."

"Nice to see you," said Lou. "How's the case going?"

Sinead took a sip of water. "Pretty well, I think. I'm still interviewing people. In fact, I've been meaning to call you. Can you recommend any sportswriters who'd be inclined to speak favorably about Adam?"

"Doll, they'll all speak favorably about Adam; he's a throwback, and the ink-stained wretches all love 'old-time hockey.' Shoot me a call, and I'll hook you up with the big boys who have some clout."

"Thanks." She glanced discreetly around the room. "Where is Adam, by the way?"

"Still in the locker room, talking to the press."

"Is he good at that?" she asked apprehensively.

"He knows what to say and what not to say, if that's what you mean."

"Good," Sinead said with relief.

"Look, honey, don't worry: the PR machine here has got his back."

"I appreciate that."

"You wanna talk to him? I'll go tell him you're here."

"Yes, that would be good," she said, trying to cover her nervousness.

"You got it. In the meantime, get yourself a donut or something. You look too thin."

Lou waddled off. Sinead tried to imagine Adam talking to the press. *He must hate it,* she thought.

She took a deep breath. The room was packed; there was no air circulating. She hoped it didn't give her a headache. Quinn sidled up to her, chewing on a bagel.

"Where's your famous client?"

"Talking to the press, apparently." Sinead took a long drink of water. "Who are all these people?"

"Family, friends, guests." Quinn peered into her eyes with concern. "You okay, Neenee? Not getting a headache, are you?"

"No, I'm okay."

"Good."

The Blades, singly and in small groups, began entering the room through a set of heavy metal double doors. "Look, do you mind if I go talk to the goalie, David Hewson?" Quinn asked. "He's friends with one of my old pals from the *Sent* I haven't heard from in a while. Thought he might have the lowdown on where the hell he's disappeared to."

"Go on."

Quinn gave her a big hug. "Any time you want to go to a game, I'm your guy."

Sinead smiled. "Thanks, big bro."

Quinn disappeared into the throng, leaving Sinead standing against the far wall of the Green Room clutching her water, which she now chugged down. She wondered how Lou was going to tell Adam she was here. *Yo, your attorney was at the game; she's in the Green Room waiting to talk to you.* She imagined Adam making a put-upon face and thinking, *Great. I just want to have a brew and go home, and now I have to talk with my lawyer.*

Five minutes later, Adam appeared, his light brown hair wet and slicked back. Sinead took another sip of water, carefully watching him. Not the chattiest of men by any means. Though he did stop to say hello to a few people, he looked uncomfortable, and all the conversations seemed to be short and sweet. It reminded Sinead of herself when she was first starting out in law; she was terrible when it came to small talk, so much so that Oliver discreetly told her one day that she was getting a reputation as a snob. Ever since then, she'd forced herself to schmooze when she had to. It still didn't come easily, but she'd mastered it. A workaholic? Yes. Intense? Yes. But a snob? No.

She checked her watch, growing impatient. Surely Adam had to know she was waiting to talk to him. Was it possible he was making her wait on purpose? Stupid thought; there was no reason for him to be manipulative.

Adam shot her a quick glance, acknowledging her presence. A few more people apprehended him on his way over. Sinead felt like she was at the end of a receiving line waiting her turn to talk to hockey royalty.

Finally, they were face-to-face.

"Hey," he said politely.

She waited for him to say more, but he didn't.

"Hi." Did he not want to talk to her? "I watched the game. I hope that makes you feel a bit more comfortable about my ability to defend you."

"Did you understand it?"

"Why don't you quiz me?" Sinead challenged.

An amused smile flickered across Adam's face. He folded his arms in front of his chest. "Well? I'm waiting."

"For what?"

"The mini lecture on how the elbowing penalty isn't going to help my case."

"I had no intention of mentioning it. At least not here and now."

"Mmm."

Sinead looked at him with concern. "You seem distracted. Is something wrong?"

"Yeah, something's wrong." Adam frowned. "I spoke with my brother earlier today. He told me you were going up to Claresholm next week to interview him."

"Why is this bothering you so much, Adam?"

"I don't like people poking around in my personal life. Talking to my brother doesn't make sense. Do you think he's going to have anything but positive things to say about me?"

"I don't know. You tell me." A tense standoff ensued. "At the very least he might be able to recommend some other people I can speak with, since you haven't," Sinead said eventually.

"That's because there isn't anyone."

"Then it'll be a short trip for me, won't it?"

"Very short," Adam replied curtly.

"How did it go with the press?" Sinead asked, changing the subject.

"Same as always."

"Meaning?" God, Mr. Taciturn had returned. It was like pulling teeth to get him to talk tonight.

"They ask me about the ref's call, I say, 'I don't think it was a penalty, but the refs have a tough job out there.' They ask me about how the team is playing, I say, 'We're really starting to come together as a unit, but we're not there yet, and we have to step things up if we want to contend for the Cup.'"

"No one asked about the lawsuit?"

Adam looked annoyed. "None of the local reporters bring it up anymore, since all I say is, 'Sorry, I can't talk about it.' Sometimes a visiting reporter brings it up, but I just say the same thing. Now, are you done quizzing *me*?"

Sinead was taken aback by his antipathy. "I wasn't quizzing you. I was just making conversation." She paused, waiting for a response. There was none, just a poker-faced stare. Obviously he'd rethought their banter of a few nights back and regretted it.

"I should get going," she said politely. She was in no mood to play "Get the sullen hockey player to talk."

"I'll be in touch soon," she told him.

Adam's expression softened for a moment. "Thanks for coming to the game."

Thanks for throwing me a bone, Sinead thought. "No problem. I know it was important to you that I see how the game is played."

Adam looked uncomfortable. "Yeah, well, thanks again."

Sinead watched him disappear back into the chattering crowd, curious to see if he stopped to talk with anyone else. He didn't. He nodded a couple of times in acknowledgment of some people, and then he was gone. Sinead took a long slug from her water bottle. She was relieved the conversation was over, but was disappointed as well as surprised that it hadn't gone the way she thought it would. So much for "greasing the wheels" with "casual conversation."

She found Quinn, told him she was leaving, and made her way outside Met Gar to hail a cab. She wondered where Adam had gone to and then chastised herself for it. *He's your client, Sinead. What he's doing right now is immaterial and irrelevant to the case.*

She closed her eyes and let the cab take her home.

7

Sinead wasn't sure what to expect of Claresholm, population 3,200. Adam's hometown was on the fringe of the Rocky Mountains. She knew it had six restaurants and one traffic light. And she knew Adam wasn't happy she was here.

She'd rented a car at the airport fifty miles away. Since she lived in the city and rarely got to be behind the wheel, she loved driving through Alberta's rolling, open ranch country. It was breathtaking. She'd booked herself into the Bluebird Motel, dubbed "Alberta's Best Kept Secret." It had more of a country inn feel to it than a motel; her room was cozy and antique-filled, with a large brass bed covered with a handmade patchwork quilt.

It was late afternoon. Sinead wasn't seeing Adam's brother, Rick, until tomorrow morning. She'd told Oliver about her conversation with Adam after the hockey game, and how antagonistic he'd been toward her about her going up to Claresholm. "Skeletons, dude, skeletons," was Oliver's pronouncement.

Kicking off her shoes, Sinead lay down on the bed and closed her eyes. She didn't know if she had the energy to go out and eat dinner, especially since she always felt so conspicuous dining alone. People in New York did it all the time: sat at a table reading a book or the newspaper. Sinead had never quite gotten the hang of it. Anytime she had to dine solo, she finished her meal as quickly as possible and left. She thought about Adam, checking out the Wild Hart on his own. Her mind kept circling back to his displeasure at her being here. She also found herself thinking about his broken engagement. Maybe the woman in question couldn't take how little he talked or expressed emotion. Actually, that wasn't fair to say. She didn't know him well enough to know if he was like that in private. "We wanted different things." God, how many times had she used that all-purpose term when people asked about her divorce? Still, she couldn't help but wonder about what kind of woman Adam would have been with.

Eager for distraction, Sinead grabbed her laptop from the foot of the bed, thankful the room had Wi-Fi. She'd be able to keep on top of her e-mail messages and look over the notes she'd gathered for Adam's case. She decided she'd order room service and make an early night of it. She wanted to be well rested when she talked to Rick Perry in the morning.

* * *

Sinead's rental car crawled along Eighth Street SW in "downtown" Claresholm, looking for the small, pale blue ranch where Adam's brother lived with his wife and two kids. She'd been so certain last night that she'd sleep well because she was so exhausted. Instead, she spent a good portion of the night awake, worrying about her conversation with Rick. What if she'd come up here for nothing?

The house was smaller than she expected, with a

mud-splashed pickup truck parked in the drive. Sinead had been careful to dress well but not too well. Too business-like, and they might be intimidated; too casual, and they wouldn't take her seriously as a professional.

She got out of the car, and immediately a dog started barking inside the house. The dog was shushed, and the front door opened. Standing there was a man who resembled Adam, if Adam let himself go: slightly overweight, but big and solid. A little boy and girl peeked out from behind him impishly. Sinead smiled, and they disappeared back into the house, giggling.

"You must be Sinead," the man said, his Canadian accent slightly thicker than Adam's. He extended his hand. "I'm Rick."

"Nice to meet you," said Sinead. "I really appreciate your talking to me today."

"Adam's not too thrilled about it, but I want to make sure he gets a fair deal."

"Exactly."

Sinead was ushered into the living room. It was small but neat, end tables littered with family pictures, a worn, green leather couch opposite a big-screen TV. The boy and girl came sliding back into the room on the wooden floor.

"This is Dylan and Carrie," said Rick.

"Hi," Sinead said, friendly.

"Hi!" Dylan replied, running off to join his sister, who'd already slid away.

"They're sweet," said Sinead. "How old are they?"

"Four and six. Adam's godfather to both of them."

"That's nice."

Rick looked uncomfortable as he stuck his hands in the back pockets of his faded jeans. "Uh, can I get you anything? Coffee? Tea?"

"Coffee would be great."

Rick gestured at the couch. "Sit down. I'll be back in

a minute." He started to leave, then turned back. "D'you mind if my wife sits in with us?"

"No, that would be great. Anything she can contribute would be helpful."

Rick nodded and continued on to the kitchen. A second later, Carrie's head popped out from around the corner. Sinead winked at her. "Hi, Carrie."

The small blonde girl entered the room shyly. "Daddy says you're here to talk about Uncle Adam."

"That's right."

"Are you his girlfriend?"

Sinead flushed. "No. Just a friend."

"Wanna see me pirouette?"

"That would be great," Sinead enthused, trying to ignore the small ache spreading through her chest. *I want a child. I want a little girl who peeks out from around corners and pirouettes.*

"Ta-da!" Carrie said with a bow when she was finished.

Sinead clapped enthusiastically. "That was terrific!"

"I know. I'm really good."

With that she darted away.

Sinead went back to her computer, reviewing her questions for Rick. He returned holding two mugs of coffee, accompanied by a tall, svelte, tired-looking blonde.

"Hi, I'm Susie," she said with a friendly smile.

"Sinead."

Rick handed Sinead her mug. "Hope the coffee's okay. I know you must be used to Starbucks."

"Rick," Susie admonished under her breath.

Sinead took a sip of the coffee. "It's very nice."

Rick sat down on the couch while Susie settled in the leather recliner opposite. Once again Sinead was struck by how strong Rick's resemblance was to Adam.

"How was your flight?" Susie asked.

"Fine."

"You ever been anyplace this rural before?" Rick asked.

"The town in Ireland where my parents grew up is pretty small."

"Huh."

Sinead couldn't escape the feeling that he was suspicious of her. Perhaps it was a family trait.

"Probably hard for you to believe Adam grew up here," Rick continued casually.

"I don't know Adam well enough to have formed that opinion," said Sinead. "Which is why I'm here."

Rick sighed heavily. "Well, let's get this show on the road."

"Do you mind if I record our conversation?"

"Why'd you need to do that?"

"So I'm not distracted typing while I interview. And it allows me to quote you with complete accuracy if I need to."

"Okay," he reluctantly agreed.

"Tell me about Adam's childhood."

"Not much to tell. I'm four years older than Adam. We were born and raised here." He paused, taking a sip of coffee. "Our mother was a housewife; our dad was an autoworker."

"Rick's an autoworker, too," Susie added proudly.

Rick shot his wife a dirty look. "*Was* an autoworker," he corrected bitterly. "I was laid off about a year ago." He paused.

"Anyway, I followed in Dad's footsteps, but Adam went the hockey route."

"Meaning . . ." Sinead coaxed.

"One of the ways to get out of a tiny town like this is by making it to the pros. Which Adam did when he was just eighteen."

"You didn't play hockey?"

"Oh, I played," said Rick. "But not well enough. Not like Adam. No one played like Adam."

Sinead ignored the resentfulness in his voice and pressed on. "Was Adam well liked?"

"Oh yeah, everyone loved Adam," said Susie. "Did he tell you he donated the money for the new hockey rink?"

"No, he didn't."

"It was completely anonymous."

Sinead's ears pricked up. "Anonymous? Can you tell me about it?"

Rick looked distinctly unenthusiastic.

"It'd be really helpful."

Rick looked put-upon. "All right. Well, obviously Susie and I knew about it, and the town council. But one of Adam's stipulations for the donation was that it be anonymous."

"Why?"

"Adam doesn't like to draw attention to himself. He's a pretty private guy."

No kidding, Sinead thought. The humility of Adam's action surprised her. He sure as hell had no humility when it came to being a hockey player.

"No one's figured it out?" Sinead asked.

"They probably have, but no one says anything about it. They know how he is, and they respect him."

"What was Adam like growing up?"

Rick looked lost. "I don't know. He was just Adam."

"Was he shy? Was he popular?"

"Not shy, just private. Kept to himself. My parents used to joke that he didn't say his first words until he was ten."

Sinead smiled at this. She could picture it, quiet Adam, concentrating on hockey.

"How old was Adam when he started playing hockey?"

Rick rubbed his chin thoughtfully. "Four, I guess. Four or five. That's when all of us start. Coaches started to come watch him when he was twelve. He knew pretty early he'd be getting out of here."

Sinead was dying to explore Rick's unmistakable strain of envy: *Couldn't you have left, too? Why did you stay?* She decided to avoid what was obviously a very sore spot.

"Was he always a hard hitter on the ice?"

Rick paused. "Yeah. I guess you could say that."

"It's what he was known for," Susie added.

"I have to ask. Did he ever get in trouble with the law?" Sinead had already asked Adam, but she wanted to double-check.

Rick snorted. "Saint Adam? No. Wait. Yeah, once: he got a speeding ticket when he was seventeen."

"What would you say are Adam's best qualities?"

"Generosity," Susie said immediately.

Rick looked irritated.

"It is," Susie insisted.

"Hardworking," Rick said. "He's always busted his ass." He took a sip of coffee. "Focused. Knew what he wanted early on, and went for it."

"Loyal," Susie continued. She paused. "He's great with kids."

"Really?" Sinead couldn't hide her surprise.

"Oh yeah. Our kids adore him. He can be very imaginative and silly when he wants to be."

Adam Perry? Silly? Sinead couldn't wrap her mind around it. She knew he had a somewhat dry sense of humor, but silly? She'd pay to see that.

"What would you say are Adam's flaws?"

"Adam has flaws?" Rick mocked.

"Don't be a jerk," Susie murmured.

Sinead sipped her coffee, waiting patiently.

Rick's eyes flickered with annoyance. "Like I said before, he can be distant."

"Aloof?" Sinead confirmed.

Susie bit her lip. "Aloof might be too strong a word. He's just cautious about who he lets in."

"Can you think of anyone else here in town I should talk to?"

"Nope," said Rick. He stood up abruptly. "Nice to meet you, Sinead. If I can do anything else that might help Adam, give me a shout."

"Will do."

He disappeared into the back of the house.

Susie looked embarrassed. "I'm sorry. Adam is a touchy subject for him."

"Why's that?"

Susie lowered her voice. "Adam's been helping us out since Rick lost his job. It's been hard on him; Rick's a proud man, and for his little brother to be paying some of the bills—he's embarrassed. It makes him feel like a loser."

Susie was looking at Sinead with interest. "You married? Kids?"

"Divorced," Sinead replied. "No kids."

"Well, maybe one day." Susie looked discomfited. "If that's what you want," she amended quickly.

"It is."

Why was she telling Susie private info she was usually so reluctant to give out? Greasing the wheels, she told herself. Plus it wasn't like she could say, "It's none of your business," after the woman had been gracious enough to let her into her home and ply her with questions. And she liked Susie. She could tell she cared about Adam, and she was probably one of the few people Adam trusted.

Sinead put her tape recorder in her shoulder bag and stood. "Thank you so much for your time. I really appreciate it."

"Oh, it was no problem. Again, I apologize if Rick seemed abrupt." She hesitated. "He's a little bit envious of Adam's success, and sometimes it comes out. It'll sort itself out," she continued, walking Sinead to the door. "They're very close, and it means a lot to Rick and me that Adam loves our kids and is so good to them."

"I have to admit, I was a little surprised when you told me Adam got silly with them. I just can't picture it."

"It's not a side of him many people have seen. I have a DVD from last Christmas if you'd like to see it."

"I'd love to." Sinead felt like she was doing something sneaky, but there was no way she was going to pass on footage of Adam Perry being silly.

Susie grabbed a laptop off an end table. In one minute, the computer was purring itself back to life. A few clicks later, there it was, the image of Adam sitting on the floor of his brother's house, letting Carrie make up his face.

"You have to have lipstick, Uncle Adam," Carrie insisted quite solemnly.

"Am I gonna look like Katy Perry when you're done?"

"Yup."

He started singing the chorus of Perry's "Hot 'N Cold" in a high-pitched voice, causing his niece to collapse in a heap of giggles.

Sinead's mouth hung open. "Oh. My. God. This is unbelievable."

"Oh, there's more."

Susie fast-forwarded to footage of Adam with Dylan. Adam was juggling three hockey pucks while singing "Oh, Canada." He taught Dylan to juggle, even though Dylan wanted to quit every time he messed up. But Adam was patient and encouraging, even with Carrie hanging off his leg begging him to do ballet with her, which he eventually did.

Susie put the computer to sleep. "That's the Adam we know and love."

"Wow." Sinead was beyond surprised. She was stunned.

"He's a good guy," Susie said warmly. "A really, really good guy."

"Yes, I can see that." She squeezed Susie's hand. "Thanks so much."

"I'll give you my cell number," Susie said conspiratorially. "That way, if you have any more questions, you can just ask me and bypass Mr. Crabby Bones."

"Thanks again, Susie."

"Oh, anytime. Anything to help Adam."

* * *

Sinead backed down the drive, taking *all* of it in. So, the only skeletons in Mr. Big Bruiser Hockey Player's closet were positive: financing the new rink and helping his brother out. That was good, though she wished he'd told her himself; it would have saved her the trip to Alberta. Even so, at least she'd gotten the information. She was slowly getting a sense of who Adam was: a somewhat enigmatic, hardworking guy whom others respected. Someone who'd known early in life what he wanted and went for it, who didn't need to be lauded for his generosity, who valued family. Someone to whom she was becoming attracted despite his being reserved. How could she not find it attractive, when she herself was the same way outside of work?

She was just about to pull away from the curb when Susie flew out the front door, waving her arms.

"Wait!"

Sinead rolled down her window. "What's up?"

"Have you talked to Ray yet?"

"Who's Ray?"

"Ray Milne. Adam's best friend. You should definitely talk to him."

Adam has a best friend? Who he conveniently forgot to mention to me?

"Could I have his number?"

"Give me a minute; I'll get it for you."

Susie ran back into the house. All Sinead could hear in her head was Oliver saying, *Skeletons, dude, skeletons.*

"Here you go," Susie said, out of breath.

"Thanks so much."

"Win that case, okay?"

"We will."

Though she suddenly had a strong feeling it might depend on Ray Milne.

8

Despite priding herself on her professionalism, Sinead was nervous when she called Ray. He was Adam's best friend; surely Adam had talked to him about the case, telling him about his female attorney whom he didn't quite trust.

Her fears were unfounded: she was greeted by a deep, warm voice at the other end of the line. At first he sounded slightly apprehensive about meeting her, but when Sinead pressed home gently that his input could help bolster Adam's case immensely, he agreed.

Driving down a rural road to Ray's, Sinead realized she really should visit her weekend house more. There was something about traveling under the moody blue sky and the way the wheat fields gave way to the mountain range in the distance that calmed her.

Ray's house was on a small dirt road off the highway. *Must be as social as Adam,* Sinead mused. She turned right onto the long, pitted, gravel drive, at the end of which was a small white ranch house. A blue van with a *Go Claresholm Hockey!* bumper sticker sat parked in front of the attached garage.

Sinead got out of the car, annoyed that the wind whipping across the fields sent her hair flying in ten different directions. The last thing she needed was to look unkempt and unprofessional. Luckily, she carried a ponytail holder with her at all times. She scraped her hair back and proceeded to the door.

The temporary calm she felt on her drive over was slowly transforming itself into unease. If it weren't for Susie, she'd never have known Ray existed. Why was that?

Sinead rang the bell, straightening her shoulders. A handsome, black-haired, blue-eyed man in an electric wheelchair appeared in the doorway.

"Ah, Sinead O'Brien, attorney-at-law," he said with a welcoming smile. "I'm Ray."

Sinead smiled politely, hoping it covered her anxiety. "I'm Sinead."

Ray pressed a button on the arm of his wheelchair so he could back up to let her in. Once inside, Sinead extended her hand to shake his and then realized, when he didn't raise his arm, that he was quadriplegic and couldn't shake hands. "Oh my God, I'm so sorry," she spluttered, mortified by her faux pas. Her face burned with embarrassment.

"No worries," Ray assured her smoothly. "Come on in."

The door closed behind them. It appeared to be controlled by some infrared device that detected when Ray was near and when he moved away.

"Have a seat," Ray offered, tilting his head in the direction of the couch.

Still feeling like an insensitive twit, Sinead sat down. She wanted to apologize again but decided to just let it go. He was probably used to dealing with people's thoughtlessness.

Sinead sat as Ray pressed another button on the arm of his wheelchair, propelling him closer to her. "I was surprised to hear from you."

"Maybe that's because I didn't even know you existed

until about an hour ago. Adam never said anything to me about having a best friend."

"Not surprised. Adam's not big on people digging into his personal life."

"That's putting it mildly. But I didn't know he was so generous. And loyal."

Sinead took a deep breath. "Ray, I really appreciate you letting me come out to see you, especially since you didn't expect it. But as I said on the phone, getting your insights into Adam's character could help the case immensely. The more complete a picture I can paint of him, the harder a time the prosecutor is going to have depicting him as some brainless, heartless hockey goon who doesn't care who he hurts."

Ray looked worried. "You really think the case will go to court?"

Sinead sighed. "I don't know. I hope not. In my opinion, it's an obvious ploy for reelection by the Philadelphia DA who's brought the charges. It's pure politicking."

Ray shook his head. "I hate that Adam's got this hanging over his head with all the stress he's already under."

"What stress?"

"Being the new captain of the Blades. They brought him in with the specific intent of helping whip the team into shape so they can take another run at the Cup. That's a helluva lot of pressure."

"I didn't know that."

"Not surprised. It's not like he talks about it. Just keeps his head down and does his job, you know."

"I know."

"Look, let's get you some water, and we'll continue talking."

"Sounds good."

Ray motored into the kitchen, where Sinead heard him talking to another man. A roommate? A few seconds later, he reappeared with a large man with a shaved head carrying a glass of water. "Hi," he said, "I'm Jasper, Ray's personal assistant."

Sinead rose to shake his hand. "Nice to meet you."

"You, too." He handed her the glass of water.

"Thanks."

"No problem." He looked at Ray. "We all set?"

"Yep."

Jasper turned back to Sinead. "Nice meeting you."

"Nice meeting you, too," said Sinead. She took a sip of water, watching Jasper disappear toward the back of the house. *Does he live here?* She wanted to ask but didn't. Too nosy.

"All right, Miss O'Brien. Fire away."

"When did you and Adam meet?" Sinead was genuinely interested.

"Playing on the Mites team," Ray said, looking sentimental. "We were seven. Even then Adam was a killer player."

Sinead winced. "Maybe not the best choice of words."

"Maybe not," Ray agreed ruefully. "But you know what I mean."

"Tell me what Adam was like growing up."

"Like I said, he was always a tough little bastard on the ice. We'd play one-on-one sometimes, and he always kicked my ass, which kinda pissed me off."

"Were other players afraid of him?"

"He made the opposition nervous, yeah. I mean he always had a reputation as a hard hitter. But he was always respected. And he was a generous player. Lots of times the coaches would want to play him constantly, but it made Adam uncomfortable. He wanted to make sure the guys on the second and third line got their ice time."

"Was he egotistical?"

"Not outwardly. But with me, yeah." Ray smiled fondly. "There was always friendly competition between us—you know, guy stuff: 'I'm gonna kick your ass, you're going down, you suck compared to me.' But he never trash-talked other players. Ever. It's just not his style."

"Was he shy?"

Rick looked thoughtful. "A little bit, when we were kids. By the time we were teenagers, he was pretty popular, even though he was kinda quiet. He had a lot of friends, mostly other hockey players."

Even though Sinead knew the basic chronology of Adam's life—Claresholm, the minors in Edmonton, NHL draft pick at eighteen, playing for Tampa then New York—she still wanted Ray's take on it all. Five minutes with him and he was already proving to be a treasure trove of useful information.

"So after high school," Sinead continued, glancing up at Ray, "Adam continued on to the minors?"

"Actually, we both did. Adam went to Edmonton, and I went to Calgary."

Sinead was intrigued. "That must have been interesting, playing against each other."

"Hell yeah," Ray said with a grin. "We got into some good scrapes."

Sinead hesitated a moment, unsure if what she wanted to ask next was inappropriate. She decided she would; the worst that could happen would be Ray telling her to mind her own business. "May I ask you a somewhat personal question?"

"In the minors," Ray supplied without hesitation. "I was paralyzed while playing in the minors."

Sinead looked down, shamefaced. "I'm sorry. I hope I wasn't staring at you or—"

"Don't apologize," Ray admonished gently. "It's natural to be curious."

Sinead looked up. "What happened?"

"Adam put a fearsome hit on me, and I went headfirst into the boards. Suffered a major fracture of the fifth vertebra in my neck. Paralyzed me from the chest down."

Sinead felt as though someone had just punched all the air out of her torso. Ray had rattled off the facts as effortlessly as someone reciting the alphabet or reading from a script. She was at a total loss for what to say. Finally, she pulled herself together. "Adam did this to you?"

"Yeah." No bitterness, no rancor.

"I . . ." Sinead paused. She was still reeling with shock. "How can you two still be best friends?"

"Because it's the nature of the game," Ray said simply. "It's not like he did it on purpose. He was just doing his job. It was totally random; it could have happened to anyone, and it could have been anyone else making the hit. It's not something players like to think about, but injuries happen. In this case, the players in question just happened to be Adam and me."

"Weren't you angry?"

"Shit, yeah. But not at Adam. I was just angry that it happened to me. Adam took it worse than I did."

Sinead still couldn't think straight. "He . . ."

"Took it hard. Still takes it hard. It changed him."

"How?"

"Made him withdraw."

"Not on the ice!"

"No, not on the ice, which is a good thing. He wanted to, but I managed to talk him out of it. Told him I'd be pissed livid if he did. Like I said, he was just doing his job."

"But he shattered your dreams."

"Not on purpose," Ray replied, unruffled.

"Wasn't it hard for you to see him go off and become this big NHL star?"

"Yeah, at first. It was what we'd both been working toward our whole lives, and I was envious he was getting to do it. He almost didn't."

"What?"

"He was so distraught after it happened he talked about

quitting hockey altogether. Said he couldn't stand the unfairness of him getting to play when I couldn't. I told him not to be an idiot; it would be a total waste if *both* of us couldn't do what we both love best. He had an obligation to get his ass out there and play for both of us."

Sinead blinked back tears. "And he did?"

"What do you think?"

"Truthfully? I don't know what to think right now. This is a huge part of Adam's history, and he's said nothing to me about it at all. It's like he didn't want me to know about you." Sinead was puzzled. "And no one here in Claresholm has ever said anything to anyone?"

"Adam is a hero here," Ray said proudly. "Everyone here wants to protect his privacy—and mine."

"Would you mind telling me more about how the accident affected him?"

"Well, like I said, he wanted to change his style of play, but I talked him out of that. The one thing I could *not* talk the stubborn bastard out of was helping me out."

"What do you mean?"

"Adam paid for this house to be built. He pays Jasper's salary, and he pays for the van. We have socialized medicine up here; it's not perfect but it's okay. He also pays for me to see private doctors if I need to." Ray looked pained. "At first I was like, 'Fuck off, man, I don't need your pity.' It really pissed me off. But eventually I saw that he *needed* to do it: not for me, but for himself. The guilt of it was overshadowing everything, even our friendship. So I let him do it."

"Does he . . . are you his only friend?"

"I'm not sure. I know I'm his only friend who is—was—a hockey player. After what happened, he pulled back from making close friends with any other players. He said he wouldn't be able to take it emotionally if he hurt someone he cared about on the ice. He's very guarded about who he lets in, both on and off the ice."

"That's abundantly clear, believe me."

"He's a great guy," Ray continued. "Always has been. A great hockey player, too. True to the way the game should be played. No wonder the NHL commissioner is on his ass."

Sinead leaned forward. *"What?"* Great. More information Adam had neglected to mention. She was going to read him the riot act when she got back to New York.

Ray frowned. "Every couple of years, the NHL brass gets a bug up their asses about trying to change their image by making the sport 'less violent.' The commissioner asked Adam to tone down his game."

"How did Adam react?"

A wide smile split Ray's face. "He told him to go fuck himself, in so many words. His GM and coach are behind him one hundred percent."

Sinead smiled politely as she imagined herself trying not to yell at Adam in her office. "Well, that's good." She took a big gulp of water. "That's all I can think of right now."

"You know, I actually enjoyed talking to you," said Ray, sounding surprised.

"Why wouldn't you?"

"Well, first there's the fact that Adam is probably going to blow a gasket when I tell him we talked."

"Blow a gasket at me? Or you?"

"Both, probably. And I was worried that I'd feel on edge. Adam told me you were kind of uptight."

Sinead's jaw set. "Those were his actual words?"

Ray looked panicked. "Uh . . ."

"Tell me. I promise I won't bust you."

Ray still hesitated. "He said you were kinda snooty. That you go digging around for facts about him, but you don't want to tell him about yourself."

"Why does he need to know about me? I'm his attorney, not his friend."

"True. I hope this doesn't offend you, but you're as good-looking as he said you were."

"Surprised, not offended." Sinead covered her momentary thrill as she concentrated on finishing her water and stood. "Thanks so much, Ray."

"When you heading back to New York?"

"Tomorrow morning."

"I coach the peewee team here in town. You should come watch the game tonight. My boys are on fire."

"Maybe I will," Sinead said. She almost committed her earlier faux pas of extending her hand to shake his, but she remembered in time and did not embarrass herself.

Ray wheeled over to the front door with her. "Drive safe now," he said as the door opened for her.

"Thanks again, Ray," Sinead said gratefully. "This has really been an immense help."

"No problem. Call me if Adam gives you a hard time. I'll set him straight."

Sinead laughed. "I'd pay to see that."

"Oh, it'd be ugly, believe me. Bye now."

"Bye, Ray."

The wind had died down to just a breeze. Sinead loved how fresh the air smelled, how pure the sun looked in the distant sky. Maybe she'd drive around for a while before going back to the hotel and reorganizing her materials.

Sinead wasn't a big believer in fate, but right now, she couldn't shake the feeling that it had been fate she found out about Ray. Of course, Adam wouldn't see it that way, the stubborn, uncooperative, maddening, caring, compassionate, handsome pain in the ass.

Ray thought *he'd* be the one to set Adam straight if need be? Wrong: that was going to be Sinead's first order of business Monday morning. And if her client didn't like it, that was just too damn bad.

9

"*Thank you for* taking time from your busy schedule to meet with me."

Sinead tried not to sound too sarcastic as she motioned for Adam to sit. His expression matched his voice on the phone last night when she'd called to set up a meeting: wary and annoyed. Sinead knew Adam was hoping that when he said the only time he could meet was seven a.m., she'd back off. Clearly he'd yet to grasp how seriously she took her job. If he'd said two a.m., she'd have been here. The sooner he figured out she was the one calling the shots, and that he couldn't keep her at arm's length any longer, the better.

Sinead had carefully applied her makeup to cover the dark circles under her eyes before leaving her apartment. She'd spent the night tossing and turning, worrying about slamming against a wall of resistance and resentfulness when she met with Adam. She also realized, as she watched the hours tick by, that Oliver had been right all along: she wanted Adam to like her. This new, somewhat unnerving realization at three a.m. ruined any chance of sleep.

Sometimes Oliver took a nap in the middle of the day after a sleepless night. Sinead decided that if she was still drooping after lunch, she might try it to see if it worked. In the meantime, she'd rely on her old faithful friend, caffeine.

Adam sat down. "How did your fact-finding mission go?" he asked. The displeasure in his voice was unnerving. *Do your job. Focus on the job.*

"Things went well."

Adam didn't respond.

"I didn't realize Claresholm was so small," Sinead continued conversationally.

"Mmm."

No chatting today, Sinead thought. *Not encouraging.* She sat down, crossing her legs. "We need to talk about my visit."

Adam waved a hand disdainfully. "Talk away."

"Let's start with Rick."

"Who you could have easily talked to over the phone."

"But then I'd never have learned you were helping pay his bills or that you were the one who footed the bill for the town's new ice rink."

Adam scowled. "Rick told you that?"

"No, his wife did."

"Shit."

"This info could be important to making your case, Adam."

"It's irrelevant."

"No, it's very relevant. Why didn't you tell me about the rink, at least? Everyone in Claresholm knows you're the one who paid for it. And while we're at it, why did you pay for it anonymously?"

"I did it because I wanted the focus on the rink, not on me as some big philanthropist. End of story."

"It shows you have a big heart. That you care about community." Adam gave her a dirty look, but Sinead continued, undeterred. "I don't care how much you hate it. I'm using the info."

Adam looked angry. "Even if I don't want you to."

"Even if you don't want me to," replied Sinead, holding her ground. "I'm building this case to *win*, and if you don't want to help me, fine. Why you're cutting off your nose to spite your face is beyond me. You are, without a doubt, the most uncooperative client I've ever had in my life."

"Is that so?"

"Yes. And I don't appreciate it."

Adam actually looked embarrassed. "I'm sorry."

"Prove it."

Adam lifted an eyebrow in surprise. "Someone's getting tough."

"I've always been tough. You just haven't wanted to deal with it."

Adam looked impressed. "I admire your tenacity. And your self-confidence."

Sinead tried to ignore the little voice in her head saying, *He does like me!* But the voice abruptly shut up when Adam, still smiling, said, "As your client, I forbid you to use the info that I'm helping Rick."

Sinead was taken aback. "You forbid me?"

"You can use the rink, if you have to. I think that's enough."

"And I think that if your case goes to court, the fact that you value family can only help," Sinead countered.

"You're being insensitive."

Sinead cocked her head, surprised. "How so?"

"Rick is a proud man. Think how he's going to feel when it gets out that his little brother is helping him out financially. He'll never forgive me. Our relationship is already rocky. You use that, and I'll lose him."

"I didn't think about that," Sinead admitted. "All right. I'll leave it out. For now."

"Thank you," Adam said, looking relieved. "I appreciate it."

"You're welcome."

For the first time since they'd "chatted" at her family's bar, Sinead felt like he was letting down his guard just a bit.

Adam was staring at her quizzically. "Can I ask you a question?"

"Depends on what the question is, Mr. Perry." Shit, did that sound flirty? She hoped it didn't.

"Do I get any say in the info you intend to use for my case? Because as you may have deduced by now, I may not want you to reveal certain things."

"Even if they're things that could keep you out of jail? Or help insure your career doesn't end?" Sinead leaned toward him. "I know what I'm doing, Adam," she reiterated, hoping to reassure him. "I assume Ray called you after I left."

Adam snorted. "Of course he did."

"You look resentful."

"Picking up on that, are you?"

Sinead bristled. "No need to be sarcastic. In my defense, let me start by pointing out that Ray could have turned me down when I asked to talk to him. So if you're angry, be angry at him."

"I am. Actually, pissed off would be more accurate."

Sinead wanted to knock on the side of Adam's head to see if it was hollow. He was being deliberately difficult. "Don't you understand how significant it is that he spoke with me, even though he knew you wouldn't like it? That says something."

"Really? What does it say?"

"It says he loves you. He doesn't want to see you get into legal trouble."

Adam shrugged. "That doesn't make me any less pissed off at him."

"You want to talk about pissed off?" Sinead returned, trying to keep her temper in check. "I'm pissed at *you*. I asked you back in the beginning if there were any skeletons in your closet, and you said no. Sorry, Adam, but paralyzing your best friend is a pretty big skeleton."

"It's no one's business," Adam maintained stubbornly.

Sinead suppressed a growl of frustration. "It's *my* business." She paused. "Ray told me everything," she said quietly.

Adam tensed. "What does that mean?"

"How you wanted to stop playing after the accident, because you thought it wasn't fair you'd be the only one doing what you both dreamed of doing. He said you contemplated changing your style of play, but he talked you out of it." She held his angry gaze. "He even told me how you help him out."

Adam glared at her. "All of that stays between Ray and me, okay?"

"He was helping me get a better handle on who you are, Adam."

"I'm the brutal bastard who paralyzed him," Adam snapped. "What else is there to know?"

Sinead was taken aback by his self-loathing.

"He doesn't hold it against you. You *know* that."

"He's a saint. If it were me, I'd hold it against him, believe me."

"No, you wouldn't."

"Oh really?" Adam looked scornful. "Tell me more about myself, Counselor."

"I found out a lot about you this weekend, Adam." Sinead edged a few inches toward him, affected by how distressed he looked. The urge to comfort him was strong. "I found out you're generous. And loyal." Sinead paused thoughtfully. "You know, no one I've interviewed has had one bad thing to say about you."

"I'm sure you could find a few if you kept digging."

"I'm sure, but the point is, people think you're a great guy. What Ray said about the incident—that you were just doing your job, that it could happen to any player at any time—is the foundation of our argument. The fact that he's your best friend and holds no malice toward you is huge."

Adam looked disturbed. "Please don't tell me you want to put Ray up on the stand."

"If a jury heard about all you do for him—"

"They'll think I'm just trying to assuage my guilt," Adam finished for her bitterly. "And they'd be right."

Sinead moved close enough to put a tentative hand on his knee. "I can't imagine what it was like for you," she said sympathetically. "What it still must be like for you."

"Screw what it's like for me! Think about what it's like for him." Adam scrubbed his hands over his face. He looked exhausted, and the day hadn't even begun.

"Ray said it turned you into a loner."

"Look," Adam said sharply. "I refuse to go through that again. Keeping a distance is fine by me."

"And what about people who don't play hockey? Do you ever get close to them?"

Adam looked skeptical. "Do you get close to people outside of work?"

Sinead was momentarily caught off guard. "Uh, my family—"

"Doesn't count. Do you have *any* friends?"

"I'm very close to Oliver," Sinead retorted.

"Doesn't count. He's your colleague."

"It counts," Sinead insisted. "Why do you want to know?"

"Turnabout's fair play, as I told you that night we were at your parents' pub. I give you personal info, you give me personal info."

"We've already exchanged information."

"Well, I want more."

Sinead licked her lips nervously. The conversation had veered off Professional Avenue and was now driving slowly down Personal Info Lane. Which was okay, if it helped draw Adam out, or so she told herself. "Like you, I'm very private. The more someone knows about me, the more vulnerable I feel, and I don't like feeling vulnerable. I'm a control freak.

"I can relate to your trying to avoid personal ties," Sinead continued. "My divorce was a very drawn-out, painful affair. It made me very apprehensive about getting involved in something that could cause me deep personal pain."

"That's why you stick to Oliver."

"Yes."

"By deep personal pain, I assume you're talking about a relationship."

Sinead felt uncomfortable. "Yes."

"Don't you ever get lonely?" Before she could balk, she realized she had asked him the same question, and he was now firing it back at her.

"Don't you?"

Adam looked stoic. "Sometimes. But that's the trade-off I had to make."

"You *chose* to make. With hockey players. I don't see why you have to be walled off from other people."

"I'm not."

"Whatever you say."

Adam looked amused. "Ray told me you were annoyed I'd described you as uptight and prissy."

"Ray told *me* you said I was good-looking."

"You are," Adam said bluntly.

Sinead's face felt hot. "Well, thank you," she murmured.

Sinead tried to ignore the quiet hum of sexual tension building in the room.

"We appear not to be discussing my case anymore," Adam noted, his gaze so direct it was unnerving.

"Yes," Sinead agreed, looking down at her lap.

The tension climbed as Adam leaned over and put his

index finger beneath her chin, tilting her face up so he could press his lips to her mouth. *This is wrong,* thought Sinead. But her body disagreed.

She was shocked when he abruptly pulled away. "I'm sorry. That was completely inappropriate."

"It's all right," she assured him.

"I'm not sure it is. It's probably best we pretend that never happened."

Sinead nodded in agreement, even though she didn't know which side was up right now.

Adam stood up. "I should go."

Sinead couldn't believe how cool and collected he looked. She wondered if inside, his brain and heart were sparring the way hers were.

"Are we done here?" he asked.

"Yes. I mean, for now." Sinead forced herself back into professional mode. "If you can think of any other information that would help your case, *tell me.*"

"I will. I can find my way out."

"All right. Bye now, Adam."

"Bye."

It seemed to take him forever to close the door. Sinead sat there, trying—and failing—to tease apart the tangled threads of her emotions. A line had been crossed, one that shouldn't have been. But did he really think she could pretend it never happened? Would *he* be able to forget?

She had to find out.

10

"Go for it."

That was Anthony's advice after Adam told him about what had happened between him and Sinead. They were in Anthony's living room, and Anthony had just trounced Adam in a game of Wii tennis. "You only won because I'm distracted, pal," said Adam. When Anthony asked him about what, Adam spilled.

"That's your answer?" Adam asked, mopping sweat off his face.

"Yeah. What other answer is there? You kissed her. She let you. Obviously there's something there."

Adam grimaced. "Thing is, I told her we should probably pretend it never happened."

"That is cold, bro."

"I know. And it's hypocritical. Because I sure as hell can't forget it happened."

"Then ask her out."

"She's my *attorney*."

"Yeah, we've established that, Einstein. So what? What's the worst that can happen? You find out you're not compatible?"

"It could damage her career. Plus we'd still have to see each other if we broke up before the case was settled. It would be awkward."

"Oh, boo-hoo," Anthony mocked, tossing a handful of peanuts down his throat. "Like that type of thing doesn't happen all the time. Jesus, Mary, and Saint Joseph—you're adults."

Adam plucked thoughtfully on his lower lip. "True."

"Look, man, you said she's smart, good-looking . . ."

"But she's also a little intense."

"Perfect for you! For your first date, you guys could have a competition, you know? Sit around and see who's more intense."

"Fuck off, Anthony."

Anthony threw a shot of water down his throat. "Just ask her out for a drink or something, Adam. If you can't do it flat out because you're too much of a coward, then we can do a double date: me and Vivi, and you and Sinead. Tell her it's to prove that you do have friends who aren't hockey players."

"Right." Why hadn't he thought of that?

"There you go, then. Anything else, moron?"

"Where would we go?"

"You leave that to your buddy here, pally," Anthony said enigmatically. "Trust me: a good time will be had by all."

"Okay. I put this in your hands, though I don't know why." He rotated his wrists, loosening them up. "You find out about that Stooges convention in L.A. in July?"

"I'm still waiting on info. But we are so there."

"Damn straight."

A Stooges convention. What would Sinead think of that? Then again, she liked jazz. Who likes jazz, for chrissakes? He had her there.

"We still on for Wednesday at my place?" Adam continued, lobbing an imaginary tennis ball against the wall. "Pizza and the second series of the show?"

"Yeah." Anthony frowned. "Mikey wants in."

"No prob."

"Forget it. He's not worthy. Plus, I want to torture him by not letting him come."

"As long as you make it clear to him that I don't share your feelings, knock yourself out."

"No problemo," said Anthony.

Anthony was right, Adam decided: a double date would prove to Sinead that he was capable of getting close to people. He was going for it. Let the chips fall where they may.

11

"Oh. A karaoke bar. I had no idea."

Adam smiled weakly as he ushered Sinead into Wally's, a karaoke bar on East Fifty-fourth Street. He'd always wanted to try karaoke but was too shy and far too uptight to risk making an ass of himself. The last thing he needed was Sinead mocking him. He'd leave the singing to Ant and Vivi.

Sinead sounded surprised when he told her he was going to prove he had friends outside the world of hockey. He made sure his invitation carried a hint of a challenge, which was why he wasn't surprised when she agreed to come out with him. Never in a million years did he imagine they were going to a karaoke bar.

They were greeted at the door by a smiling Asian maître d' to whom Anthony had given his name. Adam squinted down a dimly lit, bricked hallway. He assumed Anthony had arranged for one of the private karaoke rooms, and started toward the back. The maître d' stopped him. "Your friend is over there," he said, pointing to Anthony and Vivi, sitting at a small table in the densely packed bar.

Adam pressed his lips together grimly. "Right."

He scoped out the room: speakers in each corner, as well as the massive high-def TV at the back of the tiny stage. There was also a TV along one side of the stage where, Adam supposed, each "singer" could read the words of the songs they selected. Right now, a tipsy bleach blonde was singing Celine Dion's "I Will Always Love You." No one was laughing at her. In fact, the crowd was whistling and clapping, cheering her on. Momentary insanity gripped Adam as he thought, *Maybe I'll get up there for just one song.*

Adam felt sheepish as he glanced at Sinead, dressed casually in jeans and red scoop neck, looking fantastically sexy. "Sorry about this."

"No, no, it's fine," Sinead assured him quickly. She tore her eyes from the stage to look at him. "Really."

A big grin bisected Anthony's face as Adam and Sinead approached. "Welcome." Standing, he gestured at the walls covered in pale yellow wallpaper topped by a lime green bamboo pattern. "It doesn't get better than this, right?" Anthony's big, goofy grin returned as he turned to Sinead.

"Hello. I'm Anthony, Adam's non–hockey playing friend."

Sinead laughed quietly. "Nice to meet you."

"You, too."

Vivi rose. "I'm Vivi, Anthony's wife." She leaned over to kiss Sinead on both cheeks in the traditional French way of greeting, squeezing her hand.

Anthony clapped his hands together. "Why don't we have a few drinks, order some food, and then—sing!"

"Great idea," Adam said queasily. Drinks were fine. But there was no way he was going to get up onstage.

* * *

Sinead glanced around the room nervously. Adam and Anthony had gone to get drinks, leaving her with Vivi, whose sweetness was apparent from the get-go.

"I'm so sorry about this," she said.

Sinead furrowed her brows. "Why?"

"Because my husband is an idiot. When Anthony told me we were all coming here, I said, 'That's no place to go for a first date; it will scare her away from Adam.' But oh! That stubborn ox wouldn't listen."

"Actually, it's not a date. Adam just wanted to prove to me he has friends who don't play hockey."

"Oh." Vivi looked surprised. "Anthony said it was a date."

"Adam and I are just friends."

"Ah. So you haven't had *The Three Stooges* inflicted on you yet."

"No, thank God."

Vivi shuddered. "Well, I hope you never do. It's sheer idiocy."

"I know. My brothers used to watch it."

"Hitting, punching, poking at each other's eyes—who would enjoy such a thing?" Vivi asked disdainfully.

"I agree completely."

Another singer took the stage, a short, raven-haired man of about thirty who launched into an exuberant version of "La Vida Loca," complete with dance moves. Vivi looked at Sinead, shaking her head. "Some people are very good, some . . . not so much."

"Have you ever done karaoke?" Sinead asked shyly.

Vivi's face lit up. "Of course! I love it! It's a wonderful way to unwind."

"I've always wanted to try it, but I'm too afraid of embarrassing myself."

"Don't be silly. No one cares."

"Even so, I don't think I can." Especially not in front of Adam. Oh, God. His laughter would be so loud it would puncture her eardrums. The thought was unendurable.

"Perhaps Adam will."

Sinead tried to imagine Adam up there singing. She

couldn't, although it was a sight she'd love to see. The potential to tease him would make it worth it.

* * *

"*When the moon* hits your eye like a big pizza pie, that's amore . . .'"

"That's Amore." It figures, Adam thought, watching his friend perform onstage. Italian this, Italian that . . . still, he did seem to be having a good time, though God knows Dean Martin had to be spinning in his grave.

Sinead leaned over to him. "He's not bad."

"No, he's okay," Adam tepidly agreed.

"When are you going up?" Sinead murmured.

"I'm not. When are you?"

"I'm not."

"Why not?" Adam asked.

"Why aren't you?" Sinead lobbed back.

"I asked you first."

Sinead looked flustered. "This is silly."

"I agree."

Sinead sipped her drink. "But really, why aren't you going up?"

Adam looked caught. "I have stage fright."

"What?" Sinead gave a barking laugh. "You perform in front of thousands of people almost every night of your life!"

"And you stand up in court and use words I don't even know the meaning of. That doesn't mean I want to stand up in a room full of strangers—"

Anthony had finished his turn onstage and arrived at the table in time to hear the end of their exchange. "Enough, you guys! You sound like squabbling children."

Adam felt like a jackass.

"You should both go up there. Together."

"Why?" Sinead sounded horrified.

"Because it's *fun*," Anthony reiterated. "And believe

me, you two are a couple who look like you need to have
fun." He turned to Vivi, who appeared to be glaring at him
because he was so pushy. "I believe we were just insulted,"
Sinead said to Adam, who looked as surprised as she was.

"Seems that way."

Sinead touched her cheeks worriedly. "Do I look un-
fun to you?"

Adam laughed. "You don't look un-fun—it's—"

"I'll go up if you go up," Sinead blurted.

Adam took his time answering, trying to assess if this
were some kind of trap. "All right," he said carefully.

"Together," Sinead amended. "We have to go up
together." The desperation in her voice touched him,
because he could identify with it.

"Okay."

Sinead looked surprised. "Really?"

Adam scowled. "I said okay, didn't I?"

"I figured we'd feel less stupid if we went up together,"
Sinead reasoned.

You got that right, thought Adam. At least he'd be making a moron of himself with her, not in front of her.

"I'll go sign us up, then."

                              *   *   *

When a woman singing "I Will Survive" finished massa-
cring the song, Sinead knew it was time for her and Adam
to hit the stage. He took her hand, and for that, she was
grateful. It was steadying, which was just what she needed
right about now as her stomach took on a will of its own.

She was doing a good job blocking out the audience
when Adam whispered, "You know that song we agreed
to sing?"

"Yes?" She'd kill him if he changed his mind. She'd
been singing it in her head for the past half hour.

"Let's ham it up. We're going to be making jerks of ourselves, anyway. Why not try to have a little fun?"

She searched Adam's face. Was he putting her on? No, he wasn't.

"All right," Sinead shakily agreed. She wondered if anyone singing karaoke had ever had a heart attack and died onstage before. *Wow,* she thought to herself. *You just might make history tonight.*

* * *

"That was a blast!"

Sinead stood in front of her apartment building with Adam, still exuberant after her stage debut. What an uptight jerk she'd been, afraid to sing karaoke! It was incredible fun, especially when you got to play Olivia Newton-John to Adam's John Travolta and belt out "You're the One That I Want." She was nervous the first few seconds, but then it disappeared and it was just she and Adam and adrenaline and laughter.

"It was," Adam agreed.

"If I tell you something, do you promise you won't laugh?"

"I won't laugh."

"I've always wanted to do karaoke."

Adam's eyes widened. "Me, too! But I've always been afraid of making an ass of myself."

"Me, too."

They laughed at the coincidence, but when they finished, a polite awkwardness seemed to take over. Sinead couldn't bear the tension of standing there with him, both of them watching and waiting to see what, if anything, would happen. She needed an out, so she began rubbing her forehead. "I hate to do this, but I've got a bit of a head ache."

"Oh." Adam looked mildly disappointed. "You gonna be okay?"

"Of course." Sinead squeezed his arm. "Well, I guess you really do have friends who don't play hockey."

Adam laughed lightly. "I really do."

"So, um, see you soon."

Before Adam even had a chance to reply, she was hurrying inside.

She knew she was being a coward. No, she was being a lying coward—and rude to boot. But ending the conversation abruptly put her back in control of a situation whose parameters were beginning to crack. And to Sinead, nothing was more important than control.

12

Sinead hated when her body betrayed her: she was so tense she had to take half a migraine pill before hopping into the cab to meet Adam. She supposed she deserved it, after pretending to have one last week when she didn't. What comes around goes around, as her Mother always used to say.

She'd been shocked when he'd called and said he had some info for her that might be useful. She was even *more* shocked when Adam suggested they meet for a drink rather than at her office. Her first impulse was to run to Oliver's office to tell him, like a pathetic wallflower who'd finally been asked to the dance by the homecoming king. She restrained herself, not wanting to admit to Oliver he'd been right all along. She'd die before she told him about the karaoke bar.

Sinead's heart sank as she walked through the door of Maxie's Supper Club (the place Adam had suggested), because it was packed. Crowds made her feel stifled. She worried about getting a headache. She worried about . . . everything. *Jesus God, what kept you up last night?* her father once teased her. *The plight of bumblebees in*

Australia? But she couldn't help it. It was who she was. She'd tried meditation but had to quit because she worried about doing it right. The only thing that relaxed her, *really* relaxed her, was spending time at her house in Bearsville. It was the one place she didn't bring work with her, the only place where she truly slept well. That was why she insisted on keeping it, rather than the apartment she and Chip had shared. Oliver was right: she'd probably have fewer headaches if she cut herself some slack. She had to get up to Bearsville soon; it had been too long.

She hoped Adam was already here. The thought of having to stand in a crowd three deep was not her idea of fun. Her gaze scoured the room; he was sitting at the far end of the bar, talking to someone in a Blades jersey. He looked uncomfortable. Sinead edged toward him, relieved when the fan slid off the stool next to Adam and she was able to sit.

"Hi," she said.

"Hey."

"Fan talking your ear off?"

"Yeah. I try to be accommodating, but sometimes it gets a little weird, having strangers recite your own career stats back at you. I gave him an autograph. That seemed to satisfy him."

Sinead wondered what it must be like to be in the public eye, never knowing where or when someone is going to come up to you. She supposed you just had to accept it as part of your job.

She glanced around the bar. "Pretty popular place," she observed, stating the obvious. God, she was a moron. "My sister used to come here a lot before she got married." Like he'd *care*?

"Yeah, I heard through the grapevine it was a good place to go." Adam looked dismayed. "I had no idea it would be packed like this, though. I'm not a fan of crowds."

Sinead was relieved. "Me, neither. Want to go somewhere else?"

"Sure. Any ideas?"

Sinead racked her brain, trying to think of places she'd heard Oliver mention. Of course, she was drawing a total blank. She shrugged her shoulders lamely. "No."

"Hold on." Adam pulled out his cell. Sinead heard him say he was "having a drink with his attorney" and did the person on the other end know a "good place where they could talk." It bothered her, his calling her "his attorney," even though she had no right to feel that way. Then again, they were meeting in a professional capacity.

Adam tucked the phone back in his jeans. "C'mon," he said, tilting his head in the direction of the door. "Anthony recommended a small place not far from here called Basilica. Intimate, not very noisy. He said we could walk it."

"You trust *Anthony*?"

"Everyone deserves a second chance, and we did end up liking karaoke." He smiled at her.

"I suppose you're right."

Sinead started toward the door, annoyed when some skinny, drunken fool in a three-piece suit leered at her. She rolled her eyes. *You wish,* she thought. *Men.*

She relaxed a little as she hit the sidewalk. Air, glorious air. She took a deep breath. Adam followed a few seconds later. He, too, looked more relaxed. Relaxed and relieved.

"Sorry about that," he said again.

"Hey, at least it's not a karaoke bar," Sinead teased. "Who recommended this place, if you don't mind me asking?"

"Actually, it was your brother Quinn."

Sinead's brows furrowed in confusion. "When did you see Quinn?"

"I hang out at the Hart sometimes, remember?"

"Oh. Right."

"Did you tell Quinn you were going to be meeting me?" *Please let the answer be no,* Sinead thought. If he did tell, then the next time she saw her brother at family dinner, he was going to tease her mercilessly.

"Yeah. Told him we had some more stuff to go over."

"I can't believe he recommended Maxie's."

"Maybe he thought it wouldn't be crowded on a weeknight. Who knows?"

They fell into easy step together. "Congrats on winning in L.A.," said Sinead.

Adam glanced at her sideways. "Keeping tabs, huh?"

"I need to keep on top of whether you're spending too much time in the penalty box," Sinead answered. Which was true. Not only did she keep tabs on how Adam played, but she also had her paralegal, Damian, keep tabs on what was being written about the Blades in newspapers and online. But that was only part of the story. Sinead actually found herself growing interested in how the team was doing, especially since Ray had told her how much pressure Adam was under to "deliver."

"I was surprised you called," Sinead continued casually, trying to ignore how handsome he looked. He was wearing jeans and a simple blue oxford shirt with the sleeves rolled up to his forearms. The shirt made the color of his eyes pop. His hair was damp. For some reason, Sinead had always found men fresh from showering sexy. A brief image went zinging through her mind of him naked, water cascading over his athletic body, but a determined mental push made it sizzle away.

Adam looked puzzled. "Why were you surprised? You've been on me forever to get in touch with you if I could think of anything else that could help the case. So that's what I did."

That's when she finally noticed the raggedy green canvas bag slung over his left shoulder. She gestured at it. "I'm looking forward to seeing what you've got."

Silence. *He's not saying anything about my running inside like a chicken at the end of karaoke night. Back to professional chitchat. Well, that's the way it should be, right?*

Adam glanced at her with concern. "We were only in

Maxie's a minute, but you really looked like you were being tortured."

"I get migraines," Sinead confessed. "That's what happened the other night. Sometimes they can be brought on by too much noise and stale air."

Adam looked at her sympathetically. "One of my teammates in Tampa got migraines. There were a couple of times he had to leave in the middle of a game. He even missed a playoff game because of one."

"I can't imagine how hard it would be to play a game with a migraine." She shuddered at the thought. "There are times the pain is so bad I can't even move my head." *Why are you telling him this? He's going to think you're sickly.*

"Ever try acupuncture?"

"I didn't figure you for an alternative-therapy type," Sinead said, surprised.

Adam looked bemused. "What type did you figure me for?"

"The type who's never had any physical ailment or weakness in his life."

"I've never known anyone who's been that lucky. Professional athletes are actually willing to try any kind of treatment to get over injuries. I've hurt my back a few times, and acupuncture really helped. Maybe you should check it out."

"I'll stick to my pharmaceuticals, thank you." *Moron, now he probably thinks you're a drug addict.*

They arrived at Basilica. The place was small, with stuccoed walls and seven tables of varying size, if that. There looked to be a cast of regulars at the bar; it reminded Sinead of her parents' pub. Thankfully, it wasn't too crowded.

They were seated at a table for two in the back. A very small table. Sinead could feel her knees touching Adam's. The lighting was low, too. The atmosphere was, well, romantic. She wondered if Adam thought, too. Not that it mattered.

"Can I get you folks anything to drink?" asked a blond, blue-eyed waiter with a heavy Eastern European accent.

"Would you like to get a bottle of wine?" Adam asked.

"I can't drink wine because of my headaches," Sinead said with an apologetic wince. *God, he must think I'm a pill. A stick in the mud. Can't do this, can't do that.*

"Sorry. My buddy in Tampa couldn't, either. Forgot about that. So what would you like?"

"Martini," she told the waiter. She couldn't believe how nervous she was. It was disturbing.

"Martini for the lady," said Adam, "and a Peroni for me."

"Very good, sir. Would you like to see a menu?"

Sinead hesitated. Truth be told, she was starving, which was part of the reason she had a mild headache before going to meet Adam. But if he wasn't going to eat anything, then she'd just suck it up. "I wouldn't mind something," Adam said to her.

"Me, neither."

"The special pasta tonight is Ravioli Bolognese," said the waiter. "And we also have some very nice Veal Francese."

"I'll have the ravioli," said Sinead. As soon as she said it, she realized they were not just meeting for drinks; they were having a meal together. That required a lot of legal chitchat. *Shit.*

"I'll have the ravioli, too," said Adam.

"Very good," said the waiter, disappearing.

Sinead splayed her hands on the table. "What have you got for me?"

"I don't know if it will help, but . . ." Adam dug into the frayed satchel he'd slung over the arm of the chair, pulling out three photo albums.

"What's this?" Sinead asked, intrigued. She hadn't seen albums like this in ages. Everyone stored his or her pictures digitally now.

Adam looked uncomfortable. "Fan letters, some dating back as far as when I was in juniors. I saved the best ones."

Sinead carefully opened the first album. Unfortunately, she could barely read a thing in this damn low light. Her nose was practically touching the page as she intently perused the pages. She knew immediately that she'd hit absolute pay dirt. "Dear Adam, you've always been my hero . . ." "Dear Adam, thank you so much for visiting my son Dean in the hospital. It meant so much to him. Unfortunately, he died last week . . ." "Dear Adam, Thank you for your donation toward the new wing of our hospital. Thanks to you, research on spinal cord injury . . ." Pages and pages of thanks, hero worship, even a letter from Ray's parents. "You're like a son to us, and always will be. Please stop beating yourself up over what happened . . ."

Sinead looked up at him, moved. "These are amazing."

Adam looked uncomfortable.

"Why did you save them?"

"To remind myself I'm more than just an asshole who crippled his best friend," Adam replied bitterly.

"Adam . . ." Sinead snaked her hand across the table to squeeze his. He actually looked vulnerable. She was fully prepared for him to pull away, but he didn't. They sat there in silence, their eyes not quite meeting. "These are going to be incredibly helpful if we have to go to court," she said softly.

Adam looked pained. "I thought so."

"I really appreciate you sharing them with me," she murmured, heartfelt. "I know it must have been hard for you."

Adam forced a smile, rubbing the back of his neck.

"I'll have them scanned and get them back to you as soon as I can," Sinead promised, removing her hand.

"Right. Appreciate it."

* * *

Dinner was awkward at first. Once Adam put away the letters and they stopped talking about his case, the only place to go next was their personal lives. Adam seemed genuinely interested when she told him how she came to practice law. Still, she worried she might be boring him, as it wasn't the most riveting tale in the world: She'd wanted a profession that would be high-powered, challenging, and paid well. End of story. She didn't have a calling the way he or Quinn did. She was envious.

Adam asked about her family, pointing out that she knew all about his, so it was only fair she fill him in on the O'Brien clan. But Sinead couldn't escape the feeling that his interest went beyond simply wanting an equitable exchange of information. There was something about the way he was looking at her that betrayed him. As he slowly let his guard slip, she realized it was desire. She was confused. *He's the one who kissed you, not the other way around,* a little voice in her head reminded her. But another little voice reminded her that he was also the one who thought it best they pretend the kiss had never happened. He was sending mixed signals, and neither she nor her little voices knew what to make of it.

Eventually, they found themselves back out on the street. The mixed signals issue was really eating at her. Sinead decided to be blunt.

"Were we just on a date?" she asked. *If the answer is no,* she thought, *I'm going to dig a hole in the ground right here and jump into it.*

Adam scratched his cheek. "Do you think we were?"

Sinead blew out an exasperated breath. "You define it. You're the one who said the kiss in my office never happened. You tell me."

Adam paused thoughtfully. "I think it started out as business and then turned into a date."

"Was karaoke a date?"

"It could have been if you didn't run into your building like you were being pursued by Satan," Adam said wryly.

"I had a headache."

"Okay. Whatever you say."

Sinead ignored the challenge to her veracity, choosing instead to focus on the here and now. "I'm confused. Are we now acknowledging that the kiss happened? And if we are dating, what does that mean?"

"You think too much, you know that?"

Before Sinead could protest, Adam's mouth was on hers, burning hot with equal parts need and desire. He pulled her to him as Sinead twined her arms around his neck, taking in his taste, reveling in the feel of being in a man's arms after so long. She could easily devour him, but she held back. She did not want to look desperate, even though that's how she felt: desperate for *him.* Oliver once accused her of living half a life. It was true. She wanted a full life. One with work and a husband and a child. She wanted it all.

There was reluctance in his eyes as he tore his mouth from hers. Sinead wondered if she should invite him to her place for coffee. No. Too forward. At least for her. She was out of practice. She'd screw things up.

Realizing she wasn't going to ask him inside, Adam eventually asked her what her schedule was like.

I work seven days a week, she thought. *I work and work to fill the hole inside me where a family should be. I work to prove I'm as good as any male attorney in this city.* But pleasant warmth wrapped around her at his question. It meant he wanted to see her again.

Sinead hesitated. "It can be complicated. How about I call you?"

Adam didn't look happy. "Okay." He handed his satchel over to her.

"Thank you for trusting me with these," Sinead murmured. "I mean it."

"No prob."

He called a cab for her, then kissed her again briefly as she slid into the backseat.

"Don't work too hard," he said.

"You, either."

She watched him stroll off as the cab pulled away from the curb. They'd dined together. They'd kissed. He said it was kind of, sort of, a date. And still her mind felt muddled. She'd call Maggie and ask if she could stop by after work to talk. She needed her sister.

*   *   *

"Hi."

Maggie looked pleased as she ushered Sinead inside. Sinead had phoned her the minute she'd gotten home from her "date" with Adam, asking if she could stop by. She was surprised when Maggie invited her over for dinner the next night, sounding excited as she explained it would just be the two of them: Brendan was taking Charlie over to his uncle Joe's, allowing them some real, uninterrupted girl talk. Sinead was relieved; that was exactly what she needed.

Sinead ducked her head uncertainly as Maggie took her coat. "Brendan doesn't feel like I'm driving him out, does he?"

"Don't be crazy. This was his idea."

"Good."

Maggie motioned for Sinead to follow her through to the kitchen at the back of the old house. It was a small Victorian that Brendan was in the process of renovating himself.

"Sorry the place is such a wreck."

"It's not," said Sinead, sitting at the kitchen table. "This kitchen is pretty big."

"It is," Maggie agreed. She opened the fridge. "I've got the fixings for a Greek salad. I've also got some hummus and baba ghanouj, too. That okay?"

"More than okay."

"Good." The minute Maggie began pulling the food out of the fridge, Sinead jumped up to help.

"Neenee, sit down," Maggie admonished. "It's just a few things."

Sinead shrugged. "Okay."

"Mom sure trained us well," Maggie said dryly.

"You got that right."

Sinead watched Maggie deftly cut up the salad. Nimble hands, the same hands she used as a massage therapist before she gave it up to stay home with Charlie. Sinead knew money was tight for her sister now that she was home full-time. Maybe it was time to offer some help. She knew Brendan was a proud man, but this wasn't a gift from a stranger. It was family.

Maggie's face lit up excitedly. "Remember that grape soda we used to drink as kids? Well, I found some. It's a guilty pleasure. Want a glass?"

"Oh my God, I would love that!"

"Be prepared to get the sugar rush of your life," she warned as she handed Sinead her glass.

Sinead took a sip. The soda was just as she remembered: sickeningly sweet. Oliver would love it.

"Well?"

"Disgusting as ever and yet, I'm so glad you found it."

Maggie grinned. "Me, too."

Maggie slipped into the kitchen chair opposite Sinead. Never shy about eating heartily, at least not in front of each other, they piled their plates up high before Maggie poured out some mineral water for them. *She remembers I can't drink wine,* Sinead thought gratefully. Maggie's expression was relaxed as she took her drink.

"I'm so glad you called. We haven't had a good talk in ages. Not since Charlie's been born."

"I know." Sinead felt guilty. They indulged in small talk for a while, but eventually, Sinead felt like she just couldn't keep it in anymore. "I need to talk to you about this guy I met," she blurted out. "You're the only one whose input I really trust on this."

"Wow. A guy. *Finally.*" Maggie looked eager. "Go for it."

"Okay."

Sinead took a deep, fortifying drink of water and plunged in, telling Maggie all about Adam. When she was done, she held her breath expectantly, waiting for Maggie's pronouncement. Maggie just stared at her as if the answer was self-evident. "Go out with him."

Sinead blinked. "Just like that."

"Just like that."

"But he's my client, Mags. It's unethical. And if any of the senior partners in the firm found out, my career would be dead in the water."

"He's not going to be your client forever."

"What if we become a couple and I lose the case? Don't you think I'd lose *him*?"

"You're deliberately putting up roadblocks. Keep it simple: if you like him, date him. Go with the flow."

Sinead put down her fork. "I hate that expression! I don't go with the flow; I *control* the flow."

Maggie popped an olive in her mouth. "How's that new blood pressure medication working out for you, Neenee?"

Sinead scowled. "Shut up, Maggie."

She took a sip of her water. "All right. I'll see what happens. Look, don't say a word about this to *anyone*, especially Quinn. He's such a blabbermouth."

"My lips are sealed," Maggie promised. "Now let's get down to the good stuff . . ."

* * *

Dinner finished, Maggie set up the coffee while Sinead cut up the Irish soda bread their mother used as an excuse to drop by Maggie's house at least once a week.

"Mags?"

"Mmm?"

"I know your being a full-time mom has taken a big bite out of your income," Sinead said carefully. "Let me help."

Maggie looked over her shoulder, smiling sadly. "I appreciate the offer, but I don't think it would sit well with Brendan."

"We could say it's a loan, then."

For a moment Maggie looked like she was seriously considering it, but she soon snapped out of it. "He'll never go for it."

"But it's family. That's what families do: they help each other out."

Maggie kissed Sinead on the top of the head as she rejoined her at the table. "We'll see. I'll work on him." Her expression turned tentative. "You know, there's something I need to talk to you about."

Sinead hid her anxiety. "Sure."

"Why have you been so distant lately?" Maggie asked, looking wounded. "Is it that you don't like Charlie?"

"I love Charlie." Sinead took a deep breath, her chest actually hurting. "I'm envious of you. Can't you see that? I want to bond with him, but I feel like I don't know how. I don't think he likes me."

Maggie laughed lightly. "He doesn't like anyone right now. Just relax. These things take time."

"I hope you're right. I want to be a real aunt to him, you know?"

"That means a lot to me." Maggie took a hearty bite of the Irish soda bread. "Promise me something."

"What's that?"

"That you'll give this guy Adam a fair shot."

Sinead clucked her tongue. "Yes. Fine. But I'm the older sister here. Technically, you should be doing what I tell you, not the other way around."

"So tell me what to do, then," Maggie taunted.

"Cut me a big fat piece of soda bread and put tons of butter on it, slave."

"Now *that's* my sister."

* * *

Thoughts of Sinead were screwing with Adam's concentration. Not her fault, but still, he hated that he wasn't as present on the ice as he should have been during the game against Detroit. The Blades had won, but Adam didn't share their sense of victory.

It had been difficult for him to give Sinead the albums filled with fan letters. He'd never shown them to anyone before. Despite being proud of them, he worried that their existence made him look egotistical. As for his visiting sick kids and contributing money to hospitals, both went in the same category as financing the skating rink in Claresholm: his conditions had always been that his actions not be revealed to the public at large. He loathed publicity of this sort; in fact, he loathed publicity, period, especially the press he was getting with the assault charge hanging over his head. Every hit he made on the ice was scrutinized and dissected. It didn't inhibit him, but it was still annoying. He was going to stop reading the sports pages and watching ESPN, except for *PTI*.

At any rate, his ploy of asking Sinead for a drink under the guise of business had worked. But against his wishes, his mind kept dragging him back to the memory of kissing her. The kiss had been intense; it had been a long time since he'd felt such a connection to a woman. Yet he had some reservations about what would happen next. Just as he took his job seriously, so, too, he took his personal relationships with women seriously. He didn't want to find himself in a sticky situation.

He'd just come out of the shower and gotten dressed when Michael Dante motioned for him for follow him out into the hall.

"How you feelin'?" Michael asked.

Adam was mystified. "Fine. Why?"

"Your play seemed a little off tonight."

"Yeah, I know. Sorry about that." Adam felt bad that he'd let his team down.

"The only thing you need to be sorry about is if you're starting to tone it down because the commissioner is on your ass."

"No way," Adam assured him.

"Good. Everything else okay?"

"Fine."

"You got a girlfriend yet?"

"Not yet, but soon. Maybe."

Michael clapped him on the shoulder. "Look, all of us have off games every once in a while—even Ty did, though Christ knows he'd never admit it. I know it's hard with this case hanging over your head. But you gotta stay as sharp as you can out there. Show the league they're never gonna get rid of old-time hockey, because that's the way it's supposed to be played. Refuse to back down, and it'll inspire not only our guys, but all of Canada even more. You're already a hero to them and in the Great White North; stand your ground, and they'll follow you into hell."

Adam nodded. "Gotcha."

"Good. And good luck with your maybe girlfriend."

13

Sinead stood at her kitchen stove doing something she hadn't done in a long time: cook.

As promised, she had called Adam, even though just picking up her cell made her stomach flip. He seemed glad to hear from her. To cover her butterflies, she'd started with business, telling him she'd finished scanning his fan letters. "Would you like to pick them up at the office?" she'd asked casually, deciding that if he said yes, it meant that he'd reconsidered their "date," and they were back to "it never happened" status.

"Let's meet outside the office," he'd suggested. That's when Sinead had insanely, impulsively, invited him over for dinner. Adam agreed.

Now here she was, wrapped in a rarely worn apron, chopping vegetables with a large gleaming knife she didn't think she'd ever used before. She probably should have asked Adam what he liked to eat, but she'd forgotten, so she opted for simple: rosemary roast potatoes, roast chicken, and a salad. She'd picked up a coffee cake at Zabar's, making a mental note to send Adam home with it when the night was through; otherwise, she'd eat her way through it in a few days. Coffee cake was her weakness. Actually, baked goods of any form were her weakness. That was why she usually didn't let herself have them. *Rigid,* she chided herself. *You're so rigid. Just go with the flow.* She laughed out loud. *As if.*

Like some giddy teenager preparing for her first date, Sinead had spent hours agonizing over what to wear. She couldn't wear anything sexy even if she wanted to: pathetically, she didn't own a single item of sexy clothing. In the end, she opted for the new pair of jeans she'd bought at Bloomingdale's, and a scoop neck, yellow silk cotton jersey with elbow sleeves that Lennie Buckley had made for her a few months ago. Simple and casual.

She checked her watch: five minutes until Adam was due. Nerves had driven her to set the table an hour early. Though she couldn't drink wine, she'd picked up a bottle of New Zealand Sauvignon Blanc just in case Adam wanted some.

Sinead nearly jumped out of her skin when the buzzer sounded and the doorman announced that there was an Adam Perry here to see her. "You can send him up," she said, her heart beginning to pound like a bass drum as she quickly untied her apron, folded it neatly, and put it on the counter. *Go with the flow. Go with the flow. Go with the flow.*

Adam knocked so quietly that had she not been expecting him, she might have missed it. Sinead braced herself and then opened the door. Just the sight of him made her heart jump a notch, making smiling unavoidable.

"Hi."

Adam smiled back. "Hi."

There was an awkward moment before he leaned over to kiss her cheek. Sinead caught his scent: woodsy. She detected cedar, maybe some sweet lime. His hair was still damp from the shower. She longed to run her fingers through it, but for now, she'd have to leave that to her imagination.

Adam held out a bouquet of pink-edged daisies. "These are for you."

"Thank you." She tried to remember the last time anyone bought her flowers. God knows Chip never did, at least not in the later years of their marriage, as if he didn't have to woo her anymore. It had pained her, especially since her father still surprised her mother with flowers after forty years of marriage.

Adam whistled through his teeth, impressed with her apartment. "Wow. This is some place you've got here."

"Thank you," Sinead repeated, feeling mildly self-conscious. She did have a wonderfully large apartment on the Upper East Side. She'd worked hard to be able to buy it, but sometimes, her income embarrassed her, and she wasn't sure why. Maybe it was because deep down, she felt that it was proof that what her family said to her was right: all she'd done her whole adult life was work.

"Where do you live?" she asked Adam.

"East Twenty-eighth and Third Avenue. Pretty nondescript, but it's a fairly quiet street. Not a lot of nightlife around."

"Is that important to you?"

"Yeah. I like to wind down after games and just hang out. I'm not really a party type of guy."

"I guessed that." Sinead gestured toward the kitchen. "Um, I hope you like chicken and roast potatoes."

"Sounds great. That was actually a big favorite in my house when I was growing up."

Sinead grinned. "Me, too." She remembered the flowers in her hand. "Why don't you go sit on the couch, and I'll put these in water. Would you like anything to drink? I've got some Sauvignon Blanc."

"I'd love a glass."

"Be right back."

Sinead returned to the kitchen, rolling some of the nervousness she was feeling out of her shoulders. God, he was handsome. He had to know it. She'd tried hard not to stare at his mouth while he was talking; that beautiful, sensuous mouth that had kissed her so expertly. She put the flowers in a vase and uncorked the chilled wine, pouring him a glass as well as some water for herself. She brought the drinks out into the living room, then went back to get the flowers, placing them in the center of the coffee table. She sat down next to Adam—close, but not too close.

Adam lifted his wineglass. "Cheers."

"Cheers."

Sinead looked at her coffee table, bare except for the flowers and their two glasses, and cringed. "God, I forgot to get us some crackers and cheese. Sorry."

Adam looked baffled. "Why are you apologizing?"

Sinead felt her face flame. "It's just that I wanted things to be perfect." *And it's three minutes in, and I've already failed.*

"Anyone ever tell you that you need to relax?"

Sinead lifted her eyebrows. "Look who's talking."

Adam reeled back slightly, surprised. "What are you talking about?"

"Mr. Intense."

"Ms. Intense. Anthony said we should have an 'intense off.'"

Sinead was amused. "Oh, did he now?" She gave a small frown. "The only thing I hate about the word *intense* is that it implies being humorless, you know? Or no fun."

"I know. But it's obvious I have a sense of humor."

"Is it?"

"I'm a *Three Stooges* fan, remember?"

Sinead groaned. "God, I wish you'd never told me that." She was visited by a memory. "My brothers used to watch them all the time. Then they'd try to poke each other's eyes out. My mother was not pleased."

Adam laughed delightedly. "My brother and I used to do that, too."

"It must be a guy thing."

"Are you sure you don't want to watch a few old episodes with me?" Adam asked sardonically.

"I'll pass."

Adam sighed. "Your loss."

"You keep believing that."

Sinead took another sip of water, more to give herself something to do than out of thirst. Despite their little thrust and parry over Moe, Larry, and Curly, nerves were creeping up on her. Her mind blanked for a moment. *What should we talk about now? Business. Go to the safe topic of business.*

Sinead gestured to her antique rolltop desk in the far right corner. "Remind me: your photo albums are there." Time for another sip of water. "They're really going to help if the case goes to court, Adam."

"Yeah, well . . ."

"What's wrong?"

"I'm worried about Ray testifying in court. I hate the thought of him humbling himself for my sake."

Sinead hesitated a moment, then reached for his hand, twining her fingers through his. "I don't think this is going to end up in court. Trust me. It sounds egotistical, but Kidco hired me for a reason. While nothing is one hundred percent certain, I think I'll be able to demonstrate that there's really no case, and the charges will be dropped."

Adam ran his thumb along hers. "Christ, it's like a goddamn toothache. I hope it gets wrapped up before the playoffs."

"Ray's worried about all the pressure you're under with the Blades," Sinead said quietly.

"Ray's an old lady. Pressure is part of being a professional athlete."

"He's just concerned about you." She paused. "I am, too."

"I'm fine," Adam said testily. "Pressure comes with the paycheck. It's not a problem."

"If you say so."

He squeezed her hand. "Chicken smells good."

"Thanks." Because she was neurotic, Sinead had everything in the kitchen on a timer. She'd already cut up the salad and tossed it, putting it in the fridge so it didn't wilt before dinner.

She untangled her fingers from his, pleasantly surprised when he slid closer and put his arm around her. "This okay?" he asked.

"Yes, of course." It was more than okay. She let herself settle into the crook of his arm, then jumped up a second later. "Oh, shoot! I forgot to put music on."

"*Sinead.*" Adam's voice was affectionate yet reprimanding. "Just sit down and relax, okay? We can put music on when we have dinner."

"Okay." Sinead sat back down, but inside she was thinking: *This is a disaster so far. No, it isn't. Stop being so melodramatic.*

She let herself rest her head on Adam's broad shoulder, loving the feeling of his arm around her. *Go with the flow.* Rather than fretting about filling up the silence, she embraced it instead. They were sitting in the quiet of two people who didn't need words right now to be close. Gradually, Sinead's nervousness began to ebb, replaced by a rare sense of calm. Her mind wasn't speeding like a bullet train. She was so relaxed that when the timer rang in the kitchen, she was jolted back into real time.

"God, that almost gave me a heart attack," she said, standing up. Meanwhile, Adam remained completely unperturbed; his gaze was relaxed, almost intimate. Sinead swallowed, trying not to stare at him, or worse, say, "To hell with dinner," and lunge at him. She forced a genial smile onto her face. "Hungry?" she asked. She almost blushed. Somehow it sounded like a loaded question.

Adam's gaze locked onto hers. "Starving."

With that, Sinead knew that what she'd been fretting about earlier was completely imaginary: tonight was not going to be a disaster at all.

14

"What a great meal."

Sinead was pleased by Adam's satisfied smile as they sat down together on the couch after dinner. Things had gone well. Adam was beginning to let down his defenses, and she was, too. He asked about her marriage over dinner and she told him, though she didn't go into great detail about what it was that ultimately split her and Chip up. That was just too painful.

"I'm glad you liked the meal," she said, "but it's not like it required gourmet skills. Anyone with half a brain could have made it."

"It was still good."

"Well, thank you."

Adam's arm snaked around her, pulling her to him tight. "You thought I was a total moron when you first met me, didn't you?"

Embarrassed, Sinead buried her face in his shoulder.

"You did, didn't you?" Adam pressed, sounding amused.

Sinead looked back at him. "No. I'd just never dealt with taciturn jocks before."

"Very telling, your use of the word *jock*, not *athlete*."

"Fine, I'll admit it," Sinead said with a little huff. "I thought you were a hulking twit incapable of putting two sentences together."

Adam laughed loudly. "And when did you change your mind?"

"Who says I have?"

"I can put two sentences together right now if you want," Adam murmured.

Sinead's heart fluttered. "Okay."

He tucked her hair behind her ear, gently pressing his mouth to her ear. "I want you. Now."

"Me, too," Sinead said, trying not to tremble. She decided to be bold and kissed him lightly. If Adam was surprised, he didn't show it. Instead, he waited a few seconds before taking control, turning the bare touch of their lips into something more urgent. There was no denying the electricity passing back and forth between them, the sense that something long suppressed was finally being brought out into the light. Sinead gathered her senses together as best she could and stood, extending her hand to lead him into her bedroom.

She turned on the bedside lamp. Adam lay down so gently beside her, looking at her with such unabashed tenderness that Sinead found herself teary. *He really cares about me. I'm precious to him. And he's showing me.*

His gaze remained amorous as he put his arms around her and held her tight, his mouth leaving a trail of tiny kisses along her jawline. Sinead's eyes lazed shut. It felt wonderful, especially when his mouth moved down to the hollows of her collarbone. But sweetness wasn't what she wanted right now. She was aching with want of him. Again boldness overtook her: she grasped his face between her hands and kissed his mouth greedily, unable to hide her yearning. She wanted to devour him and be devoured in return. Groaning, Adam flipped her onto her back, and then he was on her, his luscious mouth as demanding as hers. Sinead worried about squeezing the life out of him as she clutched him tightly. She wanted to feel every inch of his body against hers, his male solidity pressing down on her, possessing her. She wanted to be unable to tell where she started and he ended.

Her craving for him was overpowering as she released him just long enough to tug on the back of his sweater. "I want this off," she whispered. "Now."

Adam laughed. "You never stop bossing people around, do you?" He bit her neck softly and then sat up, straddling her as he whipped his sweater off and tossed it on the floor. Sinead reached up, pressing her palms to his smooth, hard chest, allowing herself the luxury of feeling him. His chest was burning; or was it her hands? Adam smiled down at her so seductively that for a split second, her shyness returned as she thought: *Am I really worthy of such a look of desire?*

But clearly Adam thought she *deserved* it, as his mouth dipped down to hers, his kiss nakedly intense. Sinead pressed herself against him, physical desperation overtaking her body. Adam lifted his head to look at her; there was a ravenous look in his eye that made her blood churn excitedly, far past the point she thought possible. Adam seemed to sense it as he helped her quickly struggle out of her shirt and bra. His eyes hooded as he teased at her nipples with his mouth, his teeth gently tugging one minute, his tongue flicking the next. Sparks of pleasure cascaded through Sinead, the want of him building inside her starting to become unendurable. For the first time in years, she felt fully, truly alive.

A sharp breath overtook her as Adam's mouth slowly began its descent down her body, his kisses maddeningly light. He was torturing her and enjoying every moment of it.

As was she. Body burning, she rocked her hips against him, lightly at first, then harder. "Please," she whispered. Once again, Adam lifted his head to meet her eyes. Need was growing in him, too. She could see it on his face; hear it in his heavy breaths.

Slowly, almost gingerly, Adam undid the zipper of her jeans and tugged them down, along with her panties. Her breath held as she saw him drink her in before his fingertips created invisible trails up and down the insides of her legs and over the terrain of her hips and belly. Such delicious torment—but she wanted the torture to end.

"Make love to me," she whispered. *"Now."*

"So demanding," Adam said with a sexy smirk. "I love it."

She closed her eyes as Adam slid off her. She heard him undoing his belt, the soft sound of the rest of his clothing hitting the floor. There was the crinkle of a wrapper, and then he was back on the bed, his heated body crashing back down on hers. Sinead dug her nails into his back, gasping with pleasure when he parted her legs and eased himself inside her. His rhythm was slow and easy, but that wasn't what she wanted as she lifted her hips with each thrust and took control of the pace herself. Adam returned her frenzy, his body punching inside hers deep and hard. As the world around them burned away to just the two of them, Sinead finally achieved the relief she sought as she was swept away on pounding waves of bliss. She had barely recovered when Adam upped the tempo, and pressure began building inside her again, sweet and sharp. Mere seconds later she was overcome with roaring pleasure for a second time, her joyous screams filling the bedroom. Adam moaned, and with a final, hard thrust, filled her as he shuddered with his own release.

*   *   *

He was so quiet at first, Sinead didn't know what to think. She was cuddled in his arms, drowsing in and out of that lovely postsex haze that she'd almost forgotten existed. She assumed his silence was one of happy satiation. But the longer it went on, the more she began to worry.

"Adam?"

"Mmm?"

"Is everything okay?"

"Yes, fine." He squeezed her. "Why?"

"You're just so quiet." She felt a tiny prick of anxiety. "You're not thinking you made a mistake, are you?"

Adam opened his eyes, propping himself up on one elbow to look at her. "You're joking, right?"

"I don't know. I feel like you finally opened up to me, and now you're retreating somehow."

Adam kissed her forehead. "You're wrong. I'm just relaxing. Riding the inner tube, as Ray used to say." He peered at her curiously. "Why? Are you used to guys who are chatty after sex?"

"Not guys, guy. I've only ever been with Chip before this, and yes, he was quite the postsex yakker."

Adam looked dubious. "What did he yak about?"

"Himself, mostly."

"Figures." He caressed her hair. "I'm sorry. Generally I don't say anything if I don't think anything needs to be said."

"Don't be sorry," Sinead said. "I just want to make sure that now that we've taken this step, you're not going to dump me after one night."

"I'm not going to dump you. To be honest, I thought you might dump me."

Sinead was taken aback. "Why's that?"

"I get the sense I'm not the type of guy you usually socialize with. I don't know that a hockey player from western Canada fits in with your social scene."

"First of all, I don't have a social scene. Secondly, do I seem like a one-night stand kind of woman?"

Adam kissed her shoulder. "Nope."

One-night stand . . . "You know, if my partners find

out I'm seeing a client, I'm dead. It's considered very unprofessional—except when they do it."

"Jerks. You know where I wish we were right now?"

"Where?"

"In a cabin in the country."

"I have a country house, you know," Sinead revealed.

"You do?"

"Yeah, in Bearsville, about two hours north of the city. I haven't been there for a while."

"Why don't you go there more often?"

"I have no life outside of work." She paused. "I'm a workaholic, Adam."

Adam feigned surprise. "Really? I never would have guessed. I am, too, in case you haven't noticed."

"I have." *Which is good,* Sinead thought. *It will ensure things don't get too serious, too fast. If they even get serious, which they might not. Unless—oh, shut up, please.*

"Maybe we could go away for a weekend at your house sometime," Adam suggested.

"That would be nice." Sinead pictured them taking walks together. She'd relearn how to cook. She wouldn't bring her laptop. She'd sleep well.

"How's the hunting up there?"

Sinead sat up, staring at him in horror. *"What?"*

Adam looked dismayed. "Let me guess: you think hunting is horrible."

"It is horrible!"

"We just ate a chicken, right?"

Sinead felt cornered; she could see where this was going. "So?"

"Have you ever seen how chickens are raised? At least the deer are in the wild! They aren't being treated like shit at factories, pumped full of hormones, raised in horrible conditions before they die!"

"But it's awful to kill animals for sport!"

"It's not just for sport. If I catch any fish, we'll eat them."

"And if you kill a deer?"

"I'll gut it, dress it, and grill us some venison. Plus I can saw off the legs and make myself a nice gun rack."

Sinead blanched.

"That was a joke, Sinead."

"Thank *God*. Adam, I don't know about your coming up there to hunt." She hated when she was at her house during deer season and she'd wake to the sound of gunfire echoing off the hills. "Maybe the first time we go up to the house together, you could bypass killing things?"

"Fine." He looked at her affectionately. "No one could ever accuse you of being tepid in your views, that's for sure."

Sinead lay back down, covering her face with her hands in disbelief. "I can't believe our first postsex discussion was about deer hunting."

Adam gently pulled her hands from her face. "We can talk about *The Three Stooges* if you want."

Sinead couldn't help but smile. "You're pretty funny."

"For a bonehead."

Adam looked tender as he gathered her into his arms. "Why don't we try to get some sleep? I've got practice tomorrow morning—"

"And I've got tons of work to do." She ran her index finger down his cheek. "I've crossed a line here, you know. I vowed I would never get involved with a client. That I'd never be like *them*."

"It's no one's business."

"Technically that's true, but—"

"Earth to Sinead: we just made passionate love, and you're back to talking about work."

"God, you're right. I promise I won't do it again."

"Good." Adam kissed her forehead. "Thanks for a wonderful night."

"Thank *you*, Mr. Perry." Sinead was filled with joy and a little bit of confusion. She kept the latter at bay for now, concentrating instead on the moment and the sheer rightness of being in Adam's arms. She was remembering what it was like to live a full life, and she was happy.

15

Sinead chuckled as she walked into her parents' bar to meet Oliver, trying to ignore the knowing smirk on his face as she slid into the booth opposite him.

"Oooh, look at you: smile on your face, cheeks all aglow—you got some sugar last night, didn't you?" His observation made her apprehensive. Was there really something different about her appearance now that she was dating Adam? If so, what did that say about her previous demeanor?

"Good evening to you, too, Oliver."

"Avoidance. Means the answer is yes," said Oliver, waving crazily for Christie to come over to their table.

"It's not avoidance. It means I'm sitting in my parents' pub, starving. Can I at least have some dinner before you start cross-examining me?"

"Fair enough."

"Thank you."

Sinead took a sip of water, turning around to scan the back of the dining room so Oliver couldn't see the big, goofy grin on her face. She and Adam had gotten up extra early to make love before they both went to work, and it was lovely, languid, and slow. Sinead was worried they might drift back to sleep afterward, but then realized that was impossible. This was her and Adam, the two most conscientious people in the world. Despite their glorious dawn tumble, they were both up and out the door when they had to be. But as the day rolled on, getting up with the sun had taken its toll: Sinead was exhausted, trying to keep herself from constantly yawning.

She turned back to Oliver.

"Well?" he said.

"I want to hear about your weekend first. If you can even remember it."

"Very funny." Oliver looked thoughtful. "Well, let's see. Friday night I went to a lingerie show—"

"What?"

Before Oliver could explain, Christie came over to the table, plunking down a glass of scotch in front of him. "I take it this is what you want?"

Oliver flashed a seductive smile. "It's one of the things I want, yes."

"God, Oliver," said Sinead, embarrassed to be friends with him.

"How did last night go?" Oliver continued, his eyes indiscreetly sweeping Christie's body. "Put out any raging fires?"

"Nope."

Oliver fixed her with what Sinead supposed was his "smoky, seductive" look. "Well, I know one—"

"Bye, Oliver," Christie said, walking away.

Oliver jumped right back into his story.

"Okay, so you know that Swedish supermodel, Dani?"

Sinead braced herself. "Oh, no."

Oliver broke into a big Cheshire cat smile. "Oh, yes. I met her at a cocktail party last week, and she invited me to come to the lingerie show she was modeling in. How could I refuse?"

"Did you enjoy yourself?"

"Thoroughly—both during and after."

Sinead sighed. "Go on."

"We got to know each other a bit," Oliver said smugly, "if you catch my drift. She wanted to spend all day with me yesterday, but I said, 'Sorry, honey, places to go, people to see.' I think she's falling for me, hard."

"Yeah, right. *Anyway*."

"Spent yesterday pretty much sleeping; the little minx plumb wore me out."

Sinead groaned. *"Oliver."*

"Slept, went out for a late lunch, and then last night, me and the boys—"

"What boys?"

"A few of my friends from Yale—went and shot guns at this basement shooting gallery in NoHo. It was awesome. Ever shoot a gun, Sinead?"

"No, and I never will." Sinead gave a small shudder. "Adam has."

"Oh yeah?" Oliver looked intrigued. "You gonna tell Uncle Ollie about hockey boy, or what?"

"Finish."

"Nothing more to say. We shot guns, we went out and drank shots, and then I was a good boy and went home because like you, I needed to be at the office this morning to do some work. Your turn. Did you shtup him?"

Sinead shook her head in disbelief. "You are so crude."

"Cut the prim act and spill."

Sinead took another sip of water. "Well, you know Adam and I have been sort of dancing around the issue of our attraction."

"More like avoiding, but go on."

"We wound up having dinner one night last week— purely professional. He had some things to give me that will help the case. But then it got personal."

Oliver's eyes lit up. "Lip-locking?"

"Yes."

"What base did you get to?"

Sinead scowled. "Could we not talk about this like we're in eighth grade?"

"If you insist."

"I told him I'd call him, and I did. I wound up inviting him over for dinner last night."

"Pretty bold move for you."

"I know."

"You've never invited me over for dinner," Oliver said with a pout.

"You've never invited me over for dinner, either."

"True." Oliver's eyes flashed eagerly. "Continue."

Sinead suddenly felt shy. "We had a nice dinner and things turned romantic and well, you know . . ."

"Hot monkey sex."

"I hate you. I really do."

"Bess, is you his woman now?"

"Yes, I mean we're going to take it slow. I think. We didn't really talk about it."

Oliver took a sip of his scotch. He savored it for a moment, and then threw the rest of the drink down his throat in one gulp. "May I make an observation?"

"You will anyway, so there's no point in saying no."

"You look really happy, Sinead. Happier than I've seen you in years."

"Really?"

"Yeah, really."

Sinead pressed her lips together. "I am happy, but . . ."

"Ah, the buts. Who would you be without your buts?"

"Let me finish," Sinead said, annoyed.

"Go on."

"Well, there's the whole 'I'm his attorney' thing. I mean, it does feel weird to me."

"Does it feel weird to him?"

"He hasn't said so."

"So quit worrying. You'll get wrinkles. This could be the one, sweet pea. Go wherever it leads."

"Look who's giving love advice, Mr. Bang 'Em and Leave 'Em."

"I was born a ramblin' man. Can't be tied down." As if to prove the point, he started waving madly for Christie to return to their table.

Sinead snorted. "The only place you ramble to is the all-night pharmacy."

"Be that as it may, just relax for once in your damn life and enjoy it. Please?"

"I'm *trying*."

"Try harder, dude—I mean, dude-ess."

Sinead hesitated. "There's something else."

"What?"

"He hunts and fishes!"

Oliver looked at her blankly. "So?"

"Don't you think that's awful?"

"No. A lot of guys hunt. Deer apparently screw like bunnies, and shooting them keeps them from taking over the highways, or so I've heard."

Christie came to the table, another scotch in hand for Oliver.

"Here you go."

"Thank you, darlin'." Oliver leaned across the table and in a stage whisper said to Sinead, "Does this woman know me or what?"

"You're a regular customer, Oliver," Sinead pointed out.

"No, it's more than that," Oliver insisted, looking at Christie seductively. "It's some kind of magical . . ."

Christie walked away. "I don't get it," he said, looking genuinely baffled. "How can she be immune to my charms?"

"You're just not her type."

"What's her type?"

"Anyone but you." Sinead returned to the subject of

hunting. "So you're okay with a poor, innocent animal dying an agonizing death?"

"If it ends up on my dinner plate."

"That's what he said," Sinead muttered. "It still doesn't make it right."

Oliver blinked confusedly. "Let me make sure I'm getting this right: you consider Adam's hunting a roadblock to a serious relationship, yet you were willing to spend years with a snooty jackass who expected you to put your career on hold for kids."

"At least he didn't kill things."

"Except your spirit and self-esteem."

"I hate you. I really *do* hate you."

"Are you getting my point here?"

Sinead squirmed. "I suppose."

"Quit throwing up roadblocks before things have even started."

"It's just that we're just so different . . ."

"You're delusional. And if you had an ass, I'd kick it, I swear to God."

"I have an ass!"

"Seriously, this could be your shot at getting a good guy, no pun intended. Try to remember that, okay?"

"I will." Sinead came round from her side of the booth and gave Oliver a big hug. "Thanks. Despite being a crude, unethical lush, you do give good advice sometimes."

"And it's free! Just think: if you were my client, this would be costing you five hundred dollars an hour."

She kissed his cheek before sitting back down. "Let's order some dinner."

* * *

"Number twenty-nine, two minutes, elbowing."

It was the third period of an away game against Toronto, and so far, Adam had been sent to the penalty box twice: once for boarding, another time for charging. Both were borderline calls at best. It looked like the league had gotten to at least this set of officials about sending a message about physical play.

Adam skated over to the penalty box and sat down. Michael was screaming at the ref, who had his arms folded across his chest obstinately. "Are you fucking kidding me?" The ref was unmoved. Michael glanced up at the skybox where Ty sat, turned back to the ice, and threw his hands up in the air in disbelief.

Despite Adam's three penalties, the Blades won, 3–2. They were on a hot streak, winning eight in a row. Ty and Michael were encouraging Adam, saying his will to win was pushing the team forward just as they had hoped.

He knew Ty and Michael would want to talk to him after the game, and he was right.

"I'm not even sure there's anything to say about this," Michael said resignedly. "We all know what's up."

"Teddy Rawson paid me a visit two days ago," said Ty.

Adam and Michael waited for Ty to go on. Rawson, a former player and coach, served as Welsh's special assistant for on-ice issues. He was, in effect, the league's policeman.

"You'll love this," said Ty. "Said Welsh has been on *his* ass, pressuring him about coming down on Adam. He asked me to make Adam tone it down. Apparently Welsh has been making his life hell."

"Jesus Christ," said Michael.

"I laughed at him," said Ty. "I reminded him of the time he cross-checked that little SOB Kerry Howatt to the back of the head. 'Welsh is your problem, not mine,' I told him."

"Sorry about this shit," said Adam.

"Don't worry about it," said Ty. "I doubt Teddy will be back anytime soon. He just wants to be able to tell Welsh that he read me the riot act. This whole thing is going to blow over. The press is starting to pick up on what's going on, and even the most weak-willed officials aren't going to be able to make these calls in the playoffs."

"True," said Michael, "but in the meantime, we're regularly having to play shorthanded with our best defenseman in the box."

"Use it," said Ty.

Michael looked puzzled for a moment and then broke out into a grin. "Right. Rally around the persecuted captain. They're out to get us. Us against the powers that be. Tubs gave us that great speech back when you were the captain, Ty, remember? I think it's time for me to give one of my table-kicking rants."

Ty clapped Michael on the shoulder. "Like the old days. Old-time hockey."

"Anything new with the lawsuit?" Ty asked Adam.

"Not as far as I know," said Adam. "But I can talk to Sinead O'Brien." Adam was glad he remembered to say her full name.

"Do that," said Ty. "I'll also have the in-house guys check in with her, if they haven't been already. I would hate for that bullshit to follow us into the playoffs."

"It won't," said Michael.

"What, you've got a crystal ball?" Ty scoffed.

"I've just got a feeling."

Ty snorted as he turned to Adam. "He gets these 'feelings.' Usually they're wrong." He turned back to Michael. "Ask your cousin Gemma, the *strega*. She's got the sight, right? Maybe she knows something we don't."

"Will do," said Michael with a big yawn. "Time to get lathered up." He clapped Adam on the back. "You okay?"

"Yup," said Adam.

"Remember: we've got your back," said Michael.

He knew that. He just hoped Michael's intuition was right.

16

As promised, Michael gave the team one of his table-kicking rants at the Blades' next practice. The "us against them" strategy seemed just what was needed to get the players even more fired up. They were pissed about Adam being scapegoated, and pissed that the league was once again trying to prettify hockey's image. "They've tried it before and have always failed," Michael pointed out. "We've got to show them that no matter how many bullshit calls they make, we're not going to be cowed into changing our style of play. We play old-time hockey."

Today, Adam wondered if the team still stood behind him after they heard what he had to add. Three days before, there had been a small item in the *Sentinel* reporting that a few of the Blades' most talented young bucks, most notably Esa Saari, had shown up at a recent fashion industry gala with a gaggle of models in tow. According to the article, they then went to a private party hosted by Bon Jovi, who'd played Met Gar that night. The party went well into the morning hours. Adam did the math: that was the morning a couple of players were pitiful in practice. Adam had suspected it was because they were out partying. Now he had proof.

This had to be nipped in the bud. Now. Adam didn't give a shit if they were single and living in the most exciting city in the world. This same problem dogged the team after it won the Cup in 2002, and the necessary repair work to restore the team's reputation had been extensive.

Adam asked the coaches if they could leave the room now because he wanted to hold a players-only meeting. The coaches complied. Adam could tell from the players' expressions that they knew something serious was up; Adam wasn't known for expending precious energy and time on talking if he didn't have to. He'd also never called a players-only meeting before.

The team stood around the locker room, watching, waiting. Adam, moving deliberately slow, walked to his locker and pulled out the *Sentinel*, tossing it onto the floor, right on top of the Blades crest in the middle of the rug.

"Interesting piece in there about some of you boys," he said contemptuously. He stared at the team's latest superstar and self-proclaimed ladies' man. "Enjoy Bon Jovi's after party the other night, Saari?" Adam then turned his formidable stare on Ulf Torkelson. "How about you, Torkelson? Aren't you a bit long in the tooth to be hanging out with the squirts?" He shifted his attention to the other partygoers. "Thomas, Furness, Heinzerling? Models, huh?"

Their gazes darted away.

Adam glared at them. "What the fuck do you little shits think you're doing? We're in the home stretch of the season, and you're out fucking around! I don't give a damn what you do in the off-season, but the rest of us are busting our asses to win the Cup. When you fuck up like this, you disrespect yourself. You disrespect your fans. You disrespect hockey. And you disrespect your teammates.

The players in question hung their heads in shame—except for Saari. "But we won the game that night. Yeah, we were off our game at practice," he said, the faintest tinge of defiance to his voice. "But it was just practice."

Adam slowly walked over to where Saari was standing and came to a halt just in front of him, an inch or two closer than would be natural. "You're fucking kidding me, right?"

The tension in the room was now so thick you could choke on it.

"You seriously need me to explain this to you?" Adam continued.

"Yeah," Saari answered a bit hesitantly but unwilling to back down and lose face.

Adam said nothing. He just looked Saari in the eye, without blinking, until Saari finally lowered his gaze, unable to take the staring contest. Adam continued to stare for what felt like an eternity. Then he turned his back on Saari and walked to the center of the rug, where he stood on top of the newspaper.

"This is a *team*. No one is exempt from busting his ass: not the older guys with families, not the cocky bastards who are the current flavors of the month. There are guys on this team who have to go above and beyond every day just to make sure they stay in the league. They know the only thing standing between them and a lifetime coaching a Mites team in a two-bit town in Manitoba or Newfoundland is their effort. There are guys whose parents woke up every morning before dawn to drive them to the rink and who did without so they could afford new equipment. Players whose parents gave up family vacations so they could drive to tournaments. There are guys who would give an eye to be able to skate the Cup. And you little shits have the balls to screw off."

Shamed silence reigned.

Adam shook his head in disbelief. "Don't you have any pride—not only in what you yourself can achieve, but in what you can achieve as part of a team? What you do for a living is a privilege."

He let his fury burst through, the same anger he experienced on the ice that made him so formidable. "Listen up, you pieces of shit," he growled. "I've spent my whole life chasing the Cup, and if you think I'm going to let a pack of fucking losers rob me and everyone else in this locker room at a real shot at skating the Cup, then you are sadly mistaken.

"As of this minute, you either start treating the game with seriousness and respect, or I will personally break your scrawny necks, drag your dead carcasses onto the ice, and dump them at the blue line before the next home game.

"I forgot to mention: when you behave this way, you also disrespect me." He stood again in front of Saari. "And no one disrespects me."

With a final contemptuous look at Saari, he stepped back, looking around the room at large. "Any questions?"

The only sound was that of the players exhaling with relief.

"Good. See you at practice tomorrow."

17

"Christ, I needed this."

Adam chugged down the Heineken Anthony handed him. The Blades had lost three games in a row. Saari and the rest of the young guys were punctual to practice, but Saari projected an air of boredom, even though he was practicing up to par. Adam decided he'd let it go for now. If he rode Saari continually, there could be a backlash. He wanted the players to respect him, not think he was a dick.

He'd been seeing Sinead for a month now. They were pretty much keeping it quiet, which wasn't hard to do, since finding time to see each other wasn't easy. Sinead was still fretting a bit about their seeing each other being unethical, but Adam had discovered the way to silence her was with a kiss.

"What's on your mind, bro?" asked Anthony, cracking open his brew.

"We seem to be on a losing streak."

"It'll pass, though, right?"

"It better."

"How's it going with Sinead?"

Adam considered the question. "Pretty well, I think. It's hard to tell sometimes. We don't see each other as much as I thought we might."

"You give her the quiz yet?"

"What quiz?"

"Madonn', do you even listen to me when I talk?"

"You talk *a lot*."

"Asshole. No, listen. I developed this personality quiz. It's my belief you can tell a lot about a person by determining which of the Three Stooges they're most like."

"You're making this up, right?"

"Dead serious. For example: You and I are both Moes. We're dominant personalities. Vivi is mixed: part Moe, part Curly. I would guess, since Sinead is a high-powered attorney, that she's primarily Moe."

Adam peered at Anthony in disbelief. "Your wife consented to take this quiz?"

"Well, no, because I was pretty much able to figure out which Stooge she was on my own."

"Trust me: Sinead would ditch me if I asked her to take this quiz."

"Couples are supposed to share each other's interests, you know," Anthony pointed out.

"Sinead and I have a deal: I don't force her to endure the *Stooges*, and she doesn't force me to listen to jazz."

"How's the case going?"

"We try not to talk about it when we're on 'our' time."

Anthony nodded approvingly. "Makes sense."

Adam yawned. "I need a break. I really do. I'm thirty-five years old, Anthony. That's about ninety in hockey years. Some nights I come home from playing and I can't even move, I'm so crippled." He took a sip of beer. "I'm going to talk to Sinead about us finding some time to spend a whole weekend together."

"Sounds like a plan. Now, what do you want to watch: season one or season two?"

* * *

Sinead arrived in the office bright and early Monday morning. She checked Oliver's office. Empty.

Despite it being the early days of their relationship, she missed Adam incredibly when the team played out of town. Tonight she planned on staying late at the office, not only to keep her mind off Adam, but because she was desperate to get a leg up on her work. She'd just taken on a major class-action lawsuit against Joyce Toys, one of the largest toy manufacturers in the world. High levels of lead had been found in toddlers' toys. One of the senior partners, Jeff Kaplan, was originally going to take the case, but he was too busy. That he handpicked Sinead to take it instead meant a lot to her, but then he lowered the boom. "Are you sure *you'll* have the time? I hear you're quite close with one of the clients."

"I treat all my clients equally," Sinead said smoothly.

"Glad to hear it."

When he left, Sinead sat at her desk with her head in her hands. How the hell could he know about her and Adam? Shit. She made herself a huge mug of coffee. Oliver would know what to do.

He rolled into the office at around eight in the evening. "Hey." Oliver loosened his tie, kicked off his shoes, undid his belt, and stretched out on his couch, fingers laced behind his head. "What are you doing here? Shouldn't you be cuddled up at home with your honey, learning what a five hole is?"

"If you bothered to check your messages," Sinead said crossly, "you'd know that I was going to be here tonight. Honestly, Oliver. I don't understand how you function professionally when you only check your phone twice a day."

"Because I'm magic," he whispered, flashing his eyes dramatically. He took one hand out from behind his head, fluttering his fingers in the direction of the mini fridge across the room. "Be an angel and get me the bottle of tequila in there, will you?"

Tequila and coke. That's all the fridge was filled with. Sinead pulled the bottle out and reluctantly handed it to him. "Here you go."

"Thanks, cutie pie." Oliver lifted his head, taking a swig from the bottle. He lay back down with a sigh. "You look zonked."

"I am." Sinead nervously twirled a lock of her hair around her finger. "I think the seniors might know I'm seeing Adam."

"How?"

She told Oliver what Jeff Kaplan had said to her.

"This is so not a problem, Sinead." He took another swig. "Jeff is a clueless fuckwit, so I doubt he knows anything. But just in case, here's what you do: you go to Adam. You tell him that the big kahunas suspect something, and that you two need to split up temporarily. You split up. Then, if Jeff and the lads call you in to ask if you're screwing your client, you're not. Integrity intact. The end."

Sinead made a sour face. "The double standard really pisses me off."

"Understandably. It's even worse for you because you're the only female partner here."

Sinead's shoulders sank. "Thanks for reminding me of that, Oliver."

"Anytime." He heaved himself upright. "Trust me: it'll all come out right in the end."

Sinead was skeptical. "If you say so."

18

Sinead was confident as she made her way to Adam's apartment. He'd be in a good mood since the Blades had swept their road trip, and Oliver's plan was solid. When Adam heard why they needed to split up temporarily, he'd understand. Adam took his job as seriously as she took her own, and he had to know that given her high-strung personality, there was no way she could keep seeing him without being constantly worried about being caught.

A couple of blocks from Adam's door, Sinead realized she'd never been to his apartment before. In fact, she'd never been in this part of the city. Adam's descriptions of his surroundings were on target: the area was fairly nondescript. Still, there was a neighborhood feel to it that reminded her of the old Hell's Kitchen before the real estate brokers started calling it Clinton. People were walking their dogs, hanging out on stoops talking, doormen chatting with apartment residents. She wondered if Adam ever stopped to chat with anyone. Probably not.

The lobby of his building was pretty nondescript as well: a few well-placed plants, two black leather sectional couches for waiting guests, and a pile of magazines on a small cherrywood sideboard.

"Can I help you?" asked the doorman, a slight, balding man in his early fifties. Sinead wondered how long he'd been working here. One of the doormen in her building, Alan, had been there thirty years.

"I'm here to see Adam Perry."

The doorman nodded, buzzing Adam, while Sinead's eyes strayed to the security camera mounted high in one corner of the ceiling. She saw herself standing there in black and white. It was odd.

"Go on up," said the doorman pleasantly.

Sinead smiled. "Thanks."

Adam's apartment was in keeping with his personality: spare, the home of someone who had no patience for excess. A small, apartment-sized leather couch, an ottoman, and one end table. No rug yet. There were crates of what she assumed to be artwork leaning against the wall that hadn't been opened. And, of course, there was a television. She'd never known a man who could survive without a television.

Adam looked so happy to see her she was tempted to toss Oliver's advice out the window and go with the damn flow. But the flow had become a fast-moving, perilous torrent that could sweep her career away. She had to be careful.

Adam drew her up in his arms, kissing her full on the mouth. "Mmm. Missed you."

"Me, too." She wished she'd changed out of her work clothes before coming over. Here he was, in jeans and a well-worn sweatshirt, casual and comfortable. And here she was, Ms. Corporate. She slid out of her shoes, wiggling her toes. God, she hated wearing heels. She was going to be one of those old women with mangled feet; she knew it.

"You want to rest up for a few minutes, then go grab some dinner?" Adam asked.

"I'm not really hungry."

Adam shrugged. "Okay. We can just order in later."

"That sounds good." Sinead sank down on the couch wearily. Adam sat beside her, rubbing her shoulders.

"Hard day?"

"You could say that."

"What's up?" He sounded concerned.

She told Adam about her conversation with Jeff Kaplan. The more she talked about it, the more emotional she got, fighting off tears.

"Anyway," Sinead continued as she pulled herself together, "Oliver helped me figure out a way around it."

"What's that?"

"You and I need to split up temporarily."

Adam looked uncomprehending. "Excuse me?"

"It's simple. We split up. That way if they flat-out ask me if I'm seeing you, I won't be lying when I say no. In the meantime, I win the case. Then you and I get back together."

She smiled at him as if to say, "See? Easiest thing in the world." But her smile soon faded as she took in the look on Adam's face. He looked mildly offended.

"What's the matter?" Sinead asked.

"And what happens in between? We keep in touch via e-mail?"

"Adam."

His sarcasm threw her.

"You handled this wrong. You should have fought back and said, 'Hell yeah, I'm seeing Adam Perry. Why is it all right for all of you to date clients, but not me?'"

"It doesn't work that way."

"It will if you speak up for yourself, rather than put us through some cloak-and-dagger caper. I'm not surprised this was Oliver's idea."

"It's not cloak-and-dagger," Sinead said defensively. "And what's wrong with it being Oliver's idea? He knows how things work there better than I do. His plan is absolutely what needs to happen to make sure I don't get fired."

Adam shook his head obstinately. "I repeat: I think you need to stand up to them on this. Don't you see? If you let this double standard continue, they'll think they can cow you when it comes to other things. Plus, they'll do it to every woman after you who works for them. It's bullshit, Sinead."

Sinead blinked. This was not how she expected him to react. She thought he'd be annoyed that they had to break up temporarily, but that he'd see it made sense for her politically as well as emotionally.

Adam looked pained. "I'm disappointed in you."

Sinead felt her blood pressure spike. *"What?"*

"I thought you were someone who stood up for herself, no matter what."

"I am standing up for myself!" she said heatedly. "What if your job was on the line? You'd—"

"My job *is* on the line!" Adam snapped. "But you don't see me giving in, changing who I am to please others."

"You're not getting this," said Sinead, her frustration mounting. "This is a completely different situation. My reputation could be ruined if I rock the boat."

"Then don't let it happen. Call them on their hypocrisy."

Sinead's mouth fell open. "You're clueless."

"And you're gutless."

"How *dare* you? You have no idea what it's like to be the sole female partner in an all-male law firm, no idea at all. I've had to work twice as hard to get where I am because of my gender. I'm *always* working twice as hard. You think I'm going to risk everything I've fought for?"

"So you don't care if they maintain their double standard, as long as it doesn't affect your job. You're willing to sacrifice us."

"It's temporary! Why don't you get that?"

"And what happens when we get back together, huh? We hide it? We meet clandestinely?"

"We won't need to hide," Sinead reiterated, trying not to sound impatient. "Your case will be over. You won't be my client anymore."

Adam wasn't buying it. "And what if the case drags on for months? We're going to be apart all that time?"

"I guess." She hadn't thought of that.

Adam shook his head obstinately. "I don't think I can do this."

Sinead felt like she'd been punched. "What?"

"You heard me."

"What are you saying? That we're not worth the wait?"

"I'm talking about integrity."

Sinead rubbed her temples. "You don't get it. This allows me to keep my integrity and not lie. We're going around in circles. I don't know why you can't wait this out with me."

"Because I shouldn't have to. Because if you called them on their shit—"

"I'm not risking my career, Adam. Sorry."

"Then I guess we're done here."

"Yes, I guess we are." Sinead rose, struggling to quell the shaking she felt inside. "I'll be in touch about the case."

"Yup." Aloof Adam had returned.

"I can see myself to the door, thank you."

Adam disappeared into the kitchen.

Sinead slid her feet back into her pumps and walked to the door. She hated the sharp, hard tapping of her shoes on his bare wooden floor. *Ironic*, she thought. What she was now thinking about Adam was what he'd thought about her in the beginning: that she was sharp. Hard and brittle.

He was wrong. He didn't know what he was talking about. It was different for women. And if he couldn't get that through his excessively thick skull, well, that was his problem. She had to do what she had to do.

19

"Someone's got a puss on."

Sinead ignored her mother's comment as she dug into her mashed potatoes. It was the O'Brien Sunday dinner, and though she hadn't wanted to come, she thought it might make her feel better after what happened with Adam. It didn't.

"Work trouble?" Quinn asked, even though the inquiring look in his eyes told Sinead he was really asking something else.

"Work overload," said Sinead. "As always."

"Don't know how you're ever going to find a man if all you do is work, work, work," her mother said under her breath.

"Ma, please," said Sinead.

"What's going on?" Maggie mouthed.

"Later," Sinead mouthed back.

Her gaze drifted to baby Charlie, sitting in the same high chair she and her siblings had all used. Puréed carrots were smeared around his mouth, and he was kicking his legs happily. Sinead smiled at him tentatively. He smiled back, a big, gummy, baby smile that made Sinead happy. Maybe a connection was being made after all.

Quinn and Natalie left before dessert; they had to catch a flight to Paris. Sinead felt guilty; she still hadn't made it to the restaurant Natalie was managing. She never seemed to have time for all the things she wanted or intended or needed to do. *You don't make the time,* a small voice in her head accused. How her head hadn't exploded yet from all the voices packed inside was a mystery to her.

Charlie began whining to get out of his chair. Maggie took a washcloth to his face, wiped the mashed carrots off, and lifted him onto her lap. Sinead dipped her head tentatively.

"Mags? Maybe I—?"

Maggie smiled. "Sure."

She handed Charlie off to Sinead. He was squirmy in her arms, all restless energy. *What now?* Sinead thought, mildly alarmed.

"Hi, Charlie," she cooed. "Hey, there."

Charlie stared at her a moment, then turned back to Maggie, his chubby arms held out imploringly as he burst into tears.

"C'mere," said Maggie, wincing apologetically as she took Charlie back. "Don't take it personally. He's going through a big Mommy phase."

"I can attest to that," said Brendan. "Takes one look at my mug and starts to howl."

Sinead hoped they weren't just saying that.

"You okay?" Maggie asked.

Sinead smiled weakly. "I'm fine," she insisted. "No worries. Anyone want more coffee?"

* * *

"All right, what's up?"

Sinead and Maggie were in the kitchen, cleaning up. After dessert, they'd told their mother she looked exhausted, and that she should take a small nap. It was true; she did look tired. But getting her out of the kitchen also gave them a chance to chat privately.

"Nothing's up," Sinead said miserably.

"Adam—?"

"I was seeing Adam, and now I'm not."

"Because—"

Sinead sighed. "It's complicated."

"What isn't? Spill it."

Sinead told Maggie everything, fighting tears as she remembered Adam calling her gutless. She had never, ever in her life thought of herself that way, and the fact that it was her boyfriend who had called her that was sending her into a tailspin of self-doubt that was overwhelming.

"He's got some nerve," Maggie fumed, snapping her dish towel like a whip. "On his high horse, with no appreciation of how you've busted your ass. *'I'm disappointed in you,'*" she mimicked. "Does he have any idea how things work in the real world? What a jerk."

Sinead lifted her head to look at her sister. "What if he's right?"

"He's not right," Maggie snapped.

"I've lost him," Sinead said quietly. "Things had barely begun, and I blew it."

"Sounds like a blessing to me. And it's his loss." Maggie put a hand on her hip. "If any man ever had the balls to tell me he was disappointed in me when I was trying to save my job *and* the relationship, I'd kick those balls down the hall and tell him to go chase them."

"Normally that would be my MO, too—albeit it a bit more delicately—but this threw me for a loop."

"I can see why," Maggie said, grabbing a damp pot to dry. "But in the meantime, you need to think about yourself. Agreed?"

"Agreed," Sinead said glumly.

*   *   *

Sinead sat in Jeff Kaplan's plush office, waiting for him, Don Epps, and Terry Callahan to arrive. She knew why they wanted to see her. She could *feel* it.

"Sinead." Jeff Kaplan's voice was cordial as he entered briskly with Don and Terry in tow.

"Gentlemen." Sinead rose, shaking all their hands.

Jeff motioned for her to sit back down as he rounded his desk, while Don and Terry each sat in an antique Hepplewhite chair facing her on the couch. They might not be the biggest law firm in Manhattan, but they were one of the top-earning ones.

Jeff settled down comfortably behind his desk. "First of all, we're thrilled you decided to take on the Joyce case. We couldn't think of anyone better."

"I'd like to keep Oliver abreast of things just in case we need to litigate."

"Put that on hold, if you will. Oliver has too much on his plate right now," said Jeff.

Sinead gave a small nod. Nothing further needed to be said.

Jeff put his elbows on the desk, tenting his fingers. "How's the Perry case going?"

"It's going on a bit too long for my liking," Sinead replied. "It's obvious the DA is trying to drag it out until the elections."

"Has he got a case?"

"There have been three assault cases like this in the history of the NHL. Only one resulted in a prosecution."

"Good sign." Jeff looked troubled as he sighed deeply. "Look, I feel very awkward doing this, but I'm afraid some information has come to light that concerns us."

Here it comes, Sinead thought. "What's that?"

"Another attorney at another firm informed us that you're dating Adam Perry."

This again? Sinead thought. "It's not true," she said without hesitation.

The partners exchanged glances.

"This person claims to have seen you two together outside the office."

The only thing she could figure out was that one of the law firm's competitors saw them at the karaoke bar, at Maxie's, or at Basilica, and had gotten the wrong idea. Not that it was any of their damn business. But the legal community could be extremely cutthroat, especially when it came to someone like Sinead, who'd risen up through the ranks quickly and had an impeccable reputation both inside and outside the office.

"We've met several times outside the office for dinner to discuss the case," Sinead explained evenly. "Adam is more helpful when he's relaxed. Haven't you found the same to be true with some clients?"

They all agreed yes, that was true.

Sinead was itching to tell them that her personal life was none of their business, but she resisted. "I'm a professional. I can separate my work life from my private life."

Jeff tilted back in his chair. "You *have* always been the consummate professional, Sinead, and nothing but an asset to this office. I hope you can forgive us for questioning you about this. We just had to make sure."

"Of course." *Of course it doesn't matter when you screw your clients. You don't even have relationships with them. It's just sex.*

Well, I told the truth, Sinead thought as she walked back to her office. *I'm not seeing Adam.* The difference was, when the case wrapped, he wouldn't be there waiting for her. No one would be.

20

"Oh, man." *Anthony* was laughing so hard he was wiping tears from his eyes as he switched off the DVD player. "I do believe that is their finest work."

"Agreed," said Adam. The two had just finished a three-hour Stooge marathon, culminating in the classic episode "Punch Drunk," in which a pugilistic Curly goes berserk every time he hears the tune, "Pop Goes the Weasel." Adam couldn't count how many times he'd seen it, but it cracked him up every time. Today, however, he was laughing less than usual, and he knew why.

"Another brew?" Anthony asked.

"Sure, why not?"

"Comin' right up."

Anthony headed for the kitchen, leaving Adam alone in Anthony's living room. It was a place where Adam felt welcome. Cozy, lots of bookshelves, many of them filled with cookbooks. A picture of Anthony and Vivi on their wedding day. A photo of Michael, Theresa, and their kids. Adam made a mental note to call Rick. They hadn't talked in a while.

Anthony emerged from the kitchen, tossing him a beer. "I still can't believe Vivi and Sinead won't give the Stooges a chance."

"Yeah, well . . ." Adam cracked open his beer, pouring some down his throat. Anthony was eyeballing him closely.

"Got a bit of a dark one on today, eh?"

"What do you mean?"

"I mean you've looked like a miserable prick from the minute you walked in the door. What's goin' on?"

Adam shrugged. "Ah, you know . . . just shit."

"The lawsuit?"

"Yeah, that, and other shit." He took another sip of beer.

"Girlfriend shit?"

"Yeah," Adam admitted reluctantly. He really wasn't in the mood to talk about it, but he knew what a pushy bastard Anthony was: he wouldn't let up until Adam gave him a complete report.

Adam unenthusiastically recounted what had gone down between him and Sinead. Anthony closed his eyes while Adam talked, nodding occasionally like an old priest hearing confession. When Adam was done, Anthony's eyed popped open and he announced, "You're wrong on this one, bro."

"What?"

"Listen: you work with guys and only guys. Level playing field. That's not how it is in the real world. Wanna know why Vivi left Paris, the supposed gastronomic capital of the world?"

"Why?"

"Because being a chef there is a man's game. Female chefs don't get treated with the same respect, not only by the public, but also among chefs themselves. It's double-standard bullshit, and she didn't want to deal with it. So she came here."

"What's this got to do with me?"

"It's the same with Sinead," Anthony reasoned. "Didn't you say she's the only female partner in her firm?"

"Yeah."

"Then she must have to bust her balls to be taken seriously. I'll bet you anything that she makes less than a guy doing the same job."

"Look, get off your feminist soapbox, okay?" Adam was annoyed. "She has a chance to call these guys on their double standard, but instead, she's willing to put us on ice."

Anthony snorted. "Oh, boo-fucking-hoo. What if she calls them on their shit and she loses her job? Who's gonna support her? You?"

Adam glared at him.

"If you stick to your guns, you get respect," Anthony continued. "If she sticks to her guns and continues seeing you, she gets canned. It's as simple as that."

"It's not right," Adam insisted.

"No shit," said Anthony, looking at him like he was a moron. "But that's how it is. If that's what she needs to do to survive politically, who the hell are you to tell her you're disappointed in her? And it's not as if she's dumping you; it's just a temporary split."

"It's an issue of integrity."

"She *is* maintaining her integrity! She broke up with you so when they put her on the hot seat, she's not lying about it."

Adam frowned. "It's splitting hairs."

"That's what attorneys do. They split hairs," Anthony said heatedly. "Man, I don't know how she didn't pop you one. Seriously. I know things are really clear on the ice and in the locker room. But outside that frozen cocoon you and my brother work in, the world's not black and white. You were an asshole."

Adam was silent. Up until now, he hadn't second-guessed himself regarding his conversation with Sinead. But Anthony was messing with his ability to think clearly.

It's not a black-and-white world, asshole. But that's how he'd always viewed things.

Adam gulped down a slug of beer, eyeing his friend warily. "What would you do if you were me? And it better not involve making a flourless torte."

Anthony didn't hesitate. "I'd go to see her, swallow a huge piece of humble pie, tell her I understand why she has to do this, and that I'll wait for her."

"I know her," Adam said ruefully. "She'll tell me to take a hike."

"You'd deserve it."

Adam shot him a dirty look.

"For a guy who prides himself on being the king of the ice, you seem to be a bit frightened by the lady," observed Anthony. "WWMD: what would Moe do? That's what you need to ask yourself."

"Moe would get her in a headlock and take a hammer to her skull," Adam deadpanned. "I'm not sure that would go over too well with Sinead."

"Then apologize. It's that simple."

*   *   *

"I'm just telling you to watch your ass, Oliver."

Sinead tried to ignore the dismissive frown on her friend's face as she told him what Jeff had said at their meeting this morning: that they didn't want her bringing Oliver into the loop on Joyce Toys, and that they'd made some subtle comments about partners who lack discretion.

"I do have too much on my plate," said Oliver. He pointed at a stack of manila folders on his desk. "See those babies? I haven't even looked at them yet."

"It was the way he said 'too much,'" said Sinead. "Like an insinuation. Like it wasn't about workload."

"Here, I can use 'too much' in a sentence, too: You worry too much."

"And you worry too little," Sinead shot back. "I swear to God, if you get canned, I'll shoot myself."

"I'm not gonna get canned, baby doll. I'm the firm's star litigator. Have been for years. I pull their asses out of the fire all the time."

"Just watch it, okay? Seriously."

"If it doth pleaseth my lady, I will." He slicked back his hair with his hand. It didn't much help. He still looked slightly unkempt.

"Want a comb?" Sinead offered.

"Nah, don't need one."

"Let me at least fix your tie. It looks like a chimp knotted it."

"Fine, fine." Oliver sat down next to her on the couch, chin up, while Sinead began fixing his tie. "How'd my plan go over with Adam?"

"That's a dangerous question, considering my hands are so close to your neck."

Oliver looked taken aback. "What happened?"

"I ran the plan by him, and he blew a gasket, telling me this was my big chance to stand up to the partners, blah blah blah. He actually told me I was gutless and that he was disappointed in me. Long story short, it's over."

"Whoah, whoah, whoah." Oliver stilled her hands on his neck. "He said those things to you? *You?*"

"Yup." Sinead hated thinking about it.

"Sounds like he needs a good Oliver Casey ass kicking if you ask me."

Sinead's nerves jumped. "Please don't do that, Oliver. You would just end up bleeding all over the office. Besides, I'm still working on his case, remember?"

Oliver frowned. "Forgot."

"Yeah, well, I didn't." She was just finishing with his tie when there was a short knock, and Jeff Kaplan stuck his head in the door.

"Good to see someone is making sure you look halfway presentable in court this morning," he remarked to Oliver.

"Mornin', Jeff," Oliver said cheerily.

"Still haven't hired a new secretary?"

"In the process," said Oliver collegially. Which Sinead knew was a lie.

Jeff was unsmiling. "Try not to drive the next one away, please."

"Will do."

Jeff turned his attention to Sinead. "Got a minute?"

"Of course."

"Catch you on the rebound, snookyookums," Oliver said to Sinead with a delicate wave of his fingers as she started out the door behind Jeff.

Sinead looked over her shoulder and glared at him. His response was to blow her a kiss. Sinead just shook her head. Her mother's expression for Oliver was "a pip." And he was. Life without Oliver would be terribly boring.

Uneasiness overtook her as she walked alongside Jeff. Maybe they'd discussed it among themselves and decided they didn't believe her. She hoped not.

"You and Oliver are close," Jeff noted casually.

"We are."

"Do you have any pull with him?"

Sinead gave a short laugh. "Not really. What's up?"

Jeff pressed his lips into a hard line. "A number of people have remarked to me that they've seen Oliver falling-down drunk on several occasions. That doesn't reflect well on the firm."

Sinead hesitated a moment. "Between you and me, Jeff, I thought Oliver had special dispensation. Kind of."

"To a point," said Jeff tersely. "We knowingly put up with a great deal from Oliver; but his drinking and womanizing are getting out of hand."

"I see." Sinead felt embarrassed for her friend.

"If you could talk to him and tell him he's got to tone it

down a bit, we'd really appreciate it. We'd even pay for him to go to rehab. We don't want to lose him."

"I'll do what I can," Sinead promised. Oliver would have a fit.

She thought that was all, so she was surprised when Jeff ushered her into his office. Twice in one day.

"Sit."

Jeff's cordial expression turned serious. "I had Thomas print out the billings by partner spreadsheet." Thomas was Jeff's longtime paralegal.

"Yes?"

Jeff looked uncomfortable. "Your billing was the lowest."

"Oh." Sinead didn't know what to say.

"Sinead, I know you like to help out 'the little man,' as it were. But you've taken on too many charity cases this year. We need you to take on more corporate work, like the Perry case and Joyce Toys. Don, Terry, and I would like you to make an effort to close out your lower-billing cases as soon as possible. Settle and bargain if you have to."

"I see." *It all comes down to money,* Sinead thought. *Always has. But isn't that why you got into law? As a way to make sure you'd never, ever have to struggle the way your parents did?*

"Your problem is you've got a big heart," Jeff said warmly. "How many people from your old neighborhood still owe us money for legal work you've done for them?"

Sinead squirmed. "A few. But I know they're good for it, Jeff. Believe me."

"I'm sure they are. But I need you available to work on bigger cases. Especially with our primary litigator being so . . . busy."

"I see," Sinead said again quietly. "I promise I'll try to wrap those cases up as soon as possible, Jeff."

Her boss smiled at her. "I know you will. You've never let us down."

21

Anticipation and fear. Those were the emotions battling for dominance as Adam and the Blades sat on the bench waiting for Esa Saari, who was ten minutes late to afternoon practice. At first it was clear that everyone felt sheer annoyance; but the longer the minutes ticked on, the more anxious the players became. Coach Dante could have let them out on the ice to warm up while they all waited, but he wanted to make the point both to Saari and the team that when one of them screwed up, it screwed everyone else up. Inwardly, Adam was enraged. But outwardly, his demeanor was detached.

Little shit. Saari's continued and flagrant disregard for the Blades and the sport of hockey itself was incomprehensible to Adam, especially after the dressing down he'd already received. Did the kid really think that being an extraordinary player allowed him to be a self-centered, egotistical jerk? Saari had been good about keeping his name out of the gossip pages, but there was still a smugness about him that Adam was determined to expunge.

Adam glanced at Michael, who was standing by the

locker room door, his face red with fury. He motioned Adam over. "I wanna break that fuckin' little *farabutto*'s neck."

"Yeah, I hear ya," Adam said grimly. "Not that I know what *farabutto* means."

"You don't wanna know, believe me," said Michael, his dark eyes flashing. "The fucker is lucky Ty isn't here today. He wouldn't make it from the door of his car to the rink alive." Michael grimaced, digging his fingers into the back of his neck to massage it. "I'm going to lock the doors. Send a message."

"I have an idea," Adam offered. "Let him come in here and see how his disrespect impacts everyone. He'll get to see the resentment in their eyes."

"He's got five minutes to see resentment. Then I lock the door and he's fined and benched." Michael checked his watch again. "Jesus Christ," he muttered.

"Take some deep breaths," Adam urged. "I don't want you throwing an embolism before he gets here."

"Speaking of embolisms, that dipshit Rawson paid a visit to Ty again."

"What did he want this time?"

"Same crap. 'Adam should tone it down, blah blah blah.' I swear to Christ, you'd think they'd get it through their skulls by now it isn't gonna happen. I guess they think they can grind us down." Michael shook his head. "Morons." He regarded Adam pensively. "Any idea how your case is going?"

"It's going," Adam muttered.

"Anthony said you're getting a little tired of it dragging on."

"Yeah, I am, but what can you do?" Sometimes Adam forgot that Anthony was his coach's brother. It was weird for Adam to hear Michael recount stuff he'd told Ant when they were just hanging out.

"Stooges aren't helping your mood?" Michael ribbed.

Despite his mounting anger, Adam actually managed a grin. "A bit."

Michael touched his head. "I got a new haircut. My brother's an idiot, right? I don't look like Moe."

"Not at all."

"He's such a *gavone*."

Murmuring among the players came to an abrupt halt as Esa Saari came strolling out of the locker room. He acknowledged Michael and Adam with a pleasant nod. "Mornin', Coach. Captain."

"Get your fucking Finnish ass to the bench," Michael growled, striding purposefully toward Esa. Michael's eyes were blazing, the look on his face the same he used to make when he was a winger heading into the corners on a forecheck.

Adam thought Michael was seconds away from lunging at Saari, so he decided to intervene. "Coach, do you mind if we have a brief players-only meeting? I think the players might like to talk this out among themselves before you get involved."

Michael Dante started to calm down. He didn't say anything. He simply walked over to the bench, picked up a stick, looked to see whose it was, then put it back. Finding the one with Saari's number on it, Michael pulled it out, held it in his hands for a moment, and then in a flash broke it in half over the boards, tossing the splintered parts onto the ice.

"Five minutes," Michael told Adam, storming into the locker room.

*   *   *

Adam walked slowly toward the bench, his eyes drilling a smoking hole into Saari's broad chest. Though he didn't let it show on his face, he was pleased to see the team was eyeing their teammate with unabashed resentment. "Sorry I'm late, dudes," Saari told them. "Forgot to set my alarm."

"Yeah right," said Eric Mitchell, just audibly.

Saari turned to Adam. "Sorry I'm late, Cap," he said, looking sheepish but not sheepish enough to be believed. "I forgot to set my alarm. I know it's a bullshit excuse, but it's true. You can fine me as much as you want."

Adam just stared at him. He could feel the tension emanating from the bench tauten. They were waiting for him to tear Saari a new one. But Adam decided to approach it differently this time.

"I'm not going to fine you," Adam said, which seemed to throw Saari momentarily. "What I'm going to do is have you meet me at the Wild Hart tomorrow night at seven sharp."

"I have a date—"

"Break it," Adam said simply.

"I could do that," Saari replied as if he were doing Adam a big, fat favor.

"Not you could. You will." He motioned for the team to get on the ice. "Seven," he reminded Saari. "Don't forget."

* * *

The confused look on Saari's face as he entered the pub was priceless. Adam had deliberately sat in a back booth facing the door, not only so Saari would see him but also so he wouldn't know who Adam was with. As Saari approached the table, he watched the younger man's face go from guarded to absolute shock when he saw it was Temu Tikkanen, a great Finnish player for the NHL.

Saari was momentarily speechless as he nervously extended his hand to Tikkanen's to shake. "I— it's a pleasure meeting you. You were my biggest hero when I was growing up."

Tikkanen was unsmiling. "Sadly, it is not a pleasure to meet you."

Saari looked utterly destroyed, color draining from his

face as he turned into a stammering child in the presence of his idol. "I-I don't—"

"Sit down, Esa," said Adam firmly.

Saari sat next to Adam, looking dazed. Tikkanen was eyeing him with contempt. At first glance Tikkanen looked like just another handsome and distinguished European businessman. But the longer you looked at him, the more the scars became noticeable, and the longer you looked into his eyes, the more you could see a hardness that only came with years of physical struggle. That was the face that was staring at Saari with such displeasure that Adam almost felt sorry for the little bastard.

"You want anything to drink?" Adam offered.

Saari's eyes quickly swept the table to see what the two other men were drinking. "A beer would be fine."

Adam nodded, motioning the waiter over to order a pint for Saari. There was no small talk as the men waited for his drink to arrive. The silence had to be excruciating for Saari, especially since Tikkanen just kept staring at him. By the time Saari's beer arrived, he was staring down at the table, unable to bear the scrutiny.

Saari barely sipped his beer.

"Since you seem to have a hard time giving a shit about what I said," Adam began, "I thought Temu might help you put things in perspective."

Tikkanen finally broke his silence, but instead of speaking to Saari, he turned to Adam. "Adam, would you mind if I spoke with Saari in Finnish?"

"Not at all," Adam replied, putting his pint to his lips.

Tikkanen and Saari began speaking in their shared native tongue. "How many Stanley Cups have I won, Saari?"

"Two," Saari replied, still unable to look at his hero directly.

"Tell me why I won them."

"Because you're a great player," said Saari, his voice

quivering with admiration. "You were the first Finnish player to make it into the Hockey Hall of Fame."

Tikkanen's expression didn't change. "When you were a little boy back in Finland staring at my poster on your bedroom wall, dreaming of coming to the USA to play one day for the NHL, did you have any idea how much shit I had to put up with?"

Esa looked shamefaced. "No, sir."

"Then I'll tell you. I was the first player to represent my country here in the birthplace of hockey. They said I was soft, that all Europeans were pussies. They claimed we had no guts, that we were all flash and no substance and that if you hit us enough, we'd collapse like a house of cards. I showed them otherwise. They speared me, and I came back for more. They slashed me, and I took it, and then next time I met up with them in the corners, I made them pay. Now the league is filled with Europeans. I was one of the ones who did that. Me, Borg from Sweden, and Vlad from Russia. We worked our asses off to gain their respect, and in the end we got it.

"Adam here tells me that you're a party boy who thinks it's fine to come strolling into practice late; that you even think it's okay to slack off in practice if you produce on the ice. Which makes me want to ask you just one question: who the fuck do you think you are?"

Saari's face turned red as he shrank in his seat.

"What you fail to realize, Esa, is that you're not just playing for your team, you're playing for all of Finland. You fuck up on the ice, we all look bad. You don't respect the game, we all look bad. Are you hearing me?"

Saari swallowed nervously. "Yes."

"You make me ashamed to be a Finn. I don't like that, not after all the work I put in to proving myself. You want to be a hero to all those little boys at home who now have your poster on their bedroom walls? Set an example. Give them a reason to be proud of their country and its hockey players, so that if one of them gets a shot at playing here, they're taken seriously. Do you understand what I'm saying?"

"Yes, sir."

"If I ever hear anything about you thinking you're some hot shit young turk who doesn't have to obey the rules because he's talented, I will personally come to your flat and fuck you up so badly your career will end right there and then. We clear?"

"Yes, sir," Saari managed to squeak out.

Tikkanen sat back, satisfied, and switched back to English. "Good. You think they have any Finlandia here? Let's order some shots so I can clear the taste of bile from my mouth. Then we'll call it a night so you two can get a good night's sleep for tomorrow's practice."

22

"*Hello? Is anybody* in there?"

Sinead blinked as Maggie waved a hand in front of her face. They were in one of the booths in the Hart's dining room, having dinner. They'd been trying to get together at least one night a week. Their shared memories made for some wonderful laughs.

"I'm here," Sinead assured Maggie, even though she hadn't been for a few minutes. She was thinking about the Joyce Toys case and all the other damn cases she had to wrap up. She was also thinking about Adam, even though she hadn't seen him in six weeks.

Maggie looked dubious. "You're here now, but you weren't a few seconds ago."

"Just thinking about work," said Sinead, taking a small sip of her martini.

"And Adam."

"A bit."

"His case should be wrapped up soon, right?"

"God, I hope so."

"Then you could go out with Oliver," Maggie teased. "That's Mom's dream."

Sinead scowled. "He's not my type. Plus he's having serious issues with alcohol, which worries me a lot."

"That's too bad."

"It is. He's brilliant, and if he throws it all away because he can't get his act together, it will be awful."

"Agreed." Maggie began buttering a roll. "Look, I wanted to ask you something, and it's no biggie if you say no, okay?"

"Great opening," Sinead said dryly. "What's up?"

"I was wondering if you could watch Charlie for an hour next Wednesday night. Brendan is going to be working late, and I have an old client who was just in a car accident, and she's really in desperate need of a massage."

Sinead jumped at the chance. "Absolutely," she said, even though the prospect made her nervous.

"Thanks so much, Neenee."

Sinead took another sip of her drink. "Have you talked to Brendan about my 'loan' offer?"

Maggie looked sheepish. "I keep meaning to get around to it, but . . ."

"Don't put it off. It's important."

"I know, I know. I'll talk to him soon. I promise."

Sinead was just about to remind Maggie their parents helped Quinn with his rent when he was just starting out as a journalist when the pub door swung open, and in walked Adam.

"Shit," Sinead whispered vehemently.

Maggie turned. "What?" She spotted Adam. "Oh." She turned back to Sinead. "He better not have the balls to come over here if he knows what's good for him."

"Maggie, don't cause trouble. Please. Just block me."

"What?"

"I said block me. So he doesn't see me."

Maggie discreetly looked over her shoulder. "Too late. Christie's just handed him his beer and he's walking over here."

"Shit," Sinead repeated.

She was composed by the time Adam reached the table, even though her emotions were running as wild as undisciplined children. Coincidence he was here? Here to see her? Here just to have a couple of drinks at the bar?

"Hey," he said. His trademark greeting.

"Hello," said Sinead, reaching for her martini. Her throat had suddenly become parched.

He extended his hand to Maggie. "You must be Maggie. I'm Adam."

"I know you are."

Sinead gave her a pointed look.

"Nice to meet you," Adam said.

Maggie smiled tersely. "Nice to meet you, too."

Adam turned his intense gaze back to Sinead. "I was wondering if we could talk."

Sinead squirmed uncomfortably in her seat. "Well, right now I'm having dinner with my sister—"

"No, no, you should talk now," Maggie insisted. "Get it over with."

Sinead glared at her sister. She couldn't believe she'd said that. No, actually, she could. She just wished she hadn't.

Adam looked uneasy. "Are you sure?"

"Absolutely," said Maggie with a smile so sweet it could kill. "I need to talk to my parents about something anyhow."

Sinead wanted to sock her. "Tell Mom to hold my dinner. I'll have it in a little while."

"Right, then." Maggie turned to Adam. "It's so nice to finally be able to put a face to your name," she purred sarcastically. "I've heard so much about you."

Adam sat down in the booth opposite Sinead.

"How can I help you?" Sinead asked as if she were talking to a client—which she was.

The formality seemed to throw Adam for a moment, which puzzled Sinead. He'd appeared unexpectedly. Did he think she'd be convivial?

"I assume this is about the case?"

Adam smiled slyly. "In a way."

Sinead's heart battered against her ribs. "Explain."

Adam rolled the beer bottle between his palms. "First, I want to apologize for calling you gutless. I was talking out my ass."

"An apology from Adam Perry. I believe this is historic."

"I'm serious, Sinead," he replied, seeming distressed that she might not be taking him seriously.

"I know you are," she assured him. "And I appreciate it. Apology accepted."

Adam blew out a long breath of relief that segued into a shamed expression.

"I gave no thought to how hard you have worked to get where you are, or what you need to do to make sure nothing jeopardizes that. I reacted viscerally; the only thing my brain latched onto was that you wanted to split up with me, and once that got lodged there . . ." He shook his head, looking embarrassed.

"But I'd explained to you it would only be temporary," Sinead reminded him quietly.

"I know. But I was on my high horse and couldn't get down. Now I realize that the professional worlds we move in are very different. Mine is black and white, and yours is anything but."

"That's exactly right."

"That's probably the most eloquent I've ever been outside a locker room," Adam said self-deprecatingly.

Sinead smiled. "I'm honored to be the recipient." She suddenly felt shy. "So—?"

Adam's gaze was unblinking as he regarded her across the table. "I think I've figured out a way for us to be together without jeopardizing things for you."

"What's that?" Sinead asked cautiously.

Adam leaned across the table toward her. "We're going

to get together frequently to discuss my case, and if that leads to something else, well, it's technically not dating, right? It's just hooking up."

"But that's what all the men in the firm do. They just hook up."

"But you're not really just hooking up. You're having a relationship with me."

"So, basically, I'm lying."

"I suppose."

"You suppose?"

"C'mon, Sinead, it's perfect. Do you know how long it took my Neanderthal brain to come up with that?"

"Hours."

"Days."

"Not *technically* dating . . ." Sinead mused. "You should have been a lawyer, you know that?"

Adam grinned. "I'll admit, I am pretty proud of it." His gaze was intense yet hopeful. "What do you say?"

Sinead surprised herself. "I have to think about it. It's not that I don't want to get back with you," she assured him. "I just need time to go over it all in my mind. Explore all the angles. Make sure I'm not compromising myself."

"Spoken like a true attorney," Adam said unenthusiastically.

A great tenderness for him swept over Sinead. "You understand, don't you?"

"I guess I have to." He ran his hand through his hair. "I'm sorry. I didn't mean to sound snide."

"You didn't. Just disappointed."

"I am."

"A few days. That's all I ask."

"Fair enough."

He paused, his face more open and vulnerable than Sinead had ever seen it. "I don't want to lose you, Sinead."

Overcome with emotion, Sinead looked down at her

hands. Even her ex had never said that to her. *I don't want to lose you, either,* she thought. *But I need to make sure I examine the ramifications.*

Sinead lifted her head to gaze back at him. "A few days," she repeated quietly. "That's all I need."

* * *

"You're right. The guy's totally devious. He should be a litigator."

Sinead tried to ignore the harrowing sight of Oliver in his bright red boxers, white undershirt, and black socks as she chatted with him on his couch. He'd called in to the office that morning to say he was "working at home"—a euphemism for *hung over.* He'd been "working at home" a lot lately. Sinead decided she'd pay him a lunchtime visit.

She'd never been to Oliver's apartment, but it was exactly the way she'd always imagined it would be: an unholy mess. Being a neat freak, the mess and clutter actually made her itchy. If she could hire a team of Merry Maids to clean it, she would, but she knew Oliver would be insulted. She could hear his voice in her head: *This is how I roll, baby doll.* There was no way he brought his conquests back here; his seductive prowess *had* to take place at their abodes.

Oliver made a sour face as he chugged down a cup of coffee as thick as motor oil. "What's your hesitation?"

"I don't know," Sinead lamented. "It's just not sitting right with me."

"It's not like you're going to be stupidly blatant, right? 'Oh, yeah, here I am out to dinner holding hands with my client.' Your whole relationship will be entirely private. And before you say anything about how it makes you just as slutty as the mighty men of Kaplan, Epps, and Callahan, allow me to point out to you that you'll be having a *relationship* with this guy, not just *relations.*"

"But we'll be sneaking around. Kind of. And if the partners find out—"

"It's all bullshit, Sinead," Oliver said vehemently. "You could threaten to sue them for gender bias, you know. Just the mention of that to the outside world would dry up half the firm's billings. I think Adam's idea is great. Shit. Why didn't I think of that? It's airtight, dude-ess."

"Is it? It's splitting hairs. It's a loophole."

Oliver ran his hands over his unshaved face in frustration. "Sinead? You're an attorney. You're well acquainted with loopholes. You love loopholes. As the old song goes, loopholes are a girl's best friend." Oliver's eyes hooded. "And think about how much fun it will be, meeting for dinner and then leaving separately, only to clandestinely hook up later for some love squeezins."

"You're right."

"Of course I am. I just described my whole social life. Stick with me, kiddo. I'm always right."

"Not always."

Oliver lifted a bushy eyebrow. "Pardon *moi*?"

She had to be delicate. "You were right when you told me you were the firm's top litigator. But it's starting not to matter anymore." She winced. "Jeff commented to me recently about how you've been racking up the sick days and working at home a lot. That's not good."

Oliver heaved a long-suffering sigh. "As long as I deliver—"

"They're going to fire you if you don't cut back on your drinking and carousing," she cut in. "They asked me to persuade you to tone it down."

"Pshaw! They would never fire me."

"Jeff wasn't kidding, Oliver," Sinead admonished worriedly. How could he not take this seriously?

"Did he use the *A* word?" Oliver smirked.

"Which one? Alcoholic or asshole?"

"Alcoholic."

Pain began to throb in her chest. "You are, Oliver," she said quietly. "You might be a functional alcoholic, but you still are one. You drink every day."

"Wow," Oliver mocked. "Listen to you. When did you switch sides?"

"It's got nothing to do with switching sides," Sinead said vehemently. "It's got to do with honesty. I love you, and I don't want to see you destroy your career. It's not charming anymore, the rumpled, hungover attorney barely making it to court on time but still able to kick ass when the pressure's on. I think you need help." She hesitated. "Jeff said that if you wanted to go into rehab, the firm would be willing to pay for it."

"Fuck Jeff, and fuck you," Oliver snarled. "I've been nothing but a friend to you, and this is how you thank me? By stabbing me in the back?"

"Oliver, please try to listen to me," Sinead pleaded. "You know I wouldn't be saying any of this if it didn't worry me."

"Did you at least try to defend me to Jeff?" Oliver sneered. "Or did you kiss his ass the way you've been doing since the first day you started working there?"

"Fuck you, Oliver," Sinead snapped.

"No, fuck you."

Sinead stood up shakily. "Let's talk tomorrow when you're not hungover and irrational."

"No point. Now if you'll excuse me, I've got *work* to do."

"Right." Sinead was on her way to the door when she abruptly turned around, unable to help herself. "Just think about what I said. *Please*."

"Please shut up and get out. We've got nothing to say to each other."

Sinead left the apartment, quietly closing the door behind her. She stood in the hallway a few minutes, breathing deeply until the nausea threatening to overtake her passed. She'd never been good at fighting outside the court-room. In fact, she hated it. But she couldn't keep her mouth shut any longer. She loved Oliver; he was her best friend. And if he couldn't bear hearing the truth, then there was nothing she could do about it, which killed her. She got in the elevator, rode down to the lobby, and with a heavy heart, went back to the office.

23

Depressed from her encounter with Oliver earlier in the day, Sinead was glad when she found a minute to call Adam. At least one positive thing had come from visiting her friend, or former friend, or whatever he was: she was now willing to stop worrying about loopholes and splitting hairs, and let herself be with Adam. Even though they'd mended things the night before, he sounded glad to hear from her, as if they hadn't talked in a long time. Sinead hoped his buoyant mood wasn't the result of how well the Blades seemed to be playing. Maybe a little of it had to do with her.

When she concluded the call asking Adam if she could stop by later and he affably told her to come on over, she went directly from work to his place. It was late, and she was afraid that if she went home to change first, she might start second-guessing herself and overthink things or let weariness overtake her. The quick cab ride downtown straight from work was the perfect antidote to keep her focused on the decision she'd made.

Nervous anticipation began simmering inside her as she imagined their physical reunion and all that might entail.

She couldn't wait to press her lips against his, hear his ragged breath as he became aroused. In all the years she was with Chip, he'd never made her feel as vibrantly alive as she did the first time she was with Adam. He was as intense in bed as he was on the ice.

She smiled at his doorman, thanking him when he gave her the go-ahead to go up to Adam's apartment. She knocked twice and then opened the door. Adam grinned at her from the couch, where he sat with a big bowl of popcorn in his lap, watching *The Three Stooges*.

"Perfect timing," he said. "The episode is almost over."

"You could always finish watching it later," Sinead suggested sweetly.

Adam paused the DVD. "Come sit down next to me," he said, patting the empty space beside him. "Just two more minutes until it's done. I swear."

Sinead capitulated: she kicked off her heels, shed her trench coat, and joined him on the couch. Adam resumed playing the *Stooges*; within the space of one minute, one of them (Sinead didn't know one from the other, though she seemed to vaguely remember Quinn calling Liam "Curly") had tried to poke another's eyes out with a giant fork, one had slapped another across the head with a two-by-four, and one had hit the third in the butt with a sledgehammer. She turned to Adam with a withering expression.

"This is giving me a migraine."

Adam looked dismayed. "You don't think it's funny *at all*? Really?"

"I'm going to pretend you didn't ask that."

"Albert Einstein loved the *Stooges*."

"He did not!"

"Did." Adam switched off the TV. "Better?"

"Much." Sinead reached into the bowl of popcorn and popped a few pieces in her mouth. It was deliciously salty, just the way she liked it.

Adam casually snaked his arm along the back of the

couch as he angled his body toward her. "To what do I owe this honor?"

"I think you know."

Adam snapped his fingers. "Oh, right. You're here to discuss my case."

"Correct." Sinead licked some salt off her fingers. Lust flashed across Adam's face. *So, he finds it sexy.* She put another finger in her mouth, sucking it slowly while she gazed at Adam with a seductive smile. She was rewarded with a smoldering look in return that made her body flash with instant heat. Sinead slowly took her finger from her mouth. They were holding each other's gaze, watching, waiting to see who would bridge the gap between looking and touching. It was Adam; he leaned forward, his hand cupping the nape of her neck. "I'm sorry," he said again, his lips barely brushing hers. "You know, about not understanding how things work for you."

"Prove it."

Adam laughed, then pressed his mouth to hers, hard. Pure white heat crackled through Sinead's body as she threw her arms around his neck, returning his ardor. She loved the feeling of him pulling her closer, possessively, as if anyone dared to come near her, they'd have him to answer to.

She pushed against him, trembling but not tentative. She wanted him to know how badly she ached for him. Impatience was clawing away inside her, making her bolder than she usually would be. "I want you," she said breathily into his ear. She pulled back to look into his eyes, those eyes that were so serious and intent, and saw pure desire there. *I'm doing that to him,* she thought in amazement. *Me.*

His mouth was back on hers, bruising and wild, pushing her toward the primal. Sinead tugged up his shirt, pressing her hands against the broad expanse of chest, the perfectly muscled torso. Adam responded; his eyes lazed shut for a moment as Sinead moved her palms up and down his heated skin. Adam slowly opened his eyes, his ragged breath pausing for a moment as he laid her down on the couch. Again, Sinead watched and waited. Slowly, oh so slowly, he lowered his mouth to hers, his kisses alternately soft then savage. Sinead rocked beneath him, pressing into him, wanting him to take her right now. It was as if Adam heard her thoughts: tearing his mouth from hers, his fingers nimbly unbuttoned her blouse, tossing it to the floor. Sinead watched him, entranced by the way his eyes pooled with dark desire as he reached down to roughly push her bra up and out of his way. Sinead gasped as his mouth clamped down on her, sucking hard with a desperate groan that made her weak. Her hands glided up and down his strong shoulders, her nails pressing into the hard skin. She was close, so close. "Don't torture me," she begged.

Adam lifted his head, grinning wickedly before returning his mouth to her bare torso, hot kisses making a trail down to her hips. Sinead glanced down at him; it was killing him to wait, she knew it was. Her intuition was confirmed as Adam pushed her skirt up and slid her panties down. She was panting lightly now, the need inside her juddering through her body at a pace her mind couldn't keep up with. There was a long torturous pause; then Adam plunged his fingers deep inside her. Crying out, Sinead moved against him, silver sparks of desire playing up and down her body until she called out his name and came hard, reveling in the wild joy streaking through her.

She was just coming back to herself when she felt him lift his body from hers enough to free himself from his jeans. She held her breath, and there he was, slipping inside her, a perfect fit.

She was going to explode again. Swallowing her gasps, Sinead drew her knees up, wrapping her legs around the strong hips pumping against her. She began to quiver as his strokes became more pronounced, pushing deeper, his panting breath the sexiest sound in the world. Clamping herself tighter around him was her own undoing; she was hurled into a place of blinding, all-consuming release. Tears of joy pricked at the corners of her eyes. Happiness, abandon. She felt her inner self float up lazily like a balloon into a clear blue sky. Adam was setting her free from herself, from all the rules and pressure that had been the self-chosen parameters of her life for so long.

"You okay?" Adam rasped. He had noticed the glistening in her eyes, mistook it for pain.

"I'm wonderful," Sinead sniffled. She trailed her nails up and down his back, feeling a thrill as he closed his eyes, threw his head back, and pushed himself ever faster toward his own abandon, groaning low as he emptied himself into her and collapsed onto her, panting. Sinead ran her hands up and down his sides, the heat of his body still pulsing. She kissed the side of his face, running her hand through his sandy brown hair. When he lifted his head to look at her, she saw her own sense of freedom reflected back at her in his gaze. She slowly broke into a smile, then a delighted laugh. Adam looked at her quizzically for a moment, and then he, too, began to laugh.

"That was wonderful!" Sinead exclaimed. "That was so, so wonderful!"

Adam looked questioning, but happy. "You sound giddy."

"I *feel* giddy."

"Good." He pushed himself up on his elbows, cradled her face in his hands, planting gentle kisses all over her face. "You're the best attorney in town. Did you know that?"

"Why, thank you."

"I'd like to discuss the case a little longer, if you don't mind." Adam shifted and sat up. "How about we shower and order in some Chinese?"

"That would be great." Tell them no MSG, she almost

said, but refrained. Nothing could give her a headache tonight. Nothing.

"Spend the night," he murmured, lifting a strand of her hair and kissing it.

Sinead's heart dipped. "I can't. I don't have a change of clothing. It's probably a risky thing to do, anyway."

"Who would know?"

"I would." She kissed the tip of his nose. "When's your next free weekend?"

"A few weeks, I think."

"Let's go up to my house in Bearsville."

Adam's face lit up. "Yeah?"

"Yeah. But no guns."

"How about a fishing pole?" he asked, flashing a sly grin.

"Fine," she said, pretending to be exasperated before breaking into a broad smile. "This can work, right?" Sinead suddenly blurted. God, why did she have to ruin the moment?

Adam kissed her fingertips. "*Yes*. Just let yourself be as happy as you were a few seconds ago, okay?"

"Okay."

Of course it would work. This was a relationship between two conscientious, intelligent people. They would make it work.

24

"Don't look so scared."

Sinead gave a faltering smile as Maggie reeled off the instructions for watching Charlie. She'd arrived at her sister's early so she could tell her about reuniting with Adam. Maggie seemed genuinely happy for her, but Sinead's joy in sharing the news was slightly diminished because Maggie was distracted, frantically running around the house trying to get her things together before she left.

"Did I go over everything?" Maggie asked as she grabbed her keys. She was balancing Charlie on her hip. He was already in his pajamas, clutching a small, battered stuffed bear that Sinead remembered from their childhood.

"Yes."

Maggie walked Sinead through the Charlie drill. "He can stay up for another half hour. He likes to watch *Sesame Street*; I already have the DVD set up. When you put him down, just sit by his crib for a few minutes and rub his belly while you hum to him."

"You already told me that, Mags."

Maggie was oblivious. "He should drop off within ten

minutes. If he doesn't, kiss him, tell him good night, and leave. If he starts to howl, try to ignore it. If you can't deal with it, then take him out of the crib and hang out on the couch with him; that should calm him down. At any rate, I should be home shortly after that." She patted Sinead's shoulder. "You'll be fine." She smiled slyly. "You should have brought Adam with you."

Sinead laughed. "Oh, right. I'm sure this would be his idea of fun. Plus I don't want to get in trouble with Charlie's parents," she ribbed. Her mind flashed back to baby-sitting when she was a teenager; the one time she let her boyfriend come over after the parents left, they'd come home early and she'd gotten into a world of trouble.

Maggie seemed breathless. "You've got my cell number, right? And Brendan's?"

"Yes and yes." Sinead shooed her toward the door. "Go. You're going to be late."

"Okay." Maggie hesitated, looking mildly guilty as she kissed her son on the forehead. "You be good for Aunt Neenee, okay? Mommy will be back soon."

She handed him off to Sinead, quickly heading out the back door. Charlie was in Sinead's arms all of five seconds before he began to howl.

"Oh, shit," she whispered as he tried to wriggle out of her arms, his arms stretched toward the back door, screaming "Mommyyyyyyy!" Sinead panicked; should she let him go? Could he even walk yet? She should have asked Maggie. What if she put him down and he tried to walk and he couldn't and got hurt? God, she was an idiot.

She kept him in her arms, murmuring to him soothingly as she hustled him into the living room. "Hey, big guy, c'mon. Want to watch some Ernie and Bert? Mmm?"

Charlie seemed not to hear her as he continued to cry. Sinead carefully sat down with him on her lap, fumbling desperately with the remote, pointing it at the TV as if it were a ray gun.

"Okay, we'll watch Ernie and Bert," she trilled. She hit the DVD, and the Muppets appeared on the screen. Charlie sucked in his lower lip and stopped crying. Sinead loosened her grip a bit; he crawled off her lap and sat down beside her, mesmerized by the brightly colored puppets and their silly voices.

Thank God, she thought. If he'd kept on crying, she might have burst into tears herself. She always seemed to make him cry. There had to be something about her, some maternal warmth she lacked, that he was tuning in to. It pained her. She wanted a relationship with her nephew, she really did. But something was getting in the way of it.

He seemed oblivious to her presence now, which was good. She studied him the way you might an exotic, beautiful little animal to whom you were attracted but were afraid to get close to, because you didn't know how they might react. She swallowed, realizing what an awful mistake it would have been if she and Chip had had a child. Even if she'd won the battle of staying home part-time, it would have been a disaster, because she was clearly not cut out for this.

Charlie abruptly turned to look at her, and Sinead felt her heart lurch, fearful the mere sight of her might set him off. She smiled. "Hey, Charlie," she said gently. "I'm Aunt Neenee. Remember?"

His lower lip quivered a minute, then he went back to watching TV. She knew from the DVD Susie had shown her that Adam was wonderful with kids; maybe next time she watched Charlie, if there was a next time, she *would* bring Adam with her.

Adam. She hated having to go home after making love with him. Next time, she'd bring a change of clothing and spend the night. Oliver was right: there was something furtive about what they were doing, and that was kind of exciting. But it bothered her that they really couldn't do much beyond going out to dinner without arousing suspicion. She could watch him play hockey, she supposed, as long as she was with Quinn. But the movies or a picnic in the park or just holding hands together as they walked along the street? That was out for now. She hoped there was some movement on his case soon; she couldn't imagine having to maintain a facade of being purely professional for months on end.

Time raced by. Before she knew it, half an hour had passed, and it was time to put Charlie to bed. *God, please, don't let him begin crying again.* She turned off the TV and took a deep breath. "Bedtime, big guy," she said softly. Charlie began crawling away from her, and Sinead gingerly picked him up. He began flailing in her arms, howling for Maggie and Brendan. Sinead carefully carried him upstairs, afraid of dropping him. She was surprised to find herself on the verge of tears. *Incompetent. Please stop crying, you're scaring me. I don't know what to do.*

In Charlie's room, she turned on the night-light and carefully placed him in his crib. He pulled himself up and stood, clutching the bars of the crib as if he were in a prison cell, screaming. Should she leave him like that? Should she keep trying to put him on his back? Shit.

"Oh, don't cry, Charlie," she cooed, picking up yet another teddy bear. She hummed and made him dance along the crib railing. Charlie's tears sniffled to a halt, and he reached for the bear. Sinead handed it to him. He looked at it a minute, then tossed it, resuming his crying.

Sinead closed her eyes, trying to rub away the tension in her forehead. She knew babies weren't like this all the time, but still. Was Charlie a "handful," as her mother might say? She thought of the sacrifice she would have had to have made to have a child and told herself she was relieved things hadn't worked out with Chip. But if that were true, then why did she feel so sad?

* * *

"Hey."

Adam, deep in thought as he walked toward Met Gar, turned around to see Teddy Rawson, Commissioner Welsh's henchman, hustling toward him. Adam frowned. He needed Teddy's "You better change your game" bullshit like he needed a hole in the head.

"What's up?" Adam asked curtly.

"You got a minute?"

"Depends."

Rawson looked around. They were standing in the middle of the sidewalk, irked pedestrians parting to go around them. "C'mon. Let's have a drink in the bar outside the players' entrance into Met Gar."

"Is this the hockey commissioner's new approach?" Adam asked acidly. "Threats don't work, so now you're going to try to befriend me?"

"It's not that at all," Rawson swore. "Five minutes of your time."

"Whatever."

Adam shrugged, walking with the stocky man through the concrete plaza that surrounded Met Gar. Rawson had been a helluva player in his day, tough as nails, his willingness to drop his gloves legendary. He'd broken his nose more times than Adam could count, and the scars on his face bore testament to a player who gave it his all. He'd always respected Rawson, until he retired and became Welsh's henchman—or "Welsh's bitch," as Michael preferred to call him.

The bar was largely empty save for a few suits. Adam went to sit at the bar, but Rawson motioned him toward a table instead. "This'll be better." *Interesting,* Adam thought. Whatever Rawson was going to throw at him, he didn't want the bartender to hear it.

"What can I get you?" Rawson asked.

"Corona."

Rawson nodded and went to get their drinks. Adam took in his surroundings; the walls of the bar were decorated with huge, color photos of some of the best athletes who'd ever played hockey and basketball at Met Gar, Ty Gallagher among them. Adam's eyes lit on a team picture of the Blades on the ice, gathered around the last Stanley Cup they'd won. Envy flared up inside him. He was going to have that experience this season if it killed him.

Rawson returned with their beers, sitting down across from Adam, who was watching him carefully.

"So what's the deal?" Adam asked.

Rawson looked embarrassed. "Look, this hard-on Welsh has got for you? I don't agree with it. I think it's bullshit."

"Yeah?" Adam was skeptical.

"Yeah. The only reason I do what Welsh wants me to do is because I need this job. Otherwise, I'd go tell him to fuck himself."

"Go on. I'm listening."

"I don't know why he's got it out for you, but he does. It's like he's on a mission from God to bring you down. He's fucking obsessed with it."

"No shit. It's obvious the officials have been told to crack down and are listening to him loud and clear."

Rawson grimaced. "Yeah, I know. It's embarrassing."

"So you wanted to have a drink with me to tell me Welsh is out to get me? I've pretty much figured that out."

"No, it was important to me that you know that my doing Welsh's dirty work is nothing personal. I think you're a great player, Adam. You embody the old-time values; you play the game the way it's meant to be played. I respect you. But like I said, I need this job. Integrity isn't going to pay my bills; you hear what I'm saying? Sometimes a guy has to do what he has to do."

"I hear ya," Adam murmured, feeling bad for him.

Rawson looked relieved. "Good. Because I'd hate you to think I feel the same way Welsh does."

"Welsh . . ." Adam shook his head, puzzled. "Why me, man? There are so many goons still in the league; why does he have to go after guys who are physical but can actually play?"

"I know," Rawson agreed. "Part of the problem is, the guy's not a hockey person. He's a suit. He's a corporate lawyer. The board of governors brought him in to break the union and help them ratchet up revenues."

Adam took a slug of beer. "Yeah, well, he's a lawyer who's pissing up the wrong tree, I can tell you that."

Rawson sniggered. "He'll find that out soon enough, won't he?"

"Yep." Adam took another slug of beer. "You miss playing, Teddy?"

"Every goddamn day."

"You skated the Cup once, right?"

"Yeah. Toronto, 1967." He looked nostalgic. "Greatest night of my life. Even greater than when my daughter was born, but don't tell my wife that."

Adam laughed. "Game six of the finals that year was amazing. When you were elbowed in the face in the middle of the third period and you pulled your own teeth out on the bench and didn't miss a shift? I remember watching that game clip and thinking, 'That's how tough I want to be.'"

"And you are." Rawson took a drink. "The league has changed so much since then. It's a damn shame."

"I agree."

"Not much we can do. I wish there was some way I could help you out, Adam."

"Hey, no worries, Teddy, okay?"

"Okay." He lifted his beer bottle. "To old-time hockey," he toasted.

Adam clinked his bottle against Rawson's. "Old-time hockey."

25

"This place is amazing."

Adam stood on the deck of Sinead's weekend house, marveling at the panoramic view. The house, all wood and glass, was perched high atop a hill looking out over rolling green meadows and mountains. Adam couldn't believe she didn't come up here every free moment she had. It was beautiful and peaceful, no sound at all but the wind winding through the trees and the occasional cow mooing in the distance. No honking horns, no trucks backfiring, no fire engines . . . he loved it. Manhattan was great, but given the choice, this was where he'd choose to be.

Sinead joined him on the deck, her hair pulled back in a taut ponytail, sunglasses perched on her head. Even when she "dressed down" in jeans and a simple T-shirt, she was gorgeous. It bugged him a bit that she insisted on being the one to drive up here, but since it was her car, he really didn't have a leg to stand on. She told him he was sexist. He preferred to think of it as traditional. It felt weird being in the passenger seat. At least he'd won the battle for what music they played on the drive up. Sinead tried to foist jazz

on him, but he couldn't take it. He tried, but he couldn't. He
liked straight-on classic rock; luckily, she didn't complain.

Sinead took a deep breath. "Gorgeous, isn't it?"

"It's amazing. It must be beautiful in the winter, too."

"It is, though the driveway can be a bitch when it snows.
I can't tell you how many times we—I—got stuck going
up and down."

Adam touched her arm. "It's okay to say 'we.' It doesn't
bother me." He paused. "You still haven't told me what it
was, exactly, that finally made you two pull the plug."

"We just wanted different things," Sinead said stiffly.
"That's all."

Adam decided not to push. It was obviously a sore
subject, one she wasn't prepared to open up about yet.
He kissed her shoulder and then put his arm around her.
"Relax."

She gave him an odd look. "I am relaxed."

He kneaded her shoulder. "Relax more."

Sinead laughed, feathering her index finger along his
jawline. "This was a good idea."

"I agree."

"Does being in the country make you homesick?"

The question took Adam by surprise. "A little, I guess. I
miss people more than the place, you know?"

"How's Ray?"

Adam chuckled, shaking his head. "He's Ray. Always
busting my balls. He wants to come down if the Blades
make the playoffs."

"That would be great. And your brother?"

"I'll invite him down, but he probably won't come."

"That's too bad," Sinead murmured sympathetically.

Adam shrugged. "It is what it is."

"Mr. Stoic."

"That's me."

"Hungry?"

"Starved."

"Good. I asked the caretaker to load up the fridge with food. We'll see what he got, and then maybe tomorrow we'll decide on something we want for dinner and go into town to shop." Sinead paused. "Unless you want to eat in town tomorrow night. There are some really nice little cafés."

"Are you kidding me? The only human being I want to see this weekend is you."

Sinead blushed. "I'm flattered."

Adam sweetly kissed the side of her face. "I mean it."

She slipped out from under his arm, extending a hand to his. "Let's have lunch."

"Venison, I hope. Shot here in these very same woods."

"You're pushing it, mister. C'mon."

* * *

Sinead lay propped up on one elbow, head resting in her palm, watching Adam sleep. He'd just finished "massaging" her following a long hike, and after a more than respectable period of afterglow, he'd drifted off. Sinead envied him: she'd never been able to nap. The minute her head hit the pillow, her mind began its rapid-fire assault, bombarding her with worries and to-do lists and replays of her day. No wonder she had insomnia: she was incapable of relaxing. Until now.

I could lie here all day like this, she thought. There was something wantonly delicious about rolling around in bed naked in the middle of the day. She smiled to herself. They'd have to come up here more often.

Reaching out, she carefully pushed a lock of damp hair off Adam's forehead, noticing for the first time a small, thin scar along his hairline. An old hockey injury, no doubt. She lightly traced her index finger along the needle-thin white line. Close as she now felt to him, there was still so much to learn about him. She felt greedy; she wanted to know it all right now. But being with Adam was a little like watching a striptease: what lay beneath his surface was revealed very slowly and carefully. It tantalized, teased at the imagination. But there was no doubt in her mind that the payoff would be worth it.

She contemplated tiptoeing out of the room to call Maggie, then thought better of it. She'd wait until the weekend was over and save up all the news to tell her sister at once.

As if he knew he was being watched, Adam opened his eyes with a groggy smile. "What are you doing? You should be resting your muscles."

"I can rest them and look at you at the same time."

"Your multitasking skills impressed me from the get-go."

Sinead fit herself into the crook of his arm, resting her head on his chest. They lay there quietly. Finally, Sinead asked, "What are you thinking?" Her head popped up. "No, wait: men hate that question, don't they?"

"Pretty much, but I'll answer it, anyway." He paused. "I was thinking about retirement."

Sinead was perplexed. "Why?"

"Because when I retire, this is exactly the kind of place I want to live in."

"The house?"

"The house, the setting, all of it. I want to wake up and hear nothing but the birds and the breeze. I want to be able to walk out my front door and take a hike, or hop in my jeep and in five minutes, be able to hunt or fish."

Sinead let out a careful breath. "Kind of early to be thinking about retirement, isn't it?"

"Not for a professional athlete," Adam said, his expression slightly bitter. "I'm thirty-five; that's about eighty in hockey years. I don't want to be one of those guys who just won't let it go and winds up playing only on power plays for some European team. I want to go out on a high note—unless I end up in jail."

"You're not going to jail," Sinead scoffed. Even so, she

was beginning to feel perturbed. "So that's all you'd do all day? Hike and fish and hunt?"

"For a while," Adam mused. "Until I figured out what's next." He studied her with interest. "You?"

"Me?"

"What do you picture your retirement to look like?"

Sinead lay flat on her back, looking at the high-beamed cathedral ceiling. "Actually, I don't see why I should retire. As long as I'm active and alert and enjoy what I do, why retire?"

"I wish I had that option." He was studying her intently. "But if you did retire, you'd want to come here, right?"

"God, no," Sinead blurted. She backpedaled. "I mean, I love it here, don't get me wrong. But twelve months a year? I think I'd go crazy. There's really not much to do up here."

"Isn't that kind of the point?"

"If that's your personality," Sinead reasoned. "But it's not mine." She turned to look at him. "I'm a city girl, born and bred. I really can't imagine ever living anywhere but Manhattan."

"Even if you had a kid?"

The question took Sinead by surprise. "I don't know. I'm sure the schools here aren't very good—at least not compared to Manhattan."

"But wouldn't you rather have your kid grow up here than surrounded by steel and glass?"

"I grew up surrounded by steel and glass, and I seem to have done okay for myself," Sinead replied testily.

"True."

Sinead grew uneasy. On the one hand, she couldn't help thinking that since he was feeling her out about something light-years away (at least for her), then he was picturing their relationship long-term. But on the other hand, it was glaringly obvious they weren't on the same page, and it worried her.

"Bit early to talk about those things now, don't you think?" Sinead pointed out, hoping to lighten the mood a little bit.

"I suppose."

"Let's just go with the flow."

Adam looked amused. "Those are words I never, ever expected to hear come from your mouth."

"Believe me, I know," Sinead agreed dryly. "But maybe I'm starting to learn you can't control everything."

"I'll believe it when I see it."

"Look who's talking," said Sinead, snuggling up against him. "Maybe together we can take the intensity down a notch."

"Deal." Adam rolled toward her with a wicked grin. "You look like you need another massage . . ."

* * *

Sinead's state of relaxation lasted until she set foot in the office Monday morning. She had no sooner grabbed a cup of coffee than her assistant, Simone, frantically waved her over to her desk.

"What's up?"

"The partners came down on Oliver. He showed up here drunk out of his mind on Friday. They told him either go into rehab or he'd be fired."

"Please tell me he chose rehab. Please."

"He did, but only after making a major scene."

"I had my own go round with Oliver. Maybe this is the kick in the butt he finally needs."

"Maybe. Anyway, I e-mailed you the address and phone number of where he is."

"Thanks, Simone," said Sinead, patting her shoulder. She started for her office. "One more thing," Simone said.

Sinead turned. "What's that?"

"Mr. Kaplan said he wants to see you as soon as you get in."

"Right," Sinead said grimly as she started down the hall to Jeff's office. She was glad she didn't see Oliver's meltdown. She made a mental note to call the rehab facility as soon as she could.

She knocked on Jeff's door and then poked her head in. "You wanted to see me?"

"Yes." Jeff's tone was serious. He didn't even look up from his desk as Sinead walked in. A bolt of panic hit her. What if he knew about her and Adam?

Sinead sat on the couch opposite her boss. He looked troubled as he lifted his head to look at her.

"How was your weekend?" he asked solicitously. Sinead could see how hard he was working not to take his bad mood out on her, and she appreciated it.

"Nice."

"Do anything special?"

Oh, God, he knows. No, he doesn't. He asks you this all the time. Relax.

"I went up to the house in Bearsville," Sinead said evenly. "You?"

"Junior high soccer game. Howard did well."

"Good." Sinead sipped her coffee, waiting.

"I assume you heard about Oliver," he said carefully.

"Simone told me. How awful was it?"

"Pretty awful. He trashed his office."

Sinead winced.

"But he agreed to go to rehab, which is good," said Jeff, looking relieved. "However, it does leave us with a problem."

"Yes?"

"Oliver's pending cases. We don't know yet how long he'll be in there. In the meantime, we want you to take over two of his cases."

Sinead wasn't stunned, but she *was* surprised, especially after he'd requested she take on the Joyce Toys lawsuit.

"And those are—?"

"High-profile divorce case and a fraud case."

"The one where the Realtor failed to tell his client that he owned the property the client was buying?"

"Yes."

"I see." It was a complicated case that had been going on for months. As for the divorce case, that one was ugly as hell, with outrageous, damning accusations flying back and forth. Oliver had been getting a kick out of that one.

"You don't look enthused," noted Jeffrey.

"I'm just surprised, that's all." Sinead took another sip of coffee. "Actually, I'm flattered."

"You're incredibly capable. And now that you're wrapping up those smaller-billing cases, that should free you up to work on these, yes?"

"Definitely," Sinead fibbed. Those cases were still open; Sinead wanted to give her less affluent clients some time to pay her back. But she knew that eventually, she was going to have to collect.

Jeffrey looked pleased. "We knew you'd be up to the challenge. Plus it'll up your billing that much faster."

"I appreciate the vote of confidence."

Jeffrey splayed his hands on the desk, his expression much lighter than when Sinead had walked in.

"Anything else?" Sinead asked.

"Nope, that's it for now. We put Oliver's files in your office. Didn't want you to have to deal with the carnage in his office."

"Thank you."

"You're welcome."

He went back to the paperwork on his desk. Sinead left the office, quietly closing the door behind her. *Be careful what you wish for,* she thought. *Oliver's cases on top of the Joyce Toys lawsuit . . . shit. You can do it. You've had this much on your plate before; you can do it again. Just take it as it comes.*

* * *

"I'm doing all I can, Adam. You know that."

Sinead was working at home when Adam unexpectedly showed up. Her brain was about to burst: first Jeff pressuring her to wrap up the smaller-billing cases, then being handed Oliver's cases on top of her own, and now Adam telling her she needed to push the DA on his case, as if she didn't know that already.

It didn't help that Oliver had given her a laundry list five miles long of stuff he needed her to bring to the rehab facility, another chore on her plate. Not that she'd be able to see him until he detoxed, but she was allowed to drop stuff off for him, all of which would be searched. It was like he was moving in; she half expected him to ask her to bring his humidor.

At least she'd figured out how to wrap up the small cases around her neighborhood quickly: she used her own money to pay what they owed her. She had the cash, many of them didn't, and she refused to bug them for money they didn't have, especially since she'd known most of them since childhood. She should have done them pro bono, anyway.

She couldn't believe Adam was now getting on her case as well. When he'd called and asked to come over, her immediate assumption was negative: he'd had time to think and he'd decided to break up with her. All her life, her first instinct had always been to assume the worst. She mentioned it once to Quinn. His reply? "Welcome to being Irish."

She was honest with Adam, telling him she could only see him for a bit, and he was okay with that, or he seemed to be until she told him what he didn't want to hear.

Adam looked frustrated as he ran his hand through his hair. "You sure you've thought of everything?"

Sinead stared at him in disbelief. "Are you questioning my competence?"

"No, of course not. It's just that now, in addition to being scapegoated by refs and hounded by the NHL commissioner, I've got Ty bugging me, telling me to push you. He's really worried about this following us into the playoffs. So am I."

"And so am I. Look, you just have to deal with things being on hold for now. I can't magically wrap up the case. Yes, I can be a total pain in the ass to the DA, but apart from that, there's not too much I can do. And I hate to tell you this, but right now, your case isn't my number one priority."

"Excuse me?"

"I'm not saying it's *not* a priority," Sinead explained. "It is. But the partners just handed me a huge case, and I've taken on two of Oliver's."

"What's wrong with Oliver?"

Sinead blew out a relieved breath. "He's in rehab. Finally."

Adam looked mildly disapproving. "He seems like a really nice guy, but wrecking his life like that makes it hard to respect him."

"That's awfully judgmental," Sinead replied, surprised. "Alcoholism isn't a moral weakness, you know. It's a disease."

Adam looked dubious.

"Don't you dare say anything against Oliver," she warned. "He's my best friend. Nobody is perfect. I give him a lot of credit for finally admitting he has a problem and taking care of it."

"I suppose."

"Not everyone can be perfect like you," Sinead muttered under her breath.

Adam squinted at her. "What did you say?"

"Something not very nice." Sinead began rubbing her temples. "I'm sorry. I'm just a little cranky because I have so much to do."

"You sure you can handle all this?"

"*Yes.* Why wouldn't I?"

"I worry," Adam admitted. "I don't want you driving yourself into the ground."

Sinead tried not to bristle. "I've worked double time like this before." That's what had driven her blood pressure up the first time. And increased her headaches. Not that she would ever tell him this.

"Okay." Adam backed off, but he still looked worried. He began massaging the back of her neck.

Sinead let her head drop forward. "That feels amazing."

"You should get one once a week."

"Don't have time."

"There's always time. Just carve out—"

Sinead stilled his hand. "Ever notice you like telling me what to carve out time for?"

Adam kissed her hand. "Sorry. Part of being a control freak, I guess."

Sinead tilted her head back to look at him upside down. "I hate to do this, but I need to throw you out. I really have a ton to do."

She got up from her chair, wrapping her arms around his neck. "I wish you could stay," she murmured, nuzzling his neck.

"It's all right. I'll just head home and watch some *Stooges.*"

"Would you like a noogie before you go?" Sinead teased in a breathy voice.

"Not unless it's a code word for something else."

"I wish."

"Thursday night at my place?" Adam checked.

"Yup." She could "carve out" time for that. Hell, she could always work when she got home. She used to pull all-nighters all the time in college. Of course, that *was* over a decade ago. But she'd do what she had to do.

"Good."

His kiss was tender, so fitting with the quiet way he often had about him.

"Night," he said.

"Night."

Sinead wished she could call out, "Screw it!" and tell him to come back and spend the night; but there was no ignoring the small tower of paperwork on her desk. She sat down with a sigh and got back to work.

26

"I don't know why you're nervous. Just be yourself."

Sinead smiled weakly at Adam as they walked into Dante's, where the wedding reception for Adam's teammate, Ulf Torkelson, and his new bride—wife number two—was being held. A month had passed since Adam had indelicately tried to push her into wrapping up his case. During that time, Sinead barely had time to breathe with all the work she was juggling. At least she had something to look forward to: she was going to visit Oliver at the rehab facility for the first time tomorrow.

Sinead wasn't sure why she was so nervous. They'd skipped the ceremony. No one from Kidco Corporation was going to be here. Ty and Michael were skipping the reception; they didn't want their presence as GM and coach to inhibit the players from letting their hair down. In any case, she and Adam weren't going to display any outward signs of being a couple. Sinead supposed her anxiety went back to the shyness she'd always experienced in large social situations.

Sinead knew she'd be an object of curiosity. The players

knew virtually nothing about Adam's personal life, and there was no way any of them would come right out and ask Adam if she was his girlfriend. She still worried that they were playing this a little close to the edge, even though she couldn't imagine how it could ever get back to her bosses.

Adam gestured toward the French doors across the room. "Shall we?"

"Sure." *You can do this,* Sinead told herself. *You've mingled with doctors, attorneys, stockbrokers, the rich and famous . . . you can handle this.* She rolled her shoulders in an attempt to shake off her stress and accompanied Adam into the banquet room.

*   *   *

"Son of a bitch," Sinead heard Adam grumble under his breath as he pulled out her chair for her at their table. They were sitting with eight others: Tully Webster, his wife, Annie, and their twins, Carolyn and Jamie; Sebastian Ivanov and his girlfriend, Lennie; and Esa Saari and Kayla Black, a very well-known model. At least she knew Sebastian and Lennie.

Adam was still frowning as he sat down beside her. Of course, being control freaks and punctilious to a fault, they were the first ones there. "What's the matter?"

He gestured at the place setting for Esa Saari. "I hate that little bastard. He's an arrogant little shit, and he doesn't take the game seriously. He's gotten better, but he acts like a rock star outside the rink. He's a total party boy."

"So? You don't have to talk to him."

"I can't believe Torkelson put us at the same table."

"He probably had nothing to do with it. I think it's the bride who figures out the place settings."

"I thought couples figured it out together. My brother and his wife nearly came to blows figuring out the seating at their reception."

Sinead shrugged. "I don't really know much about it."

She paused. "At least I know Seb and Lennie," she said cheerfully.

"Sebastian's a good guy. Tough player, works hard. I don't know Lennie."

"Trust me, she's a sweetie." Sinead took a sip of the ice water that had already been poured. "Tully?"

"One of the assistant captains. Good player. Veteran. Needs to kick it up a notch if we're going to go far in the playoffs. He's getting a little tired on the ice. Don't know his wife."

Sinead cocked her head quizzically. "You only know about them as players?"

"That's all I need to know, just like that's all they need to know about me."

"So what are you going to introduce me as? Your cousin?"

"I'll just say your name is Sinead. Period."

Sinead raised her eyebrows. "And when they ask me what I do for a living?"

"Tell them the truth and let them think what they want. And like we agreed, it's not as if we're going to act like we're a couple."

"That's going to be hard," Sinead admitted, discreetly running her fingers down his arm. "You look so handsome."

"You're a disciplined person," Adam teased. "I'm sure you'll be able to restrain yourself until later tonight."

"I don't have much of a choice, do I?"

Adam grinned. "Nope."

* * *

"Where's Lennie?"

Sinead was disappointed when Sebastian arrived solo. She was looking forward to talking to her, possibly commissioning her to make a few new blazers.

Sebastian sat down across from her, looking sad. "She's at her cousin Winnie's wedding back in Saranac Lake. She couldn't miss that, and I couldn't miss this. So . . . no girl-friend."

"That sucks, my friend." Esa Saari extended a hand to Sinead, flashing a charming smile. "I'm Esa."

"Sinead."

"Very, very nice to meet you," he said. He leaned in close and said in a stage whisper, "You're here with Cap?"

"That's right," Adam answered for her with a glare of warning.

Saari sat down next to Sinead. She could see why he was such a "rock star": he was gorgeous, his confident demeanor smooth as ice. He knew how to work it.

"This is Kayla," Esa announced to the table, as his date, a flawless blonde, joined him. "We met at a private party thrown by Bon Jovi."

Sinead smiled at Kayla. "Nice to meet you. You, too," she said to the Websters. She waved across the table to the kids. "Hi. I'm Sinead. What's your name?"

The towheaded little girl suddenly looked shy. "Carolyn."

Sinead shifted her attention to the little boy, a male version of his sister. "How about you?"

"Jamie," he said bashfully, trying to turn his cloth napkin into a piece of origami.

"Cool name," said Adam.

Jamie looked up at him.

"Seriously. When I was a kid, that's what I wanted my name to be."

"What is your name?" Carolyn asked.

"Adam." His smile was charming as he asked, "Do you like to dance, Carolyn?"

Carolyn, looking mesmerized, nodded yes.

"Me, too," Adam confided. "Maybe we can dance together later."

Jamie immediately lost all interest in his napkin. "I wanna dance, too!"

"I'll dance with you," Sinead offered.

Jamie mulled it over. "Okay!" He returned to napkin folding.

Sinead was initially shocked by the way Adam just dove in and started talking to the twins. Then she remembered the footage she'd seen of him with his niece and nephew, and his love of children came back to her. Another thing they shared, except he seemed to have the golden touch, whereas she, if Charlie was any measure of success, didn't. Maybe watching him in action would prove instructive.

"How old are you guys?" Adam asked the twins.

"Six and a half," Jamie said proudly.

Adam reared back slightly, impressed. "Wow. That's pretty old. You guys must be in college, right?"

"Nooooo!" said Carolyn. "First grade!"

"Almost second," Jamie added boastfully.

"Pretty impressive," said Adam, turning to Sinead for confirmation. "Isn't that impressive?"

"Totally," Sinead agreed. "You guys look soooo much older."

Both children looked pleased.

Sinead wanted to talk to the kids some more, but Esa Saari got her ear. And once he had it, he wouldn't stop talking.

It turned out Esa and his date knew a lot of the same people as Sinead; he also wasn't shy about telling Sinead people he was dying to meet, many of whom she knew. He pumped her endlessly for info, dominating her time, making it hard for her to even chat with Adam, who looked more and more displeased the longer Esa prattled on.

Eventually, Ulf and his bride, Margo, stopped by the table.

"Thanks for coming, guys."

"Yes, thank you," said Margo in a thick Russian accent.

Sebastian Ivanov's face lit up as he began speaking to her in Russian. At one point he looked at Ulf with a smirk and burst out laughing, prompting the hulking Swede to snap, "We have to move on to the next table," to his bride, practically pulling her arm out of the socket as he dragged her away.

"What was that about, dude?" Esa asked.

"She's a mail-order bride," Sebastian revealed.

Tully Webster's mouth fell open. "No way."

"Why would I lie?" Sebastian countered. "He picked her out of a book."

"Jesus," said Esa, craning his neck to look at the couple. "I thought they hooked up pretty fast."

"Besides, who in her right mind would marry Ulfie?" Tully pointed out.

"Hey, wife number one was a pretty hot number," Tully's wife, Annie, reminded him.

"She was obsessed with Sweden. Remember? He couldn't take listening to ABBA day and night. She'd only have sex with him if he let her play 'Dancing Queen' over and over."

Sinead stifled a laugh.

"So what if this chick is mail order? People do a lot of things to get their green card," said Sebastian. "If it works for them, who are we to judge?"

"Yeah?" Saari smirked at him over his glass of champagne. "That the story with you and Lennie?"

"You're an idiot," said Sebastian. "We're not married."

"Yet."

"That's right. But keep being a wiseass, and we won't be inviting you to our wedding." They both laughed.

* * *

"Ready to dance?"

Carolyn hesitated a moment before accompanying Adam to the dance floor. Sinead looked at Jamie out of the corner of her eye; he was vehemently shaking his head no. Sinead was pretty sure that he'd change his mind once he saw what a good time his sister was having.

Sinead's gaze was set on Adam and his pint-sized dancing partner. It was a slow dance, and like so many other instances where adults dance with children, Carolyn's feet were atop Adam's. It was adorable.

Esa Saari and his girlfriend were playing such an intense game of tonsil hockey that Sinead was tempted to say, "Get a room!" She felt a tap on her shoulder and turned to see Sebastian smiling at her. "Would you like to dance?"

Sinead was just rising from her chair when Jamie's head shot up. "You said you were going to dance with me!"

"You're right." She looked at Sebastian. "Sorry, Seb. I'm already taken. Maybe later?"

"Of course," he said gallantly.

Sinead suppressed a smile as she strolled out onto the dance floor with Jamie, who had a very serious and determined look on his face as he made a beeline for his sister and Adam.

"We're dancing now," he said with a smirk. "So you two can sit down."

"Dude, there's room enough for everyone to dance," Adam assured him. The Village People's "YMCA" came on. Adam looked excited. "Watch *this*."

When the song hit the famous chorus, Adam showed them how to form the letters *Y M C A* with their arms in time to the music. Adam's teammates looked stunned. Sinead hesitated a moment, then started dancing, too. She and Adam caught each other's eye and smiled.

The four of them stayed on the dance floor for song after song. Sinead was getting tired, but she was having so much fun with the kids and Adam that she didn't want to miss a thing. She was doing the twist with a delighted Carolyn when it dawned on her that she wasn't hopeless with children. She *could* connect with them. All it took was letting your guard down, being willing to be silly, and talking to them without condescension, among other things. Her thoughts tracked back to her night with Charlie. *I was too uptight,* she thought. *Kids pick up on that.* She vowed that next time she babysat, she would try to relax, reminding herself that things did not have to go perfectly according to a rigid schedule. You had to take it moment by moment; just be there. Sinead felt like she'd discovered the secret of the universe.

27

"Is this place hell or what?"

Sinead took one look at the miserable expression on Oliver's face and burst out laughing. "You're unhinged."

They were strolling the lush grounds of Beechtree, one of the most expensive private rehab centers in the country. Though it had taken her close to two hours to drive there, she knew it was worth it the minute she set eyes on Oliver: gone was his green pallor, his paunch, the glazed look she sometimes saw in his eyes. He looked healthy.

"You look great."

"Yeah, yeah, whatever." He gestured in front of them. "Look at this. Trees. Who needs this many fucking trees?"

"It's pretty, Oliver. And serene."

"Oh yeah, serene," Oliver mocked. "I suppose you want to hear me recite the Serenity Prayer."

"Not really." Sinead squeezed his arm. "What are you so pissed about?"

Oliver threw his head back, looking at the sky. "Oh, Lord, how do I count the ways?"

"C'mon. Tell me."

"All right, all right. I'm pissed that I'm here. I'm pissed that I have to share a room with a guy who never shuts the fuck up. I'm pissed I blew my career. I'm pissed I have to go to therapy, group therapy, fill in the fucking blank. I'm pissed there's never anything good on cable."

"That it?" Sinead teased.

"You don't know what it's like, Sinead," he said miserably.

"Oliver." Sinead halted. "You were drinking yourself to death. You did not lose your career; if you did, the firm wouldn't be paying for your stay. You need to be here. You know you do."

"What I need is a whiskey, neat—joke, joke, that was a joke. Except it wasn't."

They resumed walking. "Doesn't it feel good to be sober all the time?"

"Fuck no!" Oliver scoffed. "Are you insane? It's boring. It's *real*."

"Real as in you now have to deal with certain issues, whatever they may be?"

"See, that's the thing. I don't have all that 'Daddy didn't love me and Mommy was a hooker' bullshit to sort out. I don't have any deep, dark emotional issues that drove me to drink. I just liked it. I'm detoxed now, okay? I could walk out of here with you and be perfectly fine."

"Bullshit, Oliver."

"It's true."

"Look, I know this must be scary for you—"

"It's not scary," Oliver interrupted fiercely. "It's a waste of time. You know how long the whole program is?" he asked, his voice going up an octave. "Eight weeks. Eight eight eight eight eight."

"Well, if that's what it takes," said Sinead.

"That's what they say it takes," Oliver corrected. "They don't take the individual into account. It's a one-size-fits-all program. This individual does not need eight weeks of hearing other people's sad loser stories and navel gazing."

Sinead was getting exasperated. "Just do the program and shut up, okay?"

"So even you have turned against me."

Sinead caught the impish look in his eye, and Oliver laughed.

"You're so melodramatic."

"Which is what makes me so riveting to watch in court. Speaking of which, how's it going with the divorce case?"

Sinead shuddered. "God, those two deserve each other. Last week she claimed in the paper that he locked her up in a secret dungeon. I told her that she can't just go saying these things, or he'll sue for defamation of character on top of everything else. Oh, wait, he already is." She kicked at a twig. "I think she liked working with you better."

"Of course she did. I told her all the time how hot she was. I bet you don't do that."

"No, I don't."

"And the fraud case?"

"Status quo."

"Sounds like you got a lot going on there, missy."

"I do." Mention of it made Sinead suddenly tired. It was Pavlovian: Oliver mentioned work, and she stifled a big yawn.

"You sure you can—"

"Don't you dare." Sinead pointed at him warningly. "Don't you dare finish that sentence."

Oliver raised his hands in a gesture of surrender. "Please don't hurt me, pretty lady."

Sinead linked her arm through his as they continued down a snaking gravel path toward a thicket of tall firs. God, she'd missed him. She wondered if his protestations weren't all bluster. Much like Adam, Oliver wasn't one for admitting weakness. There was no way he would ever admit there might be reasons behind his drinking, or that he was actually getting something out of therapy. Still, she could see how a calm, serene place like this would drive him nuts. Oliver lived life at warp speed, and Beechtree was very . . . still. *Adam would like it,* she thought.

"What's the buzz with you and hockey boy?" Oliver asked.

"We went to the wedding of one of his teammates last night."

"Whoa. Stop the presses." Oliver looked surprised. "You went out in public together?"

"Not as a couple. More like a date between friends. As Adam pointed out, even if his teammates did figure out I'm his attorney, it's not like they'd have the guts to ask him— or me—if there was anything else going on."

"That's not the point. That was a *très* risky move, little sister. What if word got back to the big three that you went to a wedding with your client?"

"How would word get back to them? One of the hockey players is gonna call up the firm and tell them?" As the words were leaving her mouth, Sinead felt a freeze come over her. Saari might. "Besides, you can socialize with a client without dating them."

"I'm just shocked. I thought you guys were going totally cloak and dagger."

"It was Adam's idea, not mine." Sinead sat down on a beautiful, carved wooden bench nearby, Oliver following suit.

Oliver frowned. "I hate nature."

"Adam loves it," Sinead replied, trying not to sound glum. "A lot."

"Princess doesn't sound happy."

"I'm not unhappy. It's just that when we went away for the weekend together, we somehow stumbled on to the topic of retirement, and he told me he wants to live in a place like Bearsville year round."

Oliver nudged her in the ribs. "You guys are thinking long-term, huh?"

"Not overtly," Sinead said carefully. "We're just taking

it as it comes." She frowned. "I hate that expression. That and 'Go with the flow.'"

"So if I've got this right, and I know I do because I know you, you'd rather run naked down Broadway than live in the country full-time."

"Bingo."

"Sinead, we're talking thirty, forty years away."

"I know. But it just disturbed me because it shows how different we are at heart, you know?"

Oliver snorted. "You differ on one thing. Big deal. You both love kids, right?"

Sinead softened. "Yes."

"Well, if you ask me, that's a more important issue to be simpatico on than where you'll be cashing your Social Security checks."

"But he thinks Bearsville would be a good place to raise kids! This is the type of stuff that could make or break a relationship. You have to be simpatico on *all* these big issues."

Oliver looked reflective. "You know, when Jim Beam and I were dating, our discussions never went that deep."

"I thought Johnny Walker was your guy."

"Him, too. It was a three way." Oliver tousled her hair. "Look, things have a way of working out the way they're supposed to, all right? I really believe that. Even my being here in this godforsaken—"

"Multimillion-dollar facility—"

"Is probably the way things should be karmically."

"Karmically?"

Oliver shook his head forlornly. "See, I should be drinking, right? I sound like an asshole when I'm sober. Total asshole."

"No, you don't."

"Phew." He pulled a pack of cigarettes out of the front pocket of his shirt. "You know what I mean, though, right?"

"Since when do you smoke?"

"Since I got here. Jesus, Sinead, I have to have some vice."

"Could you maybe wait till I've left?"

"Have some mercy, woman, please."

Sinead felt bad. "Fine."

Oliver lit up, appearing to take great pleasure in blowing smoke rings out of the side of his mouth. "Who knows? By the time you're both old and decrepit, he might want to stay in a city, or you might want to live in the country. You never know. C'mon, take a few deep, cleansing breaths with Uncle Ollie. You'll feel better."

Cleansing breaths? Sinead drew back. "Oh my God, can I have my friend back, please?"

"I'm trying out new, sober personalities. I call that one Yogi Oliver."

"Yogi Oliver smokes? Interesting contradiction."

Oliver's shoulders slumped. "Sure, kill my dreams." He threw the cigarette on the ground and stubbed it out. "I feel healthier already," he said sarcastically.

"So I'm being an idiot where Adam is concerned," Sinead double-checked.

"Pretty much, yeah. Stop worrying so much. It's a real buzz kill."

Sinead kissed the side of his face. "I love you, Oliver."

"I love you, too, sweetcakes. Now let's finish up this walk. The fresh air is killing me."

28

Sinead scurried around her apartment, giving it a quick tidy up before Adam arrived. He'd just called her from D.C. where the Blades were waiting to catch a plane home, asking if he could stop by for a little bit when he got in.

"I know you're really busy," he had said apologetically, which made Sinead feel bad.

"Not too busy to see you," she had assured him.

Sinead missed him. They spoke every day he was away, but it wasn't the same. It was odd: even when they were both in New York, they sometimes went three or four days without seeing each other because of their schedules. But when he was away, his absence made a huge difference to her psychologically. Perhaps it was the knowledge that if he needed her, she wouldn't be able to get to him in minutes. At any rate, she was glad he was coming home.

She went into the bathroom and splashed her face with cold water before applying a little concealer. Against her pale skin, the circles under her eyes had taken on a life of their own. She looked terrible—at least her face did. The rest of her looked pretty good in her faded skinny jeans and a black-and-white French sailor shirt.

A frisson of excitement crackled through her body when the doorbell rang, and there he was, Adam, looking sexy in jeans and olive polo shirt.

"Hey," he said, breaking into a happy grin.

"Hey." Sinead closed the door behind him. She hesitated a moment, then exuberantly threw her arms around his neck. "I really, really missed you."

Adam laughed. "Me, too." His eyes did a careful tour of her body. "You look great."

Sinead almost said, "Oh, please," but instead accepted the compliment.

Adam rested his forehead against hers for a moment, then lifted his face, his intense gaze pinning her. What happened next seemed to go in slow motion: Adam leaned in, nuzzling her neck, hot breath tickling her skin. Sinead hesitated, before letting her fingers trail seductively up his neck, tucking a stray strand of his hair behind his ear. She opened her mouth to speak, but it was too late: his lips were nipping at hers, his tongue pushing its way between her teeth.

Sinead groaned, trying to ignore Adam's seductive smile as he pulled her to him, hard. *Want you,* Sinead thought. *Want you so bad.* He was pressing hard against her. Sinead could feel him rising against her leg. All she'd have to do was undo his belt . . .

The thought of it made her feel weak. *Take him,* she thought. *For once in your life, be bold.* Pushing herself to be audacious, Sinead hurriedly pushed up Adam's shirt and began licking his chest. His head fell back with a moan as he arched into her mouth. Her own excitement growing, Sinead ran the pad of one of her thumbs over his nipples. She loved the feel of him, his taut skin, the muscles underneath. She splayed her hands on his chest, kissing him, Adam murmuring his approval.

Adam brought his head forward to look at her, his pupils dazed with desire as he grabbed her wrist. "I want you," he whispered. He didn't even wait for her to respond as he pushed her up against the wall.

"Want you," he repeated, frantically undoing his pants. Sinead watched dizzily as his clothing pooled at his feet and he kicked it away. Her breath was beginning to become fast and shallow the more aroused she became. Adam began kissing her wildly, as if he couldn't get enough of her. Sharing his desperation, Sinead freed herself of her jeans and panties, guiding him into her.

"Oh, God." Sinead gave a little cry as she wrapped her legs tightly around Adam's hips. She wanted him deep inside her, wanted to fully feel the sensation of the two of them greedy for each other.

"Missed you," Adam whispered. His hands cupped her butt, holding her up, his mouth biting her neck. And then he was whispering things in her ear she never imagined him saying, things even Chip hadn't said. Her head was spinning, her heart going like a jackhammer.

Adam resumed kissing her. He was fucking her roughly, both of them sweaty, pumping against each other. Adam bit down hard on her shoulder, and that was it; Sinead was coming with a loud scream, Adam watching with a deep thrill in his eyes. "You now," she gasped.

Adam obeyed. Fast and rough. Animal grunts. Frantic. And then he threw his head back and with one violent thrust came inside her, shuddering.

Still panting, he put his sweaty forehead against hers. For a few seconds, neither of them said anything. Eventually, Sinead slowly released her legs from around Adam's hips and lowered them to the floor. A satisfied grin lit up his face.

"Well, that was . . . uh . . ."

"Unexpected?" Sinead supplied.

"Very. Best homecoming I've ever had."

Sinead laughed, shimmying her jeans back up her hips while Adam did the same.

"C'mere."

He gathered her in his arms, tenderly stroking her face. "I love you," he said with quiet passion. "I have for a very long time."

Sinead was overwhelmed. Before Adam, she'd been telling herself she didn't care if she ever got another chance at love. But she'd been lying to protect herself, fearful of laying her heart open to another man only to have it carelessly torn apart. Adam had coaxed her back into the land of feeling. It was scary, but it was exhilarating, too.

Adam looked apprehensive. "Sinead?"

"I'm sorry. I was just thinking about how I'd talked myself into believing I didn't care if I ever fell in love again, because I was so afraid it would end in disaster like me and Chip."

"I'm not Chip," Adam reminded her quietly.

"Are you free Sunday?" Sinead suddenly asked.

"I have a practice in the morning, but after that, yeah. Why?"

"My family always gets together for a big Sunday meal. Would you like to come?"

"I'd love to."

"You might take that back after you meet my mother. She can be very pushy and blunt."

Adam tapped his chin thoughtfully. "Gee, that reminds me of someone else I know."

"Excuse me?"

"You heard me."

"All right, it's true," Sinead grumbled.

Those aren't necessarily negative traits, you know."

"Let's just wait and see if you still feel that way after you meet my mom," Sinead reiterated. She wrapped her arms around his neck again. "Stay the night?"

"On one condition."

"What's that?"

"I don't wake up at two in the morning to find you at your computer, working."

"Scout's honor," Sinead promised. "Unless I can't sleep," she amended.

"Oh, I'll help you sleep," Adam murmured seductively.

Sinead felt giddy. "Really?"

"I'm gonna see to it that you're tired out. Very tired out."

"Mmm, sounds good to me."

"Eat first? Take-out Thai? I'm starving."

"Sounds good. I'll call."

Sinead went into the kitchen, opening the drawer where she stashed all her take-out menus. She ran back into the living room impulsively.

"Say it again," she begged.

Adam smiled that slow, sexy grin of his. "I love you."

"I love you, too, Adam Perry."

She returned to the kitchen, executing a secret pirouette. She couldn't remember the last time she felt so happy. She could actually see them making a life together. It would be complicated because of what they each did for a living, but it would be real. Authentic. Who could ask for more?

* * *

"You sure I'm dressed okay?"

Sinead found Adam's question amusing as she led him up the stairs to her parents' apartment above the pub. When she'd called her folks to let them know she was bringing someone for dinner, her mother went crazy, plying her with questions. It was like being interrogated by a Celtic Torquemada.

"You look fine," she assured Adam, who was wearing jeans and a crewneck sweater. "Dinner isn't formal, you know. My dad will probably have undone his belt already in anticipation of stuffing himself, and chances are Quinn will be wearing a shirt stained with mustard or coffee. Mags will be in yoga pants, and Brendan will be in a pair of ratty old jeans, guaranteed. The only ones who will be dressed up will be my mom, who will have come directly from Mass, and my sister-in-law Natalie, who's French. She always looks dressy. And gorgeous."

Adam pinched her butt. "Not as gorgeous as you."

Sinead shooed his hand away. "Behave."

She couldn't imagine Adam not liking her family, nor could she imagine them not liking him, unless they mistook his shyness for standoffishness. Sinead turned around. "Try to talk a little, okay?" she whispered.

Adam rolled his eyes. "I'll do my best."

Sinead opened the door onto a familiar scene: her mother, Maggie, and Natalie were all chatting in the kitchen; her father, brother, and brother-in-law were in the living room watching football. It always amazed Sinead how these dinners broke down along gender lines, with the women in the kitchen and the men waiting to be called for dinner. That's the way it had always been in her family: old-fashioned.

"Look who's here," her mother said pleasantly.

Sinead kissed her mother's cheek. "Hi, Mom." She gestured at the gorgeous man standing beside her. "This is Adam."

"Lovely to meet you," said her mother, extending a hand.

"You, too." Adam handed her the small bouquet of flowers he'd bought.

"Good-looking and polite," her mother noted approvingly under her breath.

Sinead was mortified. "Ma."

Her mother feigned deafness as she went to find a vase to put the flowers in.

Sinead continued the introductions. "You've already met Maggie."

"Nice to see you again," said Maggie, sounding genuine.

Sinead had been afraid her sister would still be giving him the evil eye.

"Hey, Charlie," said Sinead to her nephew, who was balanced on Maggie's hip. She turned to Adam. "Isn't he adorable?"

"He is."

"He's a little cranky," said Maggie. "He has an ear infection and was up half the night. He's exhausted."

"Ear infections are pretty common with babies, aren't they?" Adam asked. "I remember my niece getting a lot of them when she was small."

"You're right, unfortunately," said Maggie, her eyes cutting quickly to Sinead's. She looked impressed. Sinead looked at Adam as if he were a cat that had just started to talk. She knew he loved kids, but discussing babies' ear infections was the last thing she ever expected to hear coming from his mouth.

"Can I hold him?" Adam asked.

"Sure," said Maggie slowly, again looking at Sinead. "He might start screaming, though. Just be prepared."

Maggie handed Charlie over to Adam. The sight of big, rough and tough Adam holding the baby made Sinead's breath catch. They all waited nervously for Charlie to begin howling. But he didn't. He stuck a finger in Adam's mouth and Adam pretended to bite on it and Charlie laughed.

Sinead turned away, pain flicking at her heart. Why did Charlie take to Adam and not to her? It made her envious. Then she remembered Ulf Torkelson's wedding and how she'd connected with the Webster twins. Perhaps Adam simply had more experience with babies than she had.

Adam handed Charlie back to Maggie as Sinead's sister-in-law Natalie, who'd been drying her hands at the sink, approached with a smile. Just as Sinead told Adam, Natalie, despite her simple ensemble of designer jeans, flats, and a black silk T-shirt, looked chic.

"Bonjour," she said, extending her hand to Adam. "I'm Natalie. Quinn's wife."

"Nice to meet you," Adam said.

Sinead took Adam's hand. "C'mon, I'll introduce you to the rest of the crew."

She knew it was a minor thing, but she couldn't believe how wonderful it felt to hold Adam's hand in front of people. She'd been putting as much pressure as she could on the Philly DA to drop the suit so they could "come out," but there was a fine line between professional and pest. She had to be patient.

Quinn, as usual, was watching the Jets game while texting at the same time. Her dad was in his recliner, rubbing the back that had tormented him for years, but he was too stubborn to go to the doctor. Brendan sat on the couch, relaxed as always.

Sinead brought Adam over to her father first. "Dad, this is Adam." He began to struggle out of his chair, teeth gritted against the pain.

"Don't get up," said Adam. "There's no need." He shook her father's hand. "Adam Perry."

"Charlie O'Brien."

"Bad back?"

"It's his own fault," Sinead noted. "He won't go to the doctor."

"They're all charlatans," her father maintained.

Sinead clucked her tongue. "You're impossible." She pointed at Quinn. "You already know my brother, Jimmy Olsen."

"Very funny." Quinn extended a hand. "Good to see you again, Adam."

"You, too."

"Looks like you guys have a good shot at the Cup."

"I'd agree, but I don't want to jinx it."

"I hear ya." Quinn nodded at the TV. "Jets fan or Giants fan?"

"Tampa Bay."

"Blasphemy. Get the hell out of this house now if you know what's good for you."

Brendan, in the meantime, had risen from the couch. Sometimes Sinead forgot how massive he was. He was as well-built as Adam.

"Bren, this is Adam."

"Great to meet you," said Brendan.

"You, too."

Sinead was unsure of what to do now. Leave Adam here in the den of testosterone and go back into the kitchen? Take him back into the kitchen with her? Luckily, Adam made the decision for her.

"I'm gonna hang here for a minute, okay?"

"No problem."

She knew what would happen the minute she stepped back into the kitchen, and she was right: she was swarmed.

"He's very handsome," said Natalie.

"Yes, he is," Sinead said quietly. Maggie squeezed her shoulder. She must have seen the pain on Sinead's face when Charlie took to Adam.

"He's very polite as well," Natalie continued.

"Polite or no, we'll see if this one is worthy of my daughter," her mother said with a sniff.

Sinead could feel her blood pressure go up a notch. "Ma, please don't give him the first degree. He's kind of shy."

"Well, he'll have to get over that if he wants to be part of this family."

Sinead, Maggie, and Natalie chuckled to themselves. Some things never changed.

* * *

Adam liked Sinead's family immediately. The rapid-fire, teasing banter between Sinead and her siblings . . . it had never been like that between him and Rick, at least not when they were older. Rick's resentment of him was too strong.

Like Sinead's, his parents had been hardworking, but they were much more quiet and stoic. He missed them a lot.

"Now, Adam," Sinead's mother began. Adam could feel Sinead tense beside him, so he squeezed her leg under the table reassuringly. "I understand you're Canadian."

"I am."

"I've never been there myself, but I hear Quebec is lovely."

"It is, as long as you speak French."

"Have you played hockey your whole life, son?" Sinead's father asked.

"Yup."

Sinead looked at her parents incredulously. "You guys, Mom already asked me about this stuff over the phone, and I told you."

"I want to hear it from the boy himself," her mother insisted.

Boy. Adam couldn't remember the last time someone called him that. It amused him. At any rate, the conversational ball was in his court. He was determined to make Sinead proud of him. "I grew up in a really small town in western Canada," he offered. "Unless you wanted to farm, ranch, or work in the car factory, hockey was really the only way out."

"What do your parents do?" Sinead's father asked.

"My mom stayed at home, and my dad worked in the car factory. They've both passed."

Sinead's mother reached out and patted his hand. "I'm very sorry to hear that."

"Thank you."

"You mentioned you had a niece," Maggie said with interest.

"Yeah, my brother, Rick, has two kids, a boy and a girl."

"That was lovely, the way you held Charlie. You'd probably like one or two rug rats of your own one day, eh?" Sinead's mother asked casually.

"Oh my God," Sinead groaned to Adam under her breath. She wanted to crawl under the table. "I'm so sorry."

Before Sinead could even say it, Maggie jumped in with, "You're crossing a line there, Ma."

"Sorry," Sinead's mother apologized, flashing both her daughters a look of annoyance.

Over the course of the meal, Adam felt he deftly fielded all the questions that came his way, even though he hated talking about himself.

What made him happy was that he could feel Sinead slowly relaxing beside him. Every now and then, she'd glance at him with a tentative smile, checking to see if he was okay. He wondered if she was aware of how beautiful she was. Probably not, which made her all the more attractive. He wasn't drawn to models or actresses whose egos revolved around their looks. He thought back to the first time he and Sinead had met, and how they both were so wrong about each other. He had a feeling it would become a running joke between them.

* * *

After dinner, Adam and the rest of the men were shooed back into the living room while the women cleaned up. It had been the same way at his house, too, except it wasn't football they gathered around the TV to watch, it was hockey. Ray was usually there as well, since Ray's mother was an awful cook; he'd use any excuse to eat over at Adam's house. Jesus. It seemed like it was just yesterday.

Adam sat down on the couch with Quinn. "How's the lawsuit going?" Quinn asked. "I didn't want to ask over dinner, in case it was a touchy subject."

"Still dragging on," Adam said with a frown. "Sinead's been on the DA's ass to drop the suit, but it's doubtful that'll happen until after the elections. In the meantime, the league has decided to make an example of me."

Quinn looked interested. "What do you mean?"

"Every couple of years, some of the board of governors decide they need to soften hockey's image in order to expand its appeal. They think it's too violent. They also think if they get rid of some of the hitting and the fighting, we could be as big as the NBA. So they tinker with the rules, and the refs are told to crack down. I'm the whipping boy this time around."

"But the commissioner and the league are supporting you in the lawsuit, right?"

"Publicly. In private they're hoping it forces me to change my style of play."

"Will it?"

"No," Adam replied matter-of-factly. "I can only play one way. The commission wanting to prettify hockey is something the veteran players have learned to deal with over the years. Eventually the true hockey people on the board of governors will reassert themselves. Hockey will never be as big as the NBA, because there just aren't enough people here in the States who played it when they were kids. And if you change it too much, we'll lose our traditional fan base who love it the way it is. I'm just this year's target. I know for a fact that the commissioner has it out for me personally."

Quinn chuckled mirthlessly. "I know what *that's* like. But the truth will out in the end. It might take a while, but it will. Just hang in there."

"I'm a pro at that, believe me."

"Then don't worry. With my sister handling your case, I have no doubt that scum of a DA is going down."

Adam hoped he was right.

29

"Your family is great."

Sinead was thrilled Adam liked the clan. She thought dinner had gone well, except for the few times her mother had blatantly probed his feelings about kids; she'd also brought up Chip a few times, which annoyed Sinead. Telling Adam about Chip was not her mother's prerogative, but Sinead let it go. Overall, the afternoon was a success. That was all that mattered.

They were at Adam's apartment, relaxing on the couch. Sinead had her feet in his lap, and he was massaging them, which she loved. She found massage to be one of the ultimate pleasures in life, not that she'd had one recently. She vowed she'd make time once her schedule lightened up. She'd go to Maggie. Not only was her sister a great masseuse, but it would also put some money in Maggie's pocket, which she desperately needed, especially since she'd yet to talk to Brendan about the "loan."

"I'm glad you liked them," Sinead said, pleased. "They certainly liked you."

"Good." Adam's thumbs dug deep into the balls of her feet. "Did I talk enough?"

"You were amazing. I think you said more at dinner than you've said to me the entire time I've known you."

Adam tickled her feet. "Very funny."

"What were you and Quinn talking about?"

"The case. I told him what Rawson said, about Welsh definitely having it in for me personally."

Sinead was confused. "What are you talking about?"

Adam stared at her blankly. "About the talk I had with Teddy Rawson."

"Adam?" Sinead had adopted her 'Keep cool' voice. "I have no idea what you're talking about."

"I could have sworn I told you about this."

"Whatever 'this' is, I can assure you, you didn't. Please tell me now."

Adam told her about his conversation with the ex-player, and all Sinead could think was: *Do not freak out on him. Do not read him the riot act and call him an idiot. Do not.*

She lay back, looking up at the ceiling. "If you'd told me about this when it happened, I could have wrapped things up a while ago." She propped herself up on her elbows and looked at him. "I need to talk to Teddy Rawson as soon as possible. Did Teddy give you any specific examples of things Welsh said or did that concretely demonstrated he had it out for you?"

"No."

Sinead pressed her lips together to suppress the nasty words threatening to come out of her mouth. "You didn't think to ask, did you?"

"I'm not a lawyer! I don't go around cross-examining my friends!" Adam looked worried. "Do you think Teddy would talk to you on the record?"

"No way," Sinead said without hesitation. "Remember: his salary is paid by the NHL. Welsh, as big a scum as he is, is simply their puppet."

."God, I love when you get all steely."

"We're gonna win this," Sinead declared. "I'm going to have to reinterview some of the players, but it won't be a problem."

"What's your new angle?"

"I'm not telling you! It might jinx it!"

"Another believer in the jinx. You have to tell me! I'm your client!"

"I know that." Sinead playfully wiggled her big toes. "But just trust me on this, okay?"

"Okay."

"Let's stop talking about this now. Just for today, I want to forget about work."

"Gotcha." Adam resumed kneading her feet. "Your mom seemed a little fixated on Chip at dinner."

"Sorry about that," Sinead said grimly.

"When are you going to tell me why you split up?"

"Is it important you know the gory details?"

Adam cocked his head thoughtfully. "Yeah, it is. Your marriage was a huge part of your life. Not only am I curious, but I think I have a right to know."

"You're right. We split over the issue of kids."

"What, he didn't want any and you did? Or vice versa?"

"No, we both wanted kids. We just couldn't agree on how to parent."

"What do you mean?"

"Chip thought I should be a stay-at-home mom until the child started kindergarten. That wasn't feasible: if I took five years off my career, I would completely lose momentum, and I can't afford that. I pointed out to him we had enough money for a nanny; we could have the nanny watch the baby during the day, and then we could take care of the baby ourselves at night and on the weekends.

"Chip was having none of it: he was raised by a nanny and hated it. I pointed out that his nanny was with him twenty-four hours a day for years; she basically raised him, which would not be the case with our child. It didn't matter. Eventually I said that if he felt so strongly about a parent being home, then why didn't he stay home with the baby, and I would continue working? I thought that was the perfect solution; we would both get what we wanted. Apparently, that wasn't an option, either.

"'Children need their mothers,'" he insisted. "When I made the point that they needed their fathers, too, he turned a deaf ear. He was completely inflexible on the issue. Completely."

Sinead looked up at the ceiling again. All this was very painful, not to mention stressful, for her to recount. She could feel the muscles in her head beginning to tighten, but she knew she had to finish. "It was a total standoff after that. Communication between us basically broke down. Irreparably. Eventually, we divorced. Believe me, it was for the best. So that's the story."

Adam said nothing. As the silence wore on, Sinead began to worry. She looked at him. "You're being very quiet," she murmured.

"Mmm."

"What's going on, Adam?"

Adam looked troubled. "I agree with Chip."

Sinead sat up. "What?"

"I think kids do need their mothers. Asking you to stay home for the first five years was not an outrageous demand."

"Kids need their fathers, too," Sinead pointed out calmly. She had an eerie sense of déjà vu. "There was no reason he couldn't stay home for five years if he didn't want a nanny."

"But kids bond stronger to the mother, right? That's just the natural way of things."

Sinead covered her face with her hands. "Oh my God. I can't believe you're saying this." She peered at him through the screen of her fingers. "Do you realize how backward that sounds?"

Adam was unfazed. "I'm a traditional guy. You know that."

Sinead lowered her hands. "There's traditional and then there's antiquated. Thinking the mother should be the one to stay home is antiquated. It doesn't matter which parent stays home, as long as there is a loving, caring presence there."

"I disagree."

Sinead was growing indignant. "Did you not hear the part about me losing career momentum? It's different for women, Adam. A nanny would have solved everything. A nanny wouldn't be 'raising' our child the way Chip said. Yet he was completely inflexible. Completely. His way or the highway. I'm sorry, but that's not the way things work in a marriage.

"And while I'm at it, allow me to point out that both my parents worked, and my siblings and I all turned out perfectly fine."

"They both worked because they had no other choice. I will bet you anything that if they'd had the money, your mom would have stayed home."

"Call and ask her," Sinead said heatedly. "Go on."

"Why couldn't you work part-time? As a compromise?"

"I offered to work part-time, but that wasn't enough. Besides, why couldn't *he* work part-time?" Sinead countered angrily. "I told you: it's different for women. I've had to work twice as hard to prove myself."

"Family is more important than work, Sinead."

"You think I don't know that? There are ways to have both, Adam."

They sat staring at each other. Standoff. Sinead had been in this place before with Chip. She refused to be there again.

"Are you going to talk to me?" Adam asked eventually.

"Are you going to talk to *me*?"

Adam looked troubled. "Yeah, I just . . . I don't know."

"I don't, either." Sinead rose. "I'm tired. Let's call it a night." She swallowed, her chest getting tight. "In fact, let's call it altogether. I don't think I can do this again."

Adam looked stunned. *"What?"*

"We want different things." Sinead wanted to get out of there as fast she could before breaking down.

"What about the fact that I love you?"

"I love you, too," said Sinead, choking up. "But sometimes that's not enough. Trust me." She picked her purse up off the coffee table. "I really should go."

Adam was looking at her like she was deranged. "So that's it? We're done?"

A lump formed in Sinead's throat. "Yes."

"Sinead, this is way, way premature. You're overreacting."

"How is it premature? You told me you agree with my ex-husband on the issue that ended my marriage. What are we supposed to do? Pretend you never said that? Obviously, you're not going to change the way you feel, and neither am I. So what's the point?"

Adam looked at a loss for words. "I just—I don't even know what to say."

"I'll be in touch about the case."

"Okay." He still looked stunned.

Adam walked her to the door. Sinead wished he hadn't. It would make things so much easier if he wasn't standing there beside her. The sense of unease was overwhelming.

"Thank your mother again for a great meal," said Adam awkwardly.

"I will."

"Good night."

Sinead walked out into the silent hallway, the sound of the door closing behind her echoing as loud as a sharp clap of thunder. *You have no right to feel sad,* she chided herself. *You pulled the plug.* She chanted it over and over to herself until she got home to her own place, where the mantra changed. *Stupid. Stupid, scared woman, jumping the gun. What have you done? Don't think about it now. Don't.*

She changed out of her clothes into sweats and made herself a martini. And then she did the only thing she knew how to do right, the one thing on earth she knew she wouldn't screw up. She worked.

30

"*Madonn', what the* hell were you thinking?"

Anthony's eyes were bulged out of his head as Adam told him about his breakup with Sinead. They were sitting at the bar at Dante's after closing time; usually they talked sports, politics, and Stooges. Tonight the talk was personal.

Christ, it had happened so fast it was unreal. One minute he was enjoying the warmth and hospitality of Sinead's family, the next she was dumping him. Adam hated to admit it, but it probably wasn't smart to open with the line, "I agree with Chip."

Adam took a sip of his whiskey, awaiting Anthony's pronouncement. "That's it?"

"I think you're a moron."

Adam scowled. "Don't mince words or anything."

"Seriously, dude, I know you come from bumpkin land, Alberta, but thinking it should be the mom who stays home? That's kind of fucked-up." Anthony lit up a cigar. "My brother was a stay-at-home dad for a while."

"Yeah?" Adam was dubious. "And how did that work out?"

"It didn't. Drove him wacko."

"You do realize you're bolstering my case here, right?"

"Wrong. The reason it didn't work was because he hadn't figured out how to reinvent himself when he retired." Anthony looked thoughtful as he puffed his cigar. "He used to hang out here all the time with the baby. Drove me nuts."

"Why did he hang out here?"

"Because he's a pathetic SOB, that's why." Anthony narrowed his eyes, sizing Adam up. "You wanna know what your problem is?"

"Sure." Adam was amused. Anthony loved analyzing people.

"You won't compromise. Not in work, not in your personal life, nothing."

Adam was unapologetic. "That's why I am who I am."

"*No*, that's why you lost your girlfriend in three seconds flat."

"I never said I wouldn't compromise. She didn't even give us a chance to talk about it. She just flew out the door. But you know what? I bet that even if I was willing to compromise, she wouldn't. Part of the problem is that she's a workaholic. She identifies herself totally with her job, and—"

"Don't you?"

"That's different."

"Why? Because you have a dick?" Anthony threw some scotch down his throat. "Look at it this way: what would happen if you took five years off from your career to watch a kid, and then went back to playing hockey? You think you'd still be at the top of your game? Don't think so. Same goes for her."

"I suppose," Adam grumbled.

"No, I'm right, and you know I'm right. She's got more to lose if she's the one who stays home. It sucks, but it's true. The ladies of the world have a tougher time."

"We shouldn't have even been talking about it," Adam

said with a frown. "But I wanted to know what led to her divorce, so . . ."

Adam exhaled between his clenched teeth, hoping for clarity. He felt like a dog chasing its tail. Was he right? Was she right? Were they both wrong? He'd been surprised by how quickly she was willing to just—end things. That's it. We're done. To him, it was a sign that her dislike of being vulnerable ran much deeper than she was willing to admit. It also showed how uncompromising she was.

Well, it was better like this, anyway. He could concentrate 100 percent on hockey. It wasn't like he was the only player who thought that way. Hell, Ty Gallagher had been known as "the warrior monk" throughout most of his career, eschewing a personal life to keep his focus on the game laser-sharp.

"Sinead and I splitting up is probably a godsend," he told Anthony. "Now I can concentrate on bringing the Cup to New York."

Anthony was looking at him like he was pathetic. "Jesus, you jocks are pitiful. I remember Mikey trying to convince himself of the same thing when he was on the Blades and Theresa and he were on the outs. It's just a way to make yourselves feel better about being such losers in the romance department."

Adam snorted loudly. "Says the guy whose idea of playing sports is tossing a ball of pizza dough back and forth with his sous-chef."

Anthony thrust his chin out defiantly. "Hey, I know what I know."

"You know dick, especially when it comes to being a professional athlete."

"Whatever," Anthony said dismissively. "I still think you're a moron for not insisting you guys talk it out."

"Like I said, we shouldn't have been talking about it at all. It's not like we were planning to get married or anything like that."

Anthony raised an eyebrow. "No? Is that why you met her family? Because the relationship was casual?"

"Get off my case, okay?" Adam was getting irritated. He shouldn't have brought this to Anthony to discuss. He should have gone straight to Ray—who probably would have told him the same thing: *You're an asshole, Adam.*

"Hey, you're the one who came to me, not vice versa."

"Yup. You're right." Adam drained his scotch glass. "I should run. It's late. I have practice tomorrow."

"Yeah, I gotta get up early, too: produce delivery."

They slid off the barstools.

"You should rethink this, dude," Anthony continued. "Seriously. You two were great together. Mr. and Mrs. Uptight Nutball. It was a match made in heaven. Like me and Vivi. We're Mr. and Mrs. Psycho Chef."

Adam patted his shoulder. "You have a great way with words, Ant. Thanks."

"Seriously."

"When the playoffs are done I'll see if—"

"Loser." They walked to the door. "You free Thursday night? I got a couple of other chefs coming over for a poker game. You in?"

Adam shrugged. "Sure. Why not?"

After all, he had nothing else to do.

31

Two weeks later, Sinead was sitting across from NHL Commissioner Welsh at a large, oval table in one of Kidco's conference rooms. It was early morning, and her adrenaline level was high. Welsh was tilting back in his chair, smirking. Little did he know that in a few short minutes, the smirk would be replaced with a look of distress.

"To what do I owe the honor?" Welsh asked.

"Believe me, there's nothing honorable about what's about to take place," said Sinead.

Welsh sniggered quietly.

Sinead interlaced her fingers and put her hands on the table. "I've put the Perry case together. Here's how it's going to go: I'm going to insist on a trial. I'm going to subpoena coaches and referees and players and GMs and people from the league office. I'm going to ask them to testify to whether they believe that you and the league are conspiring to prosecute Adam."

"Oh, please. No one will want to testify."

"It doesn't matter if they testify," Sinead said sweetly. "What matters is that I'm putting them on the stand, and every reporter in every city with an NHL team will be covering the trial; so will a myriad of legal reporters. So will ESPN, which will help generate interest in hockey.

"Whatever questions I ask my witnesses, they'll either say no, you and the league are not conspiring, or they'll take the fifth. Based on the interviews I've done, I'm betting they'll take the fifth. That's not good for you, Mr. Welsh. Every reporter there is going to follow up, and they're all going to reach the same conclusion: that the NHL is a corrupt, conspiratorial clique."

"You don't have the balls."

Sinead stood up, hands splayed on the table in front of her as she leaned toward Welsh, her eyes boring into his. "*Try me.* The first time someone takes the fifth on the stand, you're dead. You're over. You want Adam Perry's scalp? Go for it. But just remember it comes at a cost: yours. It's your choice."

Welsh maintained his contemptuous gaze as Sinead picked up her briefcase and walked out of the conference room. Now it was time to wait and see.

32

Sinead could barely concentrate when she got back to the office. Every time Simone told her she had a call, a tingle went through her. Just as she was beginning to give up hope that she'd get word today on what would happen, Simone told her there was a Justin Barry on the line. Sinead snatched up the phone.

"Justin."

"Sinead." Usually uptight, he sounded elated. "Congratulations! We just got word the Philly DA is dropping the charges against Adam."

"That's wonderful," said Sinead, barely able to breathe.

"He's going to give a press conference tonight at six. It'll be on ESPN. Do you mind if we tell Adam?"

"No, of course not," Sinead replied, slightly disappointed. "He should know as soon as possible."

"Hold on a minute, will you, please?" Sinead could hear Lou Capesi bellowing something in the background. Justin got on the phone with a heavy sigh. "Lou wants you to come down and celebrate with us."

Sinead hesitated a moment. "I guess I could do that."

"See you in a bit, then. And again, congrats—and thanks." Sinead was just about to hang up the phone when Justin hurriedly added, "Just one more thing."

"What's that?"

"Do you know what your fee will be?"

"I haven't tallied it up yet. But you can rest assured that the appropriate party will receive my bill by the end of the week."

Curt Justin was back. "Thank you."

Sinead put down the phone. She'd won. *She'd won.*

She ran down the hall to tell Oliver.

"I won!"

Oliver jumped up from behind his desk. "Way to go, cupcake!" He picked her up and swung her around.

"I'm kind of in shock," Sinead said breathlessly as he put her down.

"Don't lie, you flat-chested little weasel. You knew you'd win."

Sinead felt bashful. "Well . . . yeah." She picked at her cuticles. "Lou Capesi wants me to come down and celebrate."

"So go. The big guns will pop the champagne corks tomorrow."

"They're telling Adam right now."

"Better scoot down there so he can give you his special thanks," Oliver said lewdly.

"I hate you." She kissed his cheek. "I'll see you later."

* * *

The PR office at Met Gar was packed with people. Lou was running around like a maniac, wheezing so hard Sinead was afraid he'd have a heart attack. He'd ordered in a few pizzas, but Sinead didn't touch them, worried that it might make her face break out.

She was unprepared for the round of applause she received when she walked in. She thanked them humbly and then went to get herself a glass of champagne. That's when she heard another round of applause. Adam had arrived.

He made a beeline straight for her. He went to kiss her, and then at the last moment seemed to realize what he was doing and quickly switched to her cheek instead.

"This is amazing," he marveled. "Amazing." His eyes shone with gratitude. "I can't thank you enough, Sinead."

"I'm just glad things worked out in our favor." He was standing so close to her it was torture. Adam must have sensed it; he took a step back.

"How did you get Welsh to back down?"

Sinead smiled slyly. "I made him an offer he couldn't refuse."

Adam laughed. "I guess your reputation as ruthless is true." He studied her face. "You look tired," he murmured.

Sinead shrugged. "Just work." *He thinks I'm unattractive. Well, I don't care.*

"Working day and night?"

"Not like it was a few weeks back," Sinead replied, trying to ignore what she thought might be an implicit criticism. "Oliver's back."

"That's good."

"Yes, it is. The office was pretty boring without him."

"How's your family?" Adam asked cordially.

The question surprised her, but it shouldn't have. Adam Perry was the consummate gentleman. "Fine. I'll tell them you asked."

"Thanks."

"How are Ray and Rick?"

"Sounds like a cartoon," Adam mused.

"It does."

"They're both doing well. I think I may have told you Ray might come down if we make the playoffs?"

"You did."

"Rick is still looking for a job. The longer it drags on, the more angry he gets about my helping him out."

"Oh, I meant to ask you about that," Sinead blurted.

Adam furrowed his brows. "About Rick?"

"More about getting a sibling to accept financial help."

Adam listened as Sinead explained Maggie and Brendan's situation to him. When she was done, she looked at him hopefully. "Well?"

Adam grimaced. "I hate to tell you, but there's no way to get them to do it, especially if the one who's resistant is the guy, and he's proud. The first time I mentioned it just to Rick, it was no go; the second time, I mentioned it to both Rick and Susie. Susie worked on him after that, telling him to think of the kids. I know she said, 'Wouldn't you do that for Adam if the situation was reversed?' and he admitted he would, which is major, considering our relationship. Try talking to them together. If that doesn't work, see if you can get your sister to ask if he'd do it for you if the shoe was on the other foot."

"I told her that if it makes it easier for them to accept the money, it could just be a loan, not a gift."

"That's what I did."

A minute ago Sinead had wanted to run away. Now—pathetically, in her opinion—she wanted to keep the conversation going a little while longer.

"Any special plans for the summer?" she asked genially.

"I might take Dylan and Carrie for a few weeks, give Rick and Susie a break, you know?"

"Take them where?"

"Rent a cabin or something. I haven't really thought it through."

Sinead hesitated. "You're free to use my house in Bearsville."

"That's very generous of you."

"I'd rather the house were used than let it just sit there, empty."

"True," Adam said quietly.

Sinead could feel the growing sense of impatience in

the room as she and Adam stood talking. "There are tons
of people waiting to speak with you. Go on."

"Thank you," he repeated softly.

"It was my pleasure," Sinead replied, glad he'd walked
away before her eyes began to fill. She missed him, but
some things just weren't meant to be.

* * *

Once the PR celebration wound down, Adam went to work
on his skates and sticks, thinking about Sinead. Despite her
cordiality, her unease was palpable, the exhaustion on her
face worrisome. Clearly she'd been driving herself into the
ground—for him.

Adam missed her, and he could tell she missed him,
too. Maybe that was why she was so eager to tell him others wanted to speak with him, so she could get away. Like
him, she disliked displaying vulnerability. It was either
that, or she truly disliked him now. *Maybe she thinks I'm
some kind of Neanderthal, a throwback to the fifties.* She'd
ended their relationship so quickly she hadn't even given
him a chance to say that off the ice, he wasn't a "my way or
the highway" guy. Yeah, he was old-fashioned, but he was
open to compromise, depending on the situation. Well, too
late now. It *was* better this way; he'd be able to devote himself completely to the playoffs. Screw what Anthony said.
He was wrong. There's a difference between being a chef
and a professional hockey player.

Adam marveled at how his life changed overnight.
One day the lawsuit was hanging over his head like the
sword of Damocles; the next day it was gone. He wasn't
an egomaniac by any means, but he was proud of himself: he'd stuck to his guns, he'd refused to change the way
he played, and in the end, things turned out the way they
should have, and the bad guys were going to pay. He felt
vindicated. Of course, none of it would have been possible
without Sinead.

* * *

Talking to the press turned out to be less excruciating than Adam expected, especially since their questions were straightforward. Sinead was at the top of his list of people to thank. He didn't care if he sounded like a broken record; more than once he commended her on all her hard work.

He'd always hated having his picture taken, and tonight was no exception. But he bore it like a champ, reminding himself that if the Blades won the Cup, he'd be expected to do a lot of press. That he'd do happily.

Returning to the locker room after the press conference, Adam was unprepared for the reception awaiting him: his teammates began banging their sticks on the floor in salute. Adam, who rarely let down his guard around the other Blades, could not hide how moved he was and smiled broadly at their show of support.

"You did it, Cap!" David Hewson exclaimed. "You showed them what integrity looks like."

"Fuckin' A," said Eric Mitchell.

"Old-time hockey!" whooped Jason Mitchell.

Unprompted, the team started chanting, "Old-time hockey! Old-time hockey!"

"I wanna say something," Esa Saari said loudly. The players exchanged surprised glances. They all knew that Adam had torn Saari a new one at the start of the season. They also knew that it seemed to have a positive effect on their egotistical teammate: he was never late for practice, and he played as hard during practice drills as he did on the ice. He'd become a more generous player as well: it wasn't all about him showing off his extraordinary talent anymore; it was about using that talent to help build a winning team.

The team waited. Saari was looking at Adam with unabashed admiration.

"I know you and I didn't exactly get off on the right foot at the start of the season. I was an arrogant little prick.

I thought I was better than everyone else, and that the Blades should have felt grateful to have me.

"But you helped me realize that I wasn't showing proper respect for the game, as well as my teammates. Watching you, listening to you, I learned how to be a team player, and how important that is to winning. I'm not gonna lie: I thought your style of play was archaic when I first got here. Now I realize that we need a leader like you to win: someone who's willing to play his guts out every game, someone with integrity who refused to kowtow to the league."

Saari stepped forward, extending a hand for Adam to shake. "It's an honor to play with you, Captain," he said humbly, trying not to choke up. "It's an honor for all of us. Thank you."

Adam shook the young Finn's hand. "You're welcome."

At that moment, Adam admired Saari. He knew how hard it must have been for him to say all those things; the young kid turned out to have character.

Adam looked around the locker room. "You all know I'm not big on speeches. But I have to tell you all that your support during the lawsuit meant a lot to me. That's what teammates do: they watch each other's backs. This is a special team, the best one I've ever been a part of. If we keep our commitment to each other, we'll make it deep into the playoffs. And if we win the Cup . . . we will all be brothers forever. Now get dressed and get your sorry asses onto the ice to warm up. We have a game to play."

33

Sinead often worked in the office until nine or ten, but tonight she was utterly drained. Of course, that fell by the wayside when she tuned in to the Blades pregame press conference. Adam didn't seem the least bit taciturn, though she could tell he was uncomfortable. It amused her that Lou Capesi was wearing yet another stained tie. He just didn't give a damn. As someone who always had to dress impeccably, she envied him.

Adam looked so handsome standing there beside Lou. Years ago, Kidco had instituted a policy that players had to wear jackets and ties before all games, both home and away. The players all hated it, but it did lend a more professional style to the team.

She ordered in Chinese and sat in front of the TV, mindlessly surfing. But then, she put the remote down. *Oh my God*, she thought incredulously. *I want to watch the game.* It wasn't that she'd become a hockey fan; she wanted to watch Adam. And thanks to him, she now understood how the game was played. *You're pathetic,* she told herself.

The first period was just about to end (the Blades were up 1–0 against New Jersey) when her cell rang. "Hell," she muttered to herself. "Never a moment's peace." She softened when she saw it was Maggie calling.

"Hey, you," she said cheerily.

"Neenee." Maggie was crying. "I need your help."

Sinead was alarmed. "What's wrong?"

"I need you to watch Charlie. Brendan"—Maggie took a deep breath to collect herself—"sawed his left pinky off. He and his crew were rushing to cut some sheets of wood, and to make things go faster they took the safety guard off the saw, and—" Maggie broke down.

"I'll be right over."

Sinead grabbed her purse and hurried downstairs to catch a cab. Her parents were in Ireland for two weeks, which was no doubt why Maggie called her. *Please let them be able to reattach his pinky. This is Manhattan; some of the best hand surgeons in the world have to be here.*

The cab ride over to her sister's house seemed to take forever. Sinead was convinced that the traffic gods were against her: the congestion was denser than usual, and contrary to the reputation of New York cabbies, hers seemed to be in no hurry. She knew it was insane to think all of this was happening on purpose, but that's how it felt. Maggie needed her *now*; she wanted to be there already, goddammit.

Pulling up to Maggie's house, she paid and told the cabbie to wait because there would be another fare for him to take back to the city. Maggie looked anxious as she stood by the front door, shifting her weight from foot to foot, her face red and puffy from crying.

Sinead was breathless as she flew onto Maggie's porch. "I got here as soon as I could."

"Thank you," Maggie said tearfully. "Thank you so much."

"Don't be silly, Mags. This is what family is for."

"He's at Saint Luke's," said Maggie. "One of the top hand surgeons in the world is there."

"Go. Hurry up."

"Charlie's been fed, and he's in the playpen in the living room. I'll call you as soon as I know anything."

"Don't worry about me. Just worry about you."

"I love you, Neenee," Maggie said as she bounded down the porch steps.

"Love you, too."

Sinead closed the door behind her, mouth dry. She hated that she couldn't do more for her sister.

Steeling herself, she walked into the living room to be with Charlie, who was sitting in the playpen, happily playing with a set of soft, stuffed blocks.

"Hey, Charlie," she cooed cheerily.

Charlie looked at her. His bottom lip began to quiver. When he began to wail, Sinead didn't know whether to leave him in the playpen or try to calm him by rocking him in her lap. She decided to do an experiment, making monkey noises while tapping herself lightly on the top of the head. Charlie's tears came to a gulping, sniffling halt. He grinned at her, and then he began to giggle.

Sinead found herself smiling, too, as she began pulling a variety of funny faces and making silly noises. Charlie loved it, his tinkling laughter one of the most delightful sounds she'd ever heard. She bounced Charlie on her lap. She puffed up her cheeks and let him "pop" them. She sang him a few kiddie standards: "Three Blind Mice," "Old MacDonald." And witnessing his joy, feeling his warm little body against hers so relaxed and secure, Sinead had a revelation that took her breath away: it wasn't just that she was unwilling to give up career advancement to raise a child. It was also that she was unwilling to make that sacrifice for *Chip*.

It was stunning. She was so sure she loved Chip until
they started fighting over the child issue. But maybe she
didn't love him enough. Perhaps she knew deep down
inside that he didn't respect her enough to be a real partner,
and she would always be the one expected to compromise
because of his sense of entitlement. Maybe, subconsciously,
she'd been looking for a way out of the marriage.

"More!"

Sinead didn't realize that she'd stopped bouncing and
being silly. "Sorry, buddy." She resumed entertaining her
nephew, but her mind was still roiling. Adam had said he
didn't think Chip was asking too much, and she had reacted
with lightning-quick vehemence. She was furious when he'd
said family was more important than career. She agreed
with him; she just hadn't realized until now that giving up
her career was something she wasn't willing to do for Chip.

She pulled her cell out of her bag, staring at it. Should
she call Adam and ask for a second chance? Hadn't he told
her that her decision was premature and that she was overreacting? Obviously he'd been willing to discuss the issue
further as she charged out of his apartment like a crazy
person.

"What should I do, Charlie?" Sinead asked her nephew
with a forlorn sigh. "I know the law better than I can read
men. I'm scared." She buried her nose in his soft curls.
"You know what your aunt Neenee is?" She started
squawking like a chicken. Charlie laughed delightedly. *If
only life were that simple,* Sinead thought enviously. But
maybe it could be.

*   *   *

It felt like a small miracle when she finally got Charlie to go
to sleep. She was restlessly waiting for Maggie to call. The
longer the night dragged on, the more worried she became.

Finally, close to midnight, Maggie trudged wearily

through the front door. Sinead ran out to meet her in the hallway. "Well?"

"They were able to reattach his pinky." Maggie looked exhausted. "His whole crew was there waiting with me."

She peeled off her jacket, hanging it on the newel post at the bottom of the stairs, and sank down on the couch. "God, I hate hospitals."

"Doesn't everyone?" Sinead sank down beside her. "Do you want me to stay the night?"

Maggie looked touched. "You don't have to."

"You sure? It's no problem."

Maggie smiled wearily. "We'll be fine." She put her hand to her mouth, covering a big yawn. "You want a beer or something? I really need to unwind a little before I go to bed."

"That would be great."

Maggie headed for the kitchen, returning a few minutes later with two glasses of Harp. She handed Sinead her glass.

"Thanks." Sinead gulped some down, amazed at how good it tasted sliding down her throat. "Hits the spot."

She noticed Maggie's hands were shaking. Sinead reached out to still them. "It's going to be okay," she said gently.

"Yes and no," Maggie replied, her eyes welling up.

"What's going on?"

"I'm so embarrassed. We're so stupid."

"Tell me," Sinead pressed.

"Of course I'm relieved they were able to reattach Brendan's finger. But we've got no health insurance." She began to cry in earnest. "You must think we're idiots."

"*Talk to me.*"

"Actually, that's not one hundred percent accurate," she said with a sniff, swiping at her eyes. "Charlie and I are covered. Brendan isn't. It was cheaper that way. You know him: 'Don't worry, don't worry, things will be fine.' Like he's superhuman."

Sinead squeezed her hand tight. "Oh, Mags."

"It gets worse," Maggie returned despairingly. "He's self-employed, and again, to keep costs down, he decided to forgo workman's comp for himself—especially since he covers his crew."

"Mags—"

"Don't say it."

"I will say it, and if you don't listen to me, I *will* think you're stupid. I'm going to pay Brendan's hospital bills, and I'm going to pay for insurance coverage for him that includes workman's comp. It's insane for him not to have any."

Maggie was shaking her head vehemently. "He won't go for it."

"He *will* go for it, because I'm going to tell him straight-out that his family will be majorly screwed if he doesn't get coverage for himself. I'll ask him: does he really want to do that to you and Charlie? Has he thought about what would happen if anything serious happened to him? He was lucky."

Maggie swiped at her nose. "It still might not work."

"Oh, it'll work, believe me. That man loves you and Charlie more than life itself. If it makes it more palatable, I'll tell him it's a loan—speaking of which, you never talked to him about my original offer, did you?"

"No," Maggie admitted sheepishly.

"It's okay. What matters is that I'm here to help right now. And if Brendan says he's not going to accept it, I will kick his ass from here to kingdom come, so help me God."

Maggie managed a smile. "Thank you, Neenee."

Sinead hugged her. "You don't have to thank me. Ever."

Maggie took a sip of beer. "God, you never know what's waiting for you when you get up in the morning, do you?"

She sniffled again. "Enough of me and my woes. What's up with you? I'm sorry I interrupted you at work."

"I wasn't at work. I was home stuffing my face with steamed dumplings. Celebrating. I won Adam's case."

"Congratulations!" Maggie looked guilty. "You shouldn't be here covering for me! You should be out celebrating! I'm so sorry."

"You're being silly. I actually celebrated at Met Gar earlier today." She swallowed nervously. "So of course I saw Adam."

"And—?"

"It felt weird. He was so grateful, and he even kissed me on the cheek. I could tell he was kinda still attracted to me."

"But."

"There's still that roadblock in my head. The 'I agree with Chip' issue. I'm so confused."

Maggie squeezed her knee. "My turn to listen. What is it?"

Sinead groaned. "I don't want to dump this on you now; you've got enough on your plate."

"No, please, dump. I welcome the distraction." Maggie took a sip of beer. "Seriously."

"I had this realization while I was watching Charlie tonight. I know, that sounds crazy—"

"It doesn't sound crazy at all."

"We actually bonded," Sinead said happily. "I made him laugh, and he cuddled with me . . . he didn't even make a fuss when I put him down."

Maggie's gaze was gentle. "And so?"

"I realized that my reaction had to do with Chip. If Adam asked me to stay home with a child, I wouldn't have reacted so vehemently."

Maggie's eyes widened. "Wow. I mean, wow."

"I know," said Sinead, digging her knuckles deep into the back of her neck.

"What happens now?"

"Nothing."

"What do you mean, 'Nothing'?"

Sinead was torn up with misery. "I just can't face the thought of rejection. What if I tell him I made a mistake, and he doesn't want me?"

"That doesn't seem very likely."

"When I broke up with him, he told me I was overreacting and that my decision was premature."

"Maybe it was."

"I don't know." Sinead knew she sounded whiny but couldn't help it. "I think about the night I broke up with him, and obviously I wasn't reacting to Adam, I was reacting to what I'd gone through with Chip. I don't think I even gave Adam a chance to talk."

"So talk to him now."

"I'm afraid," Sinead confessed.

"You?"

"Gimme a break. You know I'm bad at this relationship stuff."

"It's because you've never put relationships first, Nee. That's not a criticism; it's just a fact."

"Well, he's the same way!"

"Is he?"

"Yes. No. Maybe." Sinead resumed rubbing her neck. "I think this might be a bad time. The Blades are making a serious run for the Cup. He probably wants to pour all his energy into that now that he doesn't have to worry about the lawsuit."

"Oh, so now you know what he thinks and feels? Quite a feat."

Sinead scowled. "Don't mock me."

"Well, don't be Miss Roadblock."

"I have to think about this."

"Stop thinking. Just *do*."

"I will, I will. In my own time."

"Well, don't leave it too long. He's a good guy; someone else will snap him up."

"Thanks," Sinead said sarcastically.

"You're welcome. Now let's veg out in front of the TV. I really need to relax."

34

You jocks are pathetic. The longer you let it go, the slimmer the chances she'll take you back.

Anthony's voice in Adam's head felt like eagle talons digging into his skull as he sat on his couch, eating milk and cookies. Yeah, yeah, he wasn't supposed to be eating junk, his body was a temple, blah blah blah. But right now, his brain didn't care. All he could think about was Sinead.

The Blades won tonight, and it was sweet—until he came to his empty apartment, and his brain began hammering away at him the way it had been for weeks. It'd been saying things he didn't want to hear but that he knew were true: winning the Cup wasn't everything. Hockey wasn't everything. Being a hockey player gave him more satisfaction and joy than he ever could have imagined. But if you stripped it down to its barest bones, the hard truth was that hockey was his career, one that would be coming to an end in the next few years.

Sinead. Shit. He shouldn't have let her just quit them and run out. But he was shocked. And then he was pissed, too proud to go to her. *Wait till after you win the Cup.*

But then he thought: Wait for what? For his life to actually begin? If his playing had suddenly become sharper now that they'd split, that would be one thing. But it hadn't. He was playing the way he always had; he was also playing with guys, Ty Gallagher included, who'd managed to win the Cup even though they had wives, girlfriends, children. The "eat, sleep, and breathe hockey" mantra was bullshit. Maybe rookies needed to hear it to keep their focus. But he was no rookie. He was a veteran player who was going to be alone the rest of his life unless he put things in proper perspective, and fast.

He drained his glass of milk. Screw the late hour. Screw waking her up. He was going to state his case now. If she thought he was nuts, so be it. It was time to stop living in some imaginary future. If he wanted her, he had to show her. *Now.*

* * *

"I'm not sure I can do that, Mr. Perry."

Adam stood at the reception desk in the lobby of Sinead's apartment building, trying to reason with the night doorman. He wanted to surprise Sinead. Rocco (Rocco the Rotund, Sinead called him) didn't want to let him up to her apartment.

"Rocco, you know me, right? Just let me up."

"I could lose my job, Mr. Perry."

"You won't lose your job," Adam assured him.

Rocco laughed at him. "Who are you? God? Suppose Sinead is pissed I let you up, and she gets me fired? You gonna pay my bills?"

"Rocco, listen to me. This is a matter of life and death. I'm not shitting you." Adam paused. "If you let me up, I'll send you and Mrs. Rocco on a vacation anywhere you want."

Rocco looked insulted. "Oh, so now you're bribing me?"

"C'mon, man," Adam begged. "How about this: I'll get

you tickets to any event at Met Gar you want for the rest of your life."

Rocco paused. "Anything?"

"Anything."

"For life?"

"For life."

"Deal."

Interesting how he didn't consider that a bribe, Adam mused.

"Can you buzz her now and tell her it's Oliver?"

Rocco shook his head. "I got a bad feeling about this."

Adam was getting desperate. "Rocco, you already agreed to this. You want me to go down on my knees, dude? *C'mon.* Time's a-wasting."

"If I wake her up, she's gonna be pissed."

"I can handle that. Just tell her Oliver's here."

"Fine." Rocco buzzed upstairs. "Sinead? Oliver's here to see you." Adam held his breath. "Go on up," said Rocco. "She's all yours."

"Did she sound like you woke her up?"

"I dunno," Rocco retorted. "Just go and leave me in peace already, okay?"

"Thanks, Rocco."

35

Oliver? Sinead was seized by a jolt of terror. Suppose he'd fallen off the wagon? Well, at least he was coming to her, not continuing his binge. *You always expect the worst. Welcome, as Quinn said, to being Irish.*

The doorbell rang, and Sinead hustled over to open it. "Oliver, I—"

Not Oliver. Adam. Adam standing there in the hall while she looked like a hag. Adam.

"Hey."

"Hey?" Sinead replied sardonically.

Adam looked flustered. "Lame, I know. I just had to see you."

"How did you get up here?"

"Rocco let me up, and please don't fire him. I really pressured him."

Sinead cocked her head inquisitively. "And you said you were Oliver because—?"

"Because I figured you wouldn't let me up if you knew it was me. Am I right?"

Sinead was silent.

"Can I come in?"

"I guess so."

Sinead's pulse was beating madly as she ushered him inside. She'd yet to clear away the cold Chinese food from earlier in the evening. *God, he'll think I'm a pig, one of those pathetic lonely women who stays in on Friday nights and stuffs her face and watches* Ace of Cakes.

"Please, sit," Sinead urged. "Unless you're not going to be here long, in which case you can stand. I guess. Either way, do you want a drink?"

Adam looked concerned. "Are you okay?"

"Yeah. Why? Of course. Fine. Why wouldn't I be?"

"Because you seem a little nervous."

"I'm not." *Don't lie.* "Actually, I am. You caught me completely off guard."

"I'm sorry."

"No, don't be, it's okay. Now." She gestured toward the couch. "Sit. Please."

"Please stop talking like a robot. You're freaking me out."

"I'll try not to," Sinead replied, amazed she could manage a smile.

They sat down in unison. Sinead could feel her pulse flutter in her throat; Adam was so close their shoulders practically touched. Perhaps it was because she hadn't seen him in a while, but he looked especially gorgeous, whereas she did not. She tucked her feet beneath her so he wouldn't see the chipped toenail polish.

"So—?" Her heart was beginning to pound, and she couldn't control it.

"I love you," Adam declared. "I love you, and I want a second chance, if you'll hear me out."

Sinead couldn't breathe for a moment. "Uh . . . okay. I'm listening."

"The night we broke up? I was a jerk. I listened to you laying out what happened between you and Chip, and never once did it strike me that in every scenario, you were the one making the sacrifices."

Sinead looked down, twisting her hands in her lap.

"I know I said I agreed with Chip. I know I told you I was traditional. But I'm not inflexible. If you hadn't run out, we'd have been able to talk about it. But you cut me off at the knees."

Adam took her hand. Sinead was shocked to see how vulnerable he looked. "All my life, all I've cared about is my career, just like you. At least you had a life outside of work. I never did. But now I realize work isn't everything. I don't even want to think about all the hours I've spent alone in my apartment worrying about strategy and training and inspiration, when I could have been out doing any number of things that have nothing to do with my job. My priorities have been fucked up, and I've missed out on a lot. Worst of all, I've missed out on you."

Sinead looked into his eyes. "Look, you're not the only one at fault here. You were right: I did overreact that night; I did end things prematurely. And like you just pointed out, I didn't even give you a chance to state your case. I'm so sorry, Adam."

Adam lifted her hand to his mouth, his lips grazing her knuckles. "I'm sorry, too."

Sinead's heart was tumbling wildly. "I've figured a few things out about myself while we were apart, too."

"What's that?"

"I was babysitting Charlie recently, and it was terrific. I'd watched him a few other times before, and for some reason, we never quite jelled. Maybe he could tell how nervous I was around him. At any rate, I've always had an awkwardness inside me that made me believe I just wasn't cut out to be a parent.

"So there I was with Charlie, and we were having a wonderful time. And I remembered you and me playing with Tully's kids, and how much fun it was." Sinead's eyes began welling up. "I realized you would have been willing to compromise and I would have been willing to stay home part-time with a child."

Words were jostling for position in her throat. "Don't you see? I wasn't reacting to you; I was having a knee-jerk reaction to what I'd gone through with Chip. As soon as you said you agreed with him, I cut and ran. And that was wrong. It was cowardly."

Adam touched her cheek. "I was the coward. I shouldn't have let you walk out the door. I should have asserted myself. But I was just so stunned; one minute we were together, the next you were running away."

"Like I said, I was reacting to past history. Again, I'm so sorry."

"It's okay."

Adam pressed his mouth to hers. The entire time they were apart, Sinead had tried to conjure the experience of being kissed by him, but the memories were nothing compared to the real thing. He tasted like love and relief and desire. She pulled away, burying her face in the crook of his shoulder. "I love you," she said softly.

Ever so gently, Adam took her face in his hands, his eyes bright and focused. "I love you, too. I swear to you, I will do whatever it takes to make this work, because the thought of living my life without you kills me." He put his burning forehead to hers. "Just be patient with me, okay? I've always put my career first."

"So have I."

"Then we'll figure it out together."

"Forever?"

"Forever," Adam whispered passionately. "And that's a promise."

36

Time feels like an assault when you're willing to push your body to the limit, Adam mused, grimacing as he slipped his sweater over his head. It was game four of the final series; if they won tonight against L.A., they'd be the Stanley Cup champions; if they didn't win, the series could drag out to an excruciating game seven. *Bring it on,* thought Adam, massaging his left shoulder where two nights before, L.A.'s Nicolai Gorky had hit him during a melee behind the Blades' goal. The pain was a mere footnote. Balls, tenacity, grit, whatever you want to call it—Adam had it in spades, and nothing was going to get in his way. Nothing.

The road to get here had been a bitch. The first round against Philadelphia went smoother than Adam had anticipated. Philly's goaltending cracked under the Blades' relentless assault, and the New Yorkers won in a sweep. They then played New Jersey in the Eastern Conference Quarterfinals in a series as hard as the Philly series was easy. It had taken every ounce of blood and guts for the Blades to beat Jersey in a seven-game series. In the second game, Adam had leveled one of Jersey's wingers, Guy Montaine, with a punishing open-ice hit. Everyone in Met Gar held their breath, waiting to see if one of the referees called a penalty. They didn't. The league had indeed backed down. Adam could play his game.

They went up against Tampa in the semis. It was a fight to the death, the games some of the most physically punishing Adam had ever played. But the Blades pulled it out in six games, and now here they were going mano a mano against L.A. on home ice in the fourth game of the finals. Adam didn't like to get ahead of himself, especially after telling his teammates to focus, but he couldn't stop imagining what it would be like to skate the Cup and be able to show Sinead, as well as his niece and nephew. Outside Met Gar, there was carefully contained insanity as fans stood pressed against the barricades, chanting, "We want the Cup!" The depth of their longing inspired Adam. He loved the high-voltage energy crackling through Manhattan as the whole city whipped itself up into Blades fever. These people knew what it was like to be Stanley Cup champions; they'd tasted this victory before, and they wanted to taste it again. Adam intended to give them what they all—himself included—wanted.

* * *

There was energy humming through the locker room, too, but it carried a faint tinge of anxiety. Some of Adam's teammates knew what it was to win the Cup, but they were no more relaxed than any of the other players. Each time was like the first time, Ty told them. Each time required the same will and determination. Adam was feeling the same thing everyone else was feeling—maybe even more, since he knew he might never have another chance at the prize that had eluded him his entire career.

"Guys."

Adam's voice was commanding as he stepped into the center of the room. By now they knew that speeches weren't his forte, and that he was more a man of action than words. But tonight, words were needed to help spur the action on. Tonight, he actually wanted to speak.

He had their complete attention. "Our bodies and spirits have taken a beating through this season, but we haven't been broken, and we will not be broken, so long as the hunger and the sheer iron will to win is there."

His eyes swept the circle of men around him, their unblinking attention exactly what he wanted.

"I've been playing in the league for seventeen years. This is the closest I've ever come to winning the Cup, and I'm not going to lie: I want it badly. But I'm not afraid of losing; I'm afraid of not wanting victory badly enough. Play as if this is the last fucking hockey game you'll ever get to play. This is hockey. Will beats skill. If we want it more than they do, we will win. *Will beats skill*.

"The Cup is sitting in the next room. Let's take it."

37

The tone of the game was set in the first period. Three minutes in, L.A. scored first, prompting a "Boooo!" so loud from the hometown crowd that Adam could feel it thrum through his bones. But the Blades responded thirty seconds later: Thad Meyers's slap shot from the right point seemed to stun not only L.A.'s goalie, Terry Cahoon, but the entire Los Angeles team as well.

Michael Dante was pulling out all the stops to close out the series this night, shortening his bench, double-shifting Saari's line, and rotating just two pairs of defensemen. Barry Fontaine wristed a rebound past Cahoon with less than a minute left in the first, putting the Blades up 2–1.

"Solid first," Adam said aloud in the locker room as he lifted his sweater and undid his shoulder pads so that one of the trainers could freeze his left shoulder, which was beginning to pulse with pain. The locker room was muted, no one wanting to jinx their first-period success. Finally, as they stood to file back to the ice, Adam broke the silence. "Will beats skill."

* * *

The Blades played like men on a mission in the second, and L.A.'s energy flagged. But Cahoon was standing on his head, keeping L.A. in the game. The tension was ratcheting up, both in the arena and on the bench. Yet Adam felt oddly calm. He was where he was supposed to be. His entire life and everything he had been through—those years of childhood hockey, traveling from town to town in the juniors, the accident with his best friend, the death of his parents, all the blood and lost teeth and pain—had all come together for this one night.

Ten minutes into the period, L.A. put a rebound past Hewson, tying the game and silencing the crowd. On the ice for the next shift, Adam saw L.A. winger Serge Fetisov coming down the right side at top speed. Adam met Fetisov and the boards at the exact same moment. Bending from the waist as he and Fetisov were about to connect, Adam thrust out his left hip, slamming into Fetisov's thighs, sending the winger airborne. The energy in the building surged as the fans rose to their feet, cheering.

* * *

No one spoke in the locker room between the second and third period . . . until Michael Dante climbed up on a bench, looked around, and in a quiet voice said, "Will beats skill."

From the moment the puck was dropped to start the third, the Blades controlled the ice. Saari played like a man possessed, but Cahoon wouldn't yield. Shots rang off the crossbar and the posts. Frustration mounted as the period entered its final moments. After a rare L.A. flurry, Adam cleared the puck the length of the ice. Saari got a jump on the flagging L.A. defense. He flew down the ice with the kind of speed that had made him a star since he was a little kid playing in a small town outside Helsinki. Getting to the puck first, he sent a blind backhand pass out into the slot. Ulf Torkelson, who'd been flowing the play, one-timed the puck over Cahoon's blocker.

The fans were on their feet, screaming.

There were only two minutes left, and the Blades had the lead. The rest of the game was a blur to Adam. L.A. pulled Cahoon for an extra skater. The desperation of the L.A. players to tie the game was topped by the desperation of the Blades to hold the lead. Blades were throwing themselves in front of pucks, diving to tip pucks out of the zone. With five seconds left, Adam dug the puck out of the Blades' left corner and lifted it as high as he could toward center ice. Seconds after it landed, the horn went off.

The Blades were the Stanley Cup champions.

38

Joy. That was the first word that came to Adam's mind. He'd dreamed of this moment for years, imagining what it would feel like, but fantasy paled compared to the real thing. The roar of the crowd was louder than anything he ever heard, the pitch of the emotion so high it bordered on hysterical.

"We want Cup! We want Cup!" The crowd was like a primitive tribe brought to frenzy by their shared relief.

Tully Webster, red-faced and exhausted as he mopped his face with a towel, nudged Adam in the ribs. "Nuts, isn't it?" he asked, referring to the crowd.

"It's great."

"Cap!" Adam turned, and an exuberant Esa Saari threw his arms around his neck. "We fucking did it! I'm allowed to party tonight, right?" he ribbed.

"As long and hard as you want, Saari."

"Yess!"

A red carpet was rolled out onto the ice, followed by a table draped in velvet. Two men in suits wearing white gloves came out, carrying hockey's holy of holies, which they carefully placed in the center of the table. When

Commissioner Welsh emerged for the presentation, a chorus of boos greeted him. But the crowd was too excited to vent their anger for long.

The commissioner's speech was short and simple. He congratulated L.A. on its season and valiant playoff run. Then he looked over at Adam.

"Captain Adam Perry, come get the Cup." Adam picked up the chalice. He held it reverently for a moment, lifted it above his head, and with a kick of his skates he was off, circling the rink, holding the grail aloft for the entire lap. When he came to where Sinead was sitting with Quinn and Oliver, he mouthed, "I love you."

Oliver mouthed back, "I love you, too," earning him an elbow in the ribs from Sinead.

One by one it was passed to everyone on the team, the men who fought together to make this moment real. Once everyone on the team had a chance to skate the Cup, it was passed back to Adam, who held it high, skating once again along the perimeter of the ice, letting fans reach over the boards to touch it and claim some of its magic.

*   *   *

Back in the locker room a few minutes later, the celebration continued. Sinead finally edged her way toward Adam.

"That was amazing!" she enthused, kissing him.

"I'm covered in sweat and champagne!"

Sinead discreetly licked his arm. "I know." She wrapped her arms around his neck. "What's next? Have you fussy boys figured out what you're doing before the Hart?"

"The official party is at Dante's."

"Would you mind if I skipped the official party and just went straight over to the pub to help my folks out?"

"Don't mind at all. You know, this would be a pretty hollow victory if you weren't in my life."

Sinead blushed. "Adam . . ."

"It's true." He gave her a quick kiss. "Go on, get out of here before your brain explodes."

"Will do. I love you, Adam Perry. And I'm so proud of you."

Adam watched as she carefully threaded her way through the ever-deepening crowd. He wondered where his family was. He was on the verge of giving up hope of seeing them when he spotted Susie and the kids squeezing through the locker room door.

"Over here!" Adam shouted, waving his hand in the air so they could see him. He decided to meet them halfway.

"Oh, Adam, we're so proud of you," Susie said tearily.

He was just about to ask about Rick when someone grabbed him in a headlock from behind, a daily occurrence when he was a child.

"Let me go, you asshole!"

Rick released him. He could have sworn his brother actually looked proud of him. "Way to go, baby bro. You earned this."

"Thanks." Adam leaned in to speak into his brother's ear. "Let's grab a minute alone later, okay?"

Rick looked at him with uncertainty. "Sure."

* * *

Adam felt like everyone in the room was demanding his attention: the press, photographers, the Kidco suits, other players . . . he treated each one respectfully, but in the back of his mind, the celebration wouldn't officially begin until the most important person in the arena arrived.

When he caught sight of Ray trying —and failing—to gain a place inside the locker room door, Adam jumped up on the nearest bench and yelled for people to make way for his best friend. Ray, with Jasper by his side, was able to motor right up to him.

"Never thought you'd do it, you fuckin' loser," Ray said with a shit-eating grin on his face.

Adam picked the Cup up off the floor. "You can only have it for a minute. I don't want your germs on it."

"Hand it over, douche bag."

Adam felt a lump form in his throat as he placed the Cup on his friend's lap, holding it steady while Ray closed his eyes, rubbing his cheek against the cold silver. *You robbed him of this. You—*

Ray's eyes were still closed when he said, "I know what you're thinking, you jack wagon. Cut it out."

Adam laughed.

Ray opened his eyes. "That's enough. You can take it away," he commanded. Adam lifted it from his lap and put it on the bench.

Michael Dante let out a loud whistle and hopped onto the bench next to the Cup. "All right, guys," he yelled. "Time to hit Dante's, then the team-only after party is at the Hart."

The locker room filled with claps and whistles. The Stanley Cup champions were ready to roll.

39

Once the locker room cleared out, Adam and Rick finally had a chance to talk.

"I really appreciate you coming," Adam told his brother, tossing him a bottle of beer.

Rick looked offended. "What? My baby brother is in the finals, and he thinks I won't be there?"

"I know this was hard for you," Adam said carefully.

Rick clenched his jaw. "Yeah, it's hard. Not because I envy what you've become, but because things aren't the way they're supposed to be. I'm the big brother; I'm supposed to be taking care of you, not the other way round."

"You have taken care of me."

Rick snorted. "Fuck off. What are you talking about?"

Adam took a slug of beer. "Who defended me to Dad when he'd bitch about spending money on 'fancy' hockey equipment, or driving me to practice when it was twenty below outside? *You.* If you hadn't run interference, I'm pretty sure he would have pulled the plug on me. But you fought for me. I owe a lot of where I am today to you."

Rick looked ill at ease.

"I know my helping out is hard on you. But that's what family's for, bro. I pull you up when times are tough; you pulled me up when times were tough. Who was fuckin' there for me when I paralyzed Ray?"

"Adam—"

"No, I'm not going to let you be modest. I would have been swallowed up by depression if it weren't for you."

The brothers looked at each other for a moment, saying nothing.

"So we're cool?" Adam asked. The brothers embraced.

"Yeah."

"Good. You ready to party?"

"Hell yeah."

"Let's head out to Brooklyn and show 'em how real Canadian boys party."

They clinked their beer bottles together. "Amen."

40

Inside the Hart, the party was already in full swing. Adam scanned the room looking for Sinead, but when he didn't see her, he assumed she was in the kitchen helping her mother. Christie was at her usual station behind the bar, along with Sinead's uncle Jimmy and her dad. There were tubs of iced champagne and beer. And music. Loud, pumping music.

Sinead's father broke into a wide grin. "Congrats, boyo."

Adam grinned back. "Thanks." He hoisted the Cup up onto the bar. Sinead's father and uncle jostled to take hold of it. Sinead's father won.

"Amazing," he marveled. "Sweet Christ, it weighs a ton."

"Give it over," said Sinead's uncle Jimmy. "You shouldn't be holding it, anyway, with your bad back."

"Eejit." Sinead's father handed the Cup over to his brother, who made a noble effort to hold it aloft but failed miserably. "You're right," he said with a small grimace as he put the trophy back on top of the bar. "Weighs more than you, Charlie."

Christie smiled warmly at Adam. "Congrats."

"Thanks. You switch shifts at the firehouse to work here tonight?"

"Yup. Wouldn't miss it for anything. Plus I'm used to being surrounded by rowdy, macho guys." She eyed the Cup. "Is it good luck to touch it?"

Adam pursed his lips thoughtfully. "Probably."

"So if I do, will it guarantee that all the guys I meet from now on aren't egomaniacs or gay?"

"Can't hurt," said Adam.

Christie touched the Cup.

"Let me know if it works," said Adam with amusement.

"Can I get you anything special?" Sinead's dad offered.

"Nah. The beer and champagne are fine."

"All right, then." Sinead's dad jerked his head in the direction of the dining room. "Get in there with your teammates, Captain."

"Will do." Adam lifted the Cup off the bar. "Sinead in the kitchen?"

"Of course she is. Waiting for you and hiding. You know that girl and parties."

Adam carried the Cup into the dining room amid loud whistles and cheers. The players reminded him of young Greek gods: powerful, in their prime. Most of them were, Adam mused. Not him. In hockey years, he truly was a dinosaur. But it didn't matter: he finally had everything he wanted, and so far, it was exceeding expectations.

He put the Cup on a table in the center of the room and headed for the kitchen.

* * *

Mrs. O'Brien's face went slack with relief at the sight of him. "Thank Christ you're here, Adam." She jerked her head in Sinead's direction. "This one is driving me mad, getting underfoot."

"I'm helping!" Sinead protested, stirring a big pot of stew on one of the industrial stoves.

"You're harming more than helping, if you ask me," her mother retorted. "Get that apron off you and go have fun with your man."

Adam kissed Sinead's cheek. "Couldn't have said it better myself."

Sinead took off the apron and squinted at Adam. "You don't look drunk."

"I'm not."

"Where are your brother and Ray?"

"They're out there. Obviously you haven't been."

Sinead frowned. "You know I'm not good at mingling."

"Don't have a choice, do you? Trust me: you'll have a good time."

* * *

Any reservations Sinead had about walking into the Blades party holding Adam's hand evaporated as soon as she saw how happy everyone was for them. Esa Saari looked especially surprised, particularly when Ray motored over to Sinead and Adam and said loudly, "Has he proposed yet?" It was immediately obvious that theirs was not a casual relationship, even though Ray's question had mortified Sinead. After that, they had to endure a few bad jokes about "attorney/client privilege," but overall, it was a great night, apart from Ulf Torkelson's wife looking Adam up and down like he was a prize bull she wanted to ride.

It was close to seven a.m. when she, Adam, and the Cup arrived at her apartment. Sinead was in that schizophrenic state where her body was physically exhausted but her mind remained sharp. It would probably be hours before she fell asleep.

She stifled a yawn as she locked the door behind them. "You tired?" she asked Adam.

He smiled wearily. "Yes and no. That was a great party."

"I was surprised you didn't get just a tiny bit drunk."

"I was buzzed," Adam protested.

"True. You *were* smiling a lot."

"That had nothing to do with booze, and everything to do with you—"

"And the Cup."

"Well . . . yeah," Adam admitted sheepishly.

Sinead kept waiting for him to put the Cup down, but he didn't. Then it dawned on her.

"You want to bring it into the bedroom, don't you?"

"Of course," Adam replied as if it were obvious.

"Would you like to sleep with the Cup, and I'll bed down in the spare room?"

"Nah. The Cup probably takes up more room than you do in the bed. I think it'll be fine on the floor beside me."

"I'm flattered."

They headed for the bedroom, which was flooded with early morning sun. Sinead hurried over to the windows and quickly pulled down the shades. The bright rays actually hurt her eyes.

Adam had planted the Cup on "his" side of the bed, close enough for him to reach out and touch.

"You're like a little kid on Christmas morning with his favorite toy." Sinead laughed, taking off her clothing as Adam stripped down as well. They slid between the sheets simultaneously, Adam tenderly wrapping her in his arms.

"I love you," he whispered as he positioned himself above her, his mouth dipping down to plant the barest of kisses on her throat.

"I love you, too." Sinead didn't worry anymore about being vulnerable. She knew, as Adam reverently kissed her all over, that he was the one she'd been waiting for.

As delicately as separating the petals of a flower, Adam pushed her knees apart. Her breath quickened; she knew what was going to happen next, and she was already wet, waiting for him. Adam slid down the length of her body, lifting his head to look into her eyes before he began flicking his tongue between her legs.

Sinead's breath quickened as excitement overtook her. Adam took his time, tongue slowly lapping, slowly circling. And then, like a stab of light to her body, he doubled the tempo. Tripled it. Sinead couldn't hold back; she arched up, her entire body quivering as she screamed with unabashed pleasure.

She slowly dropped her hips back down on the bed, still shuddering in the simmering aftermath. "Thank you," she whispered.

Adam lifted his head, looking at her with such love it stunned her. "You never have to thank me for making love to you."

Sinead reached out to cup the side of his face. "I'm not thanking you for just that. I'm thanking you for being the man you are."

"I wouldn't be if it weren't for you," Adam murmured. "I'd just be some pathetic jock with no life outside the rink. You're my life, Sinead. *You* make it all worthwhile."

Sinead was overwhelmed. Adam grinned sexily and then, getting on all fours, began nibbling his way back up her body, lingering at her breasts to unhurriedly suckle and tease. Sinead twirled her fingers in his hair dreamily. It was taking all of her self-restraint not to drag him up so they were face-to-face, where she could brutally assault his mouth with hers, pressing home the greed threatening to explode inside her.

Adam must have sensed it; he wasted no time giving her what she wanted. His breathing was hard and ragged as he pressed his lips to hers wildly for a series of hard, bruising kisses. Sinead groaned beneath him as the wonderful, tantalizing heat began once again to build inside her. She pressed against him hard, her body telling him to please, please hurry. Panting, he tore his mouth from hers, the two of them locking eyes. His body glistened with sweat, his gaze so intense and penetrating that she almost had to look away. But she didn't.

"Fuck me," she whispered. Adam obeyed, and then they were moving together, spurring each other to go harder, deeper. Sinead found the flashes of heat going back and forth between them nearly unbearable. It was stripping her raw, making a mockery of her senses. And then, finally, the beautiful, explosive, overwhelming release. But Adam wasn't there yet; a new shock of pleasure jolted her as he reached for her hands, twining their fingers together as he moaned low. Moving deep inside her, he gave himself over to his own final pleasure.

41

THREE YEARS LATER

"There's my girl."

Sinead put down her briefcase and crouched, opening her arms so her two-year-old daughter, Nina, could fly into them.

"Mommmmyyyy!"

Sinead hugged her tight, covering her face in kisses before picking her up and leaning over to kiss Adam. "How was your day?"

"Long," said Adam. He tugged on Nina's curls. "But we had fun, didn't we, Bug?"

"What did you do?" Sinead asked Nina.

"Played tag! And had a picnic in my *room*!"

"Lucky you!"

Nina wriggled to be released, so Sinead lowered her back down to the floor gently.

"Now what?" Nina asked eagerly.

"Now you let Daddy rest a little bit so he can talk to Mommy," said Adam.

"Why don't you come draw at the kitchen table while Mommy and Daddy make dinner?" said Sinead.

"Oh! Kay!" Nina ran ahead of them into the kitchen.

Sinead kicked her heels off, massaging the sole of her right foot. "God, traffic was hell."

"You say that every Thursday."

"I know."

Adam kissed her softly. "Mmm, this is my favorite day of the week."

"Me, too. I don't realize how much I miss you guys until I get in the car and start the drive home. It seems to take forever."

When Sinead found out she was pregnant soon after she and Adam married, they knew they had to find a middle ground. Sinead wanted to take maternity leave, but she didn't want to quit work completely. They decided she would stay home part-time. The rest of the time, the baby would be taken care of by a nanny.

But by the time Nina was born, things had changed radically. Adam, wanting to end his career on a high note, retired from hockey, and he was now a full-time, stay-at-home dad. Monday through Thursday, Sinead stayed in her own apartment while working in the city. Then on Thursday night, she drove up to their house in Bearsville to be with her family until Sunday night. Sometimes Adam and Nina came down to New York and stayed with her. They'd have dinner with Sinead's family, or Sinead would stay home with Nina while Adam went to see the Blades play. More often than not, though, it was just the three of them relaxing at home. Both she and Adam believed it was important that Nina see where Mommy lived part of the week and that she feel comfortable staying there. It wasn't the ideal situation, but it gave both of them what they wanted: Sinead could keep working, and Adam could live in the country.

Nina was already at the table, her face scrunched up in intense concentration as she scribbled on a piece of blank paper. "Look at her," Sinead murmured to Adam worriedly. "God, she looks so focused. I hope she doesn't take after me."

"What, type A personality?" Adam teased, pulling out a bottle of Belgian beer.

"Yeah."

With a flourish, Nina finished the picture and handed it to Sinead.

"What's this?" Sinead asked, wide-eyed with interest, even though there was nothing really discernible on the paper. It was just a bunch of squiggly lines.

"A picture of Daddy."

"Daddy doing what?"

"Dancing with monkeys."

"Wow!" Sinead said, amazed. "I didn't know there were monkeys up here."

"There are." Nina took a fresh piece of paper, and with her nose practically touching the table, began another drawing.

Sinead tapped Adam on the shoulder, where he stood opening the beer.

"What's up?"

"Look how close her nose is to the paper," she said quietly. "Do you think she might need glasses?"

Adam rolled his eyes, but he looked amused. "No. You know, thank God it's me who's the stay-at-home parent."

"Why?"

"Because if it were you, she'd be going to the doctor every three days. That is, if you were willing to take her out of the bubble."

"That's not true," Sinead insisted. She glanced back at her daughter. "Okay, it is," she reluctantly admitted, taking the glass of beer Adam handed to her.

"If it'll make you feel better, I'll give her a home eye exam," said Adam dryly. "And an intelligence test. I think she might be falling behind memorizing torts."

Sinead gave him a dirty look. "You are so not funny."

Across the table from where Nina sat doodling was a stack of the daily newspapers Adam liked to get, mainly for the sports coverage: the *Post,* the *Sentinel*, and the *Daily News*.

"How are the Blades doing?" Sinead asked, as she began taking the fixings for salad out of the fridge.

"Off to a solid start," said Adam, beer in hand, as he stared out the large kitchen window into the woods. "Jason's a good captain. Everyone knew I was just keeping the *C* warm for him. I was the bridge between the Ty and Michael generation and the new generation."

Sinead wrapped her arms around him from behind. "You miss it, don't you?"

Adam turned to look at her. "Of course I do," he admitted. "But it was good to retire at the top of my game. I didn't want to be one of those guys who don't know when it's time to hang it up. Besides, the game is really changing. Now that I'm gone, they'll easily be able to institute new rules about unintentional hits to the head."

"Bet you never thought you'd be doing this."

Adam switched places with her, standing behind her and rubbing her shoulders.

"Nope. Never in a million years. But you know what? I love it."

"You're a good dad."

"I do okay for a boneheaded jock."

Sinead playfully hit his hand. "I never thought that."

"Right. And I never thought you had a pole up your— butt."

"Good catch," Sinead whispered.

Sinead glanced back over her shoulder at Nina. She was beautiful. Perfect. Okay, maybe not perfect, especially now that she was in full-blown terrible twos mode, but still. It had been harder for Sinead to go back to work after her maternity leave than she ever could have imagined. She spent the first two weeks crying as soon as she woke up in the morning and crying the minute she left work. She was envious of Adam. But deep down, she knew she'd made the right decision. It wasn't so much a matter of losing traction in her career as it was knowing that Adam's assessment of her neurotic personality was dead on: if she were the parent staying home with Nina full-time, she'd probably make a basket case of their daughter.

"Oliver was wondering if he could come up for the day Saturday," said Sinead, peeling a cucumber.

"As long as he doesn't come bearing tons of junk food."

"He doesn't."

"He *does*," Adam countered. "By the time he left last time, I was sure it would take days for Nina to come down from her sugar high."

"That's our fault. We shouldn't have said yes every time she asked for something."

"It didn't help that Uncle Ollie was slipping her goodies on the side."

"He adores her."

"And she adores him," said Adam. "But no crap food."

"Got it."

Sinead gazed out the large kitchen window. Twilight was approaching, streaking the sky with bars of pink and gray. The leaves were starting to fall; soon it would be dark by four o'clock. But right now, there was a perfect stillness outside that matched the contentedness inside her. Sinead took in her husband's handsome profile and felt a surge of love. She looked at her daughter and couldn't believe it was possible to love another human being as much as she loved Nina.

It didn't come naturally to her, but after all was said and done, she knew the reason she was so blessed: it was because she'd stopped trying to control everything, choosing instead to go with the flow. As long as she remembered that, she knew life would always be as wonderful as it was right now, no matter what challenges the future might bring.

Go ahead. Try…

Just a Taste

By *New York Times* bestselling author

Deirdre Martin

Since his wife's untimely death, Anthony Dante has thrown himself into his cooking, making his restaurant, Dante's, a Brooklyn institution. So far, his biggest problem has been keeping his brother, the retired hockey star, out of the kitchen. But now, a mademoiselle is invading his turf.

Stunning Vivi Robitaille can't wait to showcase her taste-bud-tingling recipes in her brand new bistro, Vivi's. Her only problem is an arrogant Italian chef across the street who actually thinks he's competition.

The table is set for a culinary war—until things start getting spicy outside of the kitchen…

M300T0109

It's a...

Total Rush

Free spirit Gemma Dante wishes her love life were going as well as her New Age business. So she casts a spell to catch her Mr. Right. But when the cosmic wires get crossed, into her life walks a clean-cut fireman who's anything but her type.

Sean Kennealy doesn't know what to make of his pretty neighbor who burns incense. He only knows that being near her sparks a fire in him that even the guys at Ladder 29, Engine 31 can't put out.

From
New York Times Bestselling Author

Deirdre Martin

penguin.com

Double the Pleasure

A contemporary romance anthology featuring
New York Times bestselling author

Lori Foster
and
Deirdre Martin
Jacquie D'Alessandro
Penny McCall

Four sizzling all-new stories of fun and games between friends and lovers, including a novella featuring the return of those sexy Winston men—this time, identical twin brothers who use their knock-out mirror-image good looks to switch places and have a little fun with the girls of their dreams.

penguin.com

From the national bestselling author of
FLAT-OUT SEXY

Erin McCarthy

HARD *AND* FAST

He has what it takes to set her heart racing . . .

Praise for Erin McCarthy's novels

"Sizzling hot."
—*Romance Junkies*

"Funny, charming, and very entertaining."
—*Romance Reviews Today*

penguin.com